COFFIN MAKER

MARK L. FOWLER

COFFIN MAKER   MARK L. FOWLER

Published in 2014 by FeedARead.com Publishing

Copyright © Mark L. Fowler

The author or authors assert their moral right under the Copyright, Designs and Patents Act, 1988, to be identified as the author or authors of this work.

All Rights reserved. No part of this publication may be reproduced, copied, stored in a retrieval system, or transmitted, in any form or by any means, without the prior written consent of the copyright holder, nor be otherwise circulated in any form of binding or cover other than that in which it is published and without a similar condition being imposed on the subsequent purchaser.

A CIP catalogue record for this title is available from the British Library.

COFFIN MAKER   MARK L. FOWLER

1. THE LAST MOMENTS OF SOLITUDE

I love them I hate them.

The Coffin Maker sat hunched over his journal, the monumental *History of Death,* wondering if this book didn't represent his greatest achievement.

Even greater than making coffins?

Even greater than boxing up the human race?

It was a tough call.

The fingers of his right hand were hammering at the side of his desk, while his left hand strangled the pen that he held like a dagger over the page.

I love them I hate them.

Had he done it? Had he finally written the perfect sentence?

Something in the room twitched. The Coffin Maker looked up from his journal. "What was that?" he whispered, his ears straining at the echo of his voice as it returned the question, scanning for imperfections that might reveal a hidden presence.

His question unanswered he turned back to look again at the words still drying on the page of his beloved book.

I love them I hate them.

There was no doubt about it. He *had* done it. Perfection. The Poet of Death's finest hour. What balance. What symmetry. Not a syllable, not even a letter, misplaced.

He shook his head at the miracle of it. "Why can't humanity be so succinct?"

The stillness flinched, again breaking the spell, the Coffin Maker's eyeballs grating in their sockets as

COFFIN MAKER   MARK L. FOWLER

his searchlight gaze trawled every nook and cranny of the high-ceilinged room.

Revealing nothing.

Something was coming, though. He could feel it.

He waited, not moving a bone.

Nothing came.

Not yet.

Not quite.

At last he turned back to the page, again admiring his beautiful words. What more was there to say about the human race? Over the centuries he'd watched them pulling backwards and forwards over scraps of knowledge, stuffing it all vainly into their little editions, filling page after page with tired speculation about time and space and freewill and gods and devils. Yet did a single sentence in any of those feeble-minded volumes reveal even a glimpse of the Divine Plan?

"$1+1=2$. That's all they know. And some of them aren't so sure about that!"

For the third time the Coffin Maker's concentration was breached, the room seeming to turn inside out, as though an immense hand had entered to its extremities, and was now withdrawing, taking the fingers of the glove back with it and folding them within the palm.

Tiredness, thought the Coffin Maker, determined to resist. But the force of curiosity was too strong. And so for the third time he looked up from his journal, his senses straining into the black silence. In

COFFIN MAKER   MARK L. FOWLER

Earthly terms it felt like a storm coming. Yet no storms had ever reached the Kingdom of Death.

A thought entered the Coffin Maker's head. A question.

Do I love them?

He looked down at the page.

Gasped.

His words.

His beautiful words.

Soured.

Somehow leaked their wisdom.

I love them. I hate them.

Suddenly the questions were piling up.

Love? How can Death, if that's what I am, love the thing that it works so tirelessly to destroy?

And can I even say that I hate them? I'm doing a job. Doing what I was created to do. Love and hate don't come into it. So where did these words come from...?

Anger rose up through his marrow, pulsing beneath his parchment skin.

"This is what comes of trying to write about mankind. There's nothing to fathom. They're born and they'll die. In the process they've ruined another perfect day."

Fighting to retain some composure, he reminded himself that he still had his solitude. His precious, priceless solitude.

Then it happened.

As though the first flake of snow was falling in the Kingdom of Death. There, floating down past the window.

COFFIN MAKER   MARK L. FOWLER

Scrambling from his desk, he pressed a cold face against the glass, following the uninvited object with fierce disbelief as it sailed casually to the ground.

It wasn't a snowflake, rather a sheet of paper.

A note?

Who in creation would send him a note?

The Creator?

What games was the Creator playing?

Unless...

Was this the day..?

The Creator finally sending – revealing –

The Divine Plan!

In an instant the Coffin Maker's mean carcass was scurrying outside to investigate.

No winds blow in the Kingdom of Death, and the Coffin Maker didn't have to chase after the paper. There was no teasing gust to keep it all the time an inch out of reach. It simply lay there, waiting for him, bearing its message in coloured lights.

He picked up the note, the iron in his gun-grey eyes sparking as he read it.

Looking out across the infinite wastelands, he felt tears of rage bubbling inside. This desolate kingdom was his, his alone and had been from the beginning. What had changed?

His pride spluttered and beneath it something darker stirred.

He held the note to his skull, against the furnace stoking up inside. But the paper would not ignite. Fire had not yet come to the Kingdom of Death, though it would, soon enough.

COFFIN MAKER   MARK L. FOWLER

Every bone in his skeleton-frame was vibrating with such violence that he thought he might topple under the weight of his own fury. Storm clouds of raw plutonium, sufficient to obliterate worlds, settled across his face.

The note fell from his fist. He watched it go. It lay on the seething ground, twinkling back at him.

Apprentices?
Why?
And why now..?

2: WHAT THE COFFIN MAKER MISSED

Father Henry made up a hearty fire in his study, and was settling down to work on his sermon when Bishop Stones arrived.

"To what do I owe this honour?" asked the priest, nervously. "Can I get you a coffee, perhaps?"

"I'll come straight to the point," said Bishop Stones, squeezing his considerable hindquarters into the seat nearest the fire, before opening his briefcase. "You've been a fine servant of God for many years, Father Henry."

"That sounds ominous."

"It's about this 'Coffin Maker' business. This book of yours."

"Oh, that," laughed the priest, his ruddy face turning scarlet.

"Hoping to supplement your income?"

"Hardly that. Though I thought I might serialise it in the parish magazine," he added, instantly regretting the joke. "So how did you come to hear about my little...project?"

From under raised eyebrows, Stones softly growled. "God works in mysterious ways. I was visiting a parishioner, since you ask."

The bishop removed a large brown folder from his briefcase. "Your *little project*, Father Henry. Some seventy thousand words, no less." He extracted from the folder a manuscript bound with a fearsome elastic band. "I take it this isn't an only copy?"

Father Henry held the bishop's searching stare for as long as he could stand it, before lowering his eyes

… and reaching into the bottom drawer of his writing desk. "It does need a bit of work," he said, taking out his own copy, "before I'd inflict it on the rest of my flock."

The eyebrows were up again. "Is this book a response to the death of your sister?" asked the bishop, removing the thick elastic band from his copy of the manuscript.

"My intention was never to be blasphemous," said Father Henry.

"I'm sure it wasn't. The devil works in mysterious ways. Look, the whole tone of the thing troubles me greatly. You seem to be treating subjects like death and evil like they're some kind of joke. And it's so wretchedly uneven: one minute you employ an inflated style that I presume is an attempt at irony; the next you seem to be straying into the territory of - saints preserve us – gothic horror!"

Father Henry let out a burst of involuntary laughter.

Stones glared. "Have I said something amusing?"

"I hadn't realised that you were such a literary critic."

The laughter died a swift, agonising death.

"Are you sure I can't interest you in a coffee...?"

Ignoring the offer of refreshments for the second time, the bishop launched a further attack.

"I find your basic cosmology confused and confusing. Perhaps you spent too much time studying philosophy and not enough time on theology. On the one hand you seem to be invoking a battle between God and the devil, while on the other tying the subject of evil to popular psychology - self-delusion, the divided self and all of that nonsense."

The bishop's nostrils flared. "Am I in the presence of a divided mind, Father Henry? Are you undergoing an existential crisis?"

Bishop Stones was on a roll. "Is the agony of choice knocking at your door and disturbing your inner sanctum? Is the Coffin Maker meant to represent you? Have you become *Everyman*?"

A smirk settled across the larger man's face, though he was far from finished. "Have you externalised the beast and the angel that co-exist within you? Or am *I* the model for the Coffin Maker? Did you trim him down to a pile of bones so that I wouldn't recognise myself? We could both of us do with shedding a few pounds - is that the subtext? Are you suggesting that the Church needs to slim down from past indulgences?"

"I never meant to cause offence," said the priest, sweat running freely down his face. "I thought my book might...help."

"Help who?"

"Those whose lives have been touched – blighted - by death and loss."

"Your sister's child - John? Coming up for thirteen, I believe?"

"It isn't easy for a youngster - facing the death of a parent, I'm sure you can imagine -"

"There's nothing wrong with *my* imagination, Father Henry. I think the point is this: you have duties as a priest, important and profound duties."

"I'm aware of that."

COFFIN MAKER   MARK L. FOWLER

"Are you?"

Bishop Stones turned the pages of the manuscript. I mean to say, just listen to this. *"'As elusive as Heaven or Hell, and existing as one of God's best kept secrets, The Kingdom of Death braced itself for the immediate shattering of the Coffin Maker's solitude. A lesser place might have crumbled, but the Kingdom was vaster than even the Coffin Maker could know, and resilient enough to take the burden of his fury."*

Father Henry tried to interject, but Stones raised a hand and read on. *"'Coffin inhabited only the dry oasis disrupting the emptiness of the Kingdom, the place he called the Coffin Complex. This assortment of buildings, all seemingly touched by a finger of madness, formed the broken heart of the Dead Land.*

"'From the hallucinogenic violence of the architecture, any reasonable mind might believe that all death in the world was controlled from this place...'"

Bishop Stones looked across at the glistening priest. "I could *almost* believe that such a place and character exist. And before you take that as a compliment, I will remind you again of your station in this life. The world's in enough of a mess without the clergy throwing in its own flights of fancy. It's time we got back to basics."

The bishop turned the page, shaking his head. *"'Under the invisible shadow of the Kingdom of Death, a blue and green world turned, rolling through the wildness of space like a child's lost ball, never daring to flinch from its finite path around the parental Sun.*

COFFIN MAKER   MARK L. FOWLER

"'Billions of people did what they did, being born, dying, getting on with the business of life. Not one of them knew that a walking talking skeleton, inhabiting a nebulous and gothic land, had started receiving letters. Not one of them knew that the Coffin Maker existed.'"

Father Henry was wondering if Stones intended reading out the entire manuscript. Then the caustic voice paused. Stones, his eyes riveted to the page, shook his head with the gravity of a hanging judge. "Must I go on?"

"I'd rather you didn't."

It was all the encouragement he needed.

"...'No human being was ever a stranger to looking into the sky, with the peculiar and vivid feeling that someone, somewhere was watching. 'From ancient peoples gathered in remote clusters, to the modern multitudes huddled in fairy tale cities, all who have claimed membership of the human race have known in their hearts and bowels what it is to be centre-screen. To look into an unsuspecting sky and, for that strange moment, not simply to feel it, but to know *it. Yet what they didn't know was that the Coffin Maker was the watcher in the sky, scrutinising their every move from the legions of monitors he kept trained on the blue and green world.'"*

Stones smacked the manuscript. "It's not exactly orthodox, is it? What the blazes are you trying to say?"

The priest, at a loss as to why his inquisitor appeared unaffected by the heat in the room, thought that he was about to melt. And on top of everything, his stomach was rumbling louder even than the bishop's.

Best to get it over with, and retreat into the solace of a good supper.

"I wanted to show Death as a bumbling fool, not to be feared, rather to be pitied. I think there can be great comfort in that."

"Go on," said the bishop, not appearing at all convinced.

"I wanted to remind people that 'good' and 'evil' are moral choices that we all have to make, and keep making. That life and death and all that it entails is not an abstract metaphysical battle, remote from the lives of ordinary people."

The bishop dropped the manuscript onto the hearth, and it landed with a loud, startling slap. "And where's God in all this? You're a priest, not a science-fiction writer. I'm sorry about your sister, but I can't condone this sort of thing. And I don't see that a grief-stricken boy can possibly gain comfort from this kind of morbid nonsense. Maybe you've some grieving of your own still to do. Maybe you need to think about taking some time off."

The bishop stood up. "I've said what I came to say."

Father Henry couldn't help but feel relieved to hear it.

"One more thing," said Bishop Stones.

"I don't want to keep you," said the priest.

"I've been hearing whispers about this 'Colonel Gouge' baloney. They seem to be generating from this parish. I don't expect to hear reports of them being amplified from the pulpit - am I making myself clear?"

COFFIN MAKER   MARK L. FOWLER

Stones bent to pick up the copy of the manuscript from the hearth, looking deliberately into the flames burning steadily in the grate as he did so, before handing the pages to Father Henry. "I leave it to your judgement, of course, but in my opinion you make a better priest than novelist. It would be a tragedy to see you fall between callings. And if I might be allowed one final observation: if you're not careful, I think that fire will begin to die very quickly. Goodnight."

The Coffin Maker trained a monitor on Zone Thirty-Nine. How was it possible, how could he have missed it - missed anything! There was no place to hide from death on that exposed globe.

But still he had missed it.

The seed.

And now that seed, big as a man and uglier in the heart, was blowing itself across the Earth and over the border to Zone Thirty-Nine. And in the border-lands of that so-called 'great nation', its work was beginning.

And he'd missed it. Missed it, he had no doubt, because of the threatened shattering of his solitude.

Yet of all the zones in the world, why Thirty-Nine? It was the last place to expect the unexpected. A nation of quiet comforts and stable riches. It had its problems, its battles and its poverty, but it also had President Doveman. And by all accounts from that Globe of Sorrows, that Planet of Damned-Fools, Doveman was a leader hating war and loving humanity. Naive and lovable, man of the people, the future looked so bright over the country that mandatory prescription shades seemed only a term of office away.

COFFIN MAKER   MARK L. FOWLER

That's what the posters said.

Gullibility, thought Coffin. It was destined to remain as integral a part of the human condition as blessed mortality itself.

And not a coffin ride from the presidential palace where President Doveman had enjoyed the past twelve months of quiet power, there stood a church. A church boasting a spire that reached into the sky, pointing the way blindly toward Heaven, and boasting a priest who, by his own admission, would not be content until he'd seen every last one of the faithful safely through those mythical gates.

All Saints where, in the words of Father Henry, "miracles happened daily". All Saints where, according to the guidebook, 'the spirit soared through prayer and architectural magnificence'.

But what the guidebook didn't say was that this 'miracle in stone' could be examined inch on inch by the greatest earthbound detective carrying the largest magnifying glass in history, and still not yield the slightest clue that this would be the nourishing ground for the seed that the Coffin Maker had missed.

The seed that Father Henry and two of his wretched congregation seemed hell-bent on demonising out of all proportion. The place where it would all bear fruit.

Even before receiving his first letter in the entire history of life and death, Coffin had held quiet suspicions about that church, boasting as it did three men, the legendary priest included, all prophesying wildly about an evil seed blowing toward them.

And that ridiculous manuscript.

Of course they didn't know about the note; couldn't possibly know anything of the Kingdom of Death. It was no more than an inspired fluke. All that worthless manuscript proved was that, if the fools wrote enough rubbish, eventually they were bound to stumble across a truth.
But they would never know it was the truth.

Father Henry's stomach was rumbling fit to wake the dead, and he knew well enough that only a supper of unprecedented proportions could restore the peace of mind required to finish his sermon.

The most important sermon that he had ever been called to deliver. The world was set to change and the duty had fallen on him to give out the first call to arms.

Taking both copies of the manuscript he knelt before the dwindling fire and asked that Bishop Stones might one day understand why Colonel Gouge could no longer go unmentioned in the House of God.

Thumbing through the pages, thinking about his sister, and about her young son, John, he came across a section that made him smile.

'If the mortal world was oblivious to the fact that a heap of bones had finally made it onto the divine mailing list, it didn't rob the event of its significance. Didn't lessen the impact or dilute the consequences. That the Kingdom of Death received its first postal delivery mattered. For billions of people, all blissfully ignorant of the facts, the shattering of the solitude of the Coffin Maker by sending him two apprentices mattered.'

Father Henry looked for a last time into the dying flames. He knew what he had to do. The baton had to be passed on.

The book belonged to John now, and John alone would decide its fate – and perhaps much more besides.

The room was warm enough.

He stood up. There was a supper to fix and a sermon to complete and by God he didn't mean to stint on either.

3: THE HISTORY OF DEATH

The shattering of the Coffin Maker's solitude was swift, and the Kingdom of Death, surviving the enormity of the event, sprang to curious life with two fresh buds to flank its lonely thorn.

They were not easy days in the Kingdom of Death, and yet, as Coffin was later to reflect, perhaps they should have been. In the light of what lay ahead, and in what was already reaping its first poisoned harvest down on the Planet of Fools, they were days of carefree joy.

Yet savour them he did not, instead busying himself in a gathering rage that found release only in work. There was no finer cure for the negative emotions, in his book, than hammering nails into coffins. It was not a job, not even a vocation - it was *lifeblood.*

If the taking of his solitude hadn't been torment enough, the odours had put the tin hat on it. Bare moments after reading the note, his nostrils had began twitching. There had never been anything to smell in the Kingdom of Death; odour had been a peculiarly mortal phenomena.

He'd wondered whether the shock of the note had affected his sanity, because unless he was mistaken, sweet violets were mixing with the sour scent of decaying flesh and sending the results straight to his brain. He knew the importance mortals seemed to attach to smells, but what were they doing here?

Was some twisted sense of humour at work?

COFFIN MAKER   MARK L. FOWLER

He had turned to see the smells solidify, and it all happened quicker than the management of a sudden death.

Standing there, apart, like blatant opposites gratefully disconnected, the contrasting vapours rising off them without shame, without apology - his two apprentices.

He had needed no introduction, their names somehow, mysteriously, emblazoned on his mind. Taking form from the scent of violets stood Hieronymus, and arising from the stench of putrefied flesh, Beezle.

Coffin was not impressed with his new arrivals. Their odours had quickly dissipated, but their presence had remained. As their employer he could only think of firing them; as their teacher, of beating their heads together; and as a father - he tried not to even think of that. With the meagre leisure time that he allowed himself, he busied his agitated bones, filling the pages of his journal with the Poetry of Death.

It isn't humans alone who fail to see the beautiful ironies of death. The wonderful poetry of death. The craftsmanship that goes into death.

He had to admit it: bang on target again. Which was more than could be said for the fool responsible for letting an entire island of doomed flesh and blood survive a beautifully executed earthquake. On the sun baked island of Zone Twelve, thousands were already paying homage to strange gods for saving their lives.

COFFIN MAKER   MARK L. FOWLER

It was incompetence that had saved them. And it left him close to putting his hammer through the skulls of his apprentices, both eager as they were to heap the blame on the other. Couldn't he leave them alone for a single minute? He'd done all the hard work; he'd set the thing up. All they had to do was hammer some nails. All they had to do was do as they were told.

"You'll never work together again," he told them.

They hadn't seemed at all concerned at this. Relieved, possibly.

It was around this challenging time that Coffin decided 'three' was his unlucky number. The feeling was magnified by something in Zone Thirty-Nine that he couldn't quite get the measure of. Perhaps, he reflected bitterly, it was simply that the place had too many threes hiding inside it.

Something's happening down there. Comes around. Sent to test me. But it's never been up early enough to fool the Coffin Maker. Changes its appearance. Fancies itself. But I'm there at the birth and I'm not taken in by the 'innocent' baby and I don't miss the slug beneath the skin. Humans - blind to the cruelty forming. The malice festering. Can't even recognise evil when it comes as one of their own. And it always does. Time after time. Can't spot the imposter. But I can. And I've hung its countless names like trophies in the pages of this journal. But do I get any thanks? Does the human race get down on its knees and thank me for saving its

COFFIN MAKER   MARK L. FOWLER

skin? So it's back. Zone Thirty-Nine this time. And the human race oblivious again.

Coffin sat back to admire the page. Sometimes, most times, his sheer style amazed him.

Smugness tried to make itself comfortable on the sharp edges of his face. But though the look showed determination to stay, its discomfort grew until it could take the pain no longer, grateful to hand its place to an expression better suited to so much bone.

What's different this time? In all that wretched green Earth what makes Zone Thirty-Nine so special? Ten threes in thirty. Three threes in nine. A lot of threes.

A scowl broke from his eyes, pouring a grisly light on the surrounding bone.

As if I haven't enough to worry about. Hieronymus and Beezle. What do they remind me of? A paltry human tale. Beauty and the Beast.

The ferocity of the light subsided and he sighed. What was the Creator playing at? Had He run out of things to do? Was He bored enough to start playing games?

Coffin had a mind to take the day off and go looking for the Divine Plan. To find that philosophical Holy Grail that so obsessed the humans. If he wasn't so busy running around supervising two numbskulls. If he wasn't so busy trying to supervise death in the world.

If he didn't have Zone Thirty-Nine to worry about.

COFFIN MAKER   MARK L. FOWLER

He wanted his solitude back.

Grieving for the past, he turned back a million pages of his journal. Page one. That exquisite, incomparable beginning. Reading those first entries brought a tremor to his knuckle heart as he remembered the first day, being introduced to the first humans in the finest garden setting on the entire miserable planet.

What a glorious first day. Life and Death shaking hands.

How noble he'd felt. The Poet of Death. Life's constant companion. Life's dark cousin, deserving of respect, not vilification and scorn. It was all there on those first pages - even the self-portrait.

Plucked fresh from the firmament, character and features stamped at the anvil. None of the terrors of youth. Old beautifully old. Thick white hair sitting like a cloud of angels on a bone patchwork face giving a home to two explosions of metal that would forever haunt his gun-grey eyes. So deeply made that infinity would never move a hair or a wrinkle. Mere time would neither play addition nor subtraction with the finely carved character lines that had welcomed a rare spirit aboard at the first drawing of breath.

Ah - it took a poet to recognise a poet. Coffin then and Coffin now.

As he read on, re-living the trembling excitement that both sides had felt that day, he basked in the trust and friendship that had poured between them. They had truly been in love, Life and Death. Yet as he turned the pages of the *History of Death*, he saw

COFFIN MAKER   MARK L. FOWLER

how quickly the balance had broken, and how profoundly the love affair had soured into conflict.

He hurried through the pages, turning hundreds, thousands of years at a time, tracing the patterns through the centuries.

The descent.

Approaching the last pages, he halted at the brink of the Twentieth Century with a sense of foreboding, before moving with great deliberation through the years of what mankind had called the 'Great Wars'.

He thought back to those final moments of the Second World War, and the way he had allowed himself a smile at the end of that wildly ambitious campaign, applauding his own audacity in realising a supreme artistic vision, an apex of craftsmanship.

He thought how, in the intense ambiguity of the moment, with exuberance wilting under the weight of uncertainty and blossoming regret, how it had crossed his mind that maybe he'd taken coffin making to a dangerous summit, leaving no place to look but down.

Down from his place of exile, shunned and forever misunderstood by the human race.

The tragedy of it.

Yet his faithful recordings documented how he had quickly abandoned such thoughts, re-assuring himself that he was no enemy of mankind, but still its friend.

There was no denying he had shown them the way to mass destruction, allowed them to indulge their barbarous instincts to the full; but he'd never have to lead them so far again. The lessons were learnt, surely.

COFFIN MAKER   MARK L. FOWLER

Once and for all. Not even the human race could be so utterly stupid that it needed to learn such lessons again.
Could it?
The feelings of euphoria in those last moments of that monumental slaughter had signified the farthest point in a long journey out of paradise. It was there in black and white, in his own hand.

Time to start heading back towards the joy of that first great day when Life and Death held hands like lovers.

So why did it feel like he was heading back into the void? Was he being punished? Or were those idiots – those mortal fools – back on the brink? Were Hieronymus and Beezle the manifestations of his sin – or mankind's incurable folly?
Was this his punishment for missing the coming of the seed?
Or was there an apocalypse brewing as payment to the human race for their refusal to change? To learn?
Coffin slammed his journal shut and summoned his apprentices. It was time to get a few things straight.

His youthful charges made their separate ways through the labyrinthine corridors connecting their hastily constructed quarters with the unknown paths that led down to the ancient catacombs. Above these dark and subterranean corners of the Kingdom of Death lay the corridors leading to Coffin's own quarters, consisting of a flat circle of empty rooms, a lonely moon face from which two ugly jug ears had been badly sewn.

COFFIN MAKER   MARK L. FOWLER

From the left ear walked Hieronymus, from the right Beezle.

Coffin waited in the room at the northern tip of the moon; the room with a fine coffin-wood table that supported his journal; the room with a fine coffin-wood framed window that allowed him to look out on the rest of the Coffin Complex.

North from his window stood the Triangle: at the far point was the soaring giant, the gothic imbecility that was the Tower; to the left out of his window, the Vaults and to the right the Dome. Whenever Coffin dwelt on the Triangle for too long, his bones would vibrate, and so over time he had almost entirely cured himself of the habit.

As his unwanted charges dutifully entered the room, he noted that they no longer brought with them any odours. *Getting used to them? Used to their incompetence!*

He welcomed them with a roar of seething disgust. "Get in here I haven't all day damn you listen and learn. Coffin making is a craft."

He held a hammer in one hand and a nail in the other. "These are the tools of the trade. These are the Servants of Death. I build a coffin and a life ends. It ends the moment I drive in the last nail. No-one told me this. Instinctive knowledge."

The barking was starting to hurt his throat, yet he refused to weaken. Today was a turning point. No more tomfoolery.

"The coffin must accommodate all aspects of the person at that instant or they slip free, back into the world, and I have to start again. Timing is everything.

COFFIN MAKER   MARK L. FOWLER

Coffin making is an art, a magical art, and no mere magician trying to stuff a genie back into a bottle ever worked so hard. I didn't make things this way."

He placed the tools down, carefully, and glared into the faces of his two apprentices. "All men are mortal!" he thundered. "That was the extent of my training. And not a word, sign or round of applause since. Nothing!"

He was shaking. "Don't you have work to do?"

The apprentices turned and started to move away. Carefully gauging the effect, Coffin turned the volume down to a whisper. "One more thing." He watched them stop, turn back around. "You'll find me particular with words.

He let the volume out again. "I don't expect you to absorb my vocabulary all at once but you will observe immediately that there is no place here for 'God'. You will, should the need arise, use the term, 'Creator'. Now familiarise yourself with the zones and let countries be damned."

Coffin savoured their confusion. Funny the way they wouldn't look at each other; wouldn't join their frustrations together. They appeared separated by worlds.

As they again made to leave, Coffin held up a hand, halting them with five long bones of arthritic elegance. He returned to a grating whisper, hoarse and painful. "Remember this: Never give me cause to become angry. You wouldn't like it. Now go."

In the silence he opened his journal and wrote,

COFFIN MAKER   MARK L. FOWLER

Feels like Hieronymus and Beezle have always been here. No sign of them leaving. What did I do to deserve them? An eternity alone. Blissful time that should have been mine forever. And nothing more than a note to herald their arrival. Worrying about this has led me to miss the seed of whatever's come to Zone Thirty-Nine.

His temper beat its wings.

Why can't mankind take responsibility for gate keeping what comes into its own world? They don't deserve me.

He was ready for work. Real work. His bones were itching. The time for words was over.
    For now.
    Just one more paragraph.
    His face grated into a grim frown.

I have a bad feeling. Three is bringing me bad luck. Three simple deaths. A priest. A man too old to be climbing trees. A soldier. What are these simplicities to the Coffin Maker?

He placed his pen down and began beating the side of his desk with both hands. When he could stand the pain no longer, he picked up his pen again.

Three coffins. If it wasn't for the pleasure it would deny me I'd leave them for Beauty and the Beast. Find out whether prettiness or ugliness is the more incompetent. No! Unthinkable. Too important these three.
    But why?

COFFIN MAKER   MARK L. FOWLER

The unease was growing. Coffin closed his journal and collected his hammer and a selection of nails. It was time to work off the bad feeling.

First he trained the monitor that peered deep into the heartland of Zone Thirty-Nine, bringing up the focus on a cassocked priest, rotund and ruddy. "The fatal flaw," muttered Coffin as he watched the priest devouring a gigantic supper.

"Gluttony."

Time pressed forward at the hand of the Coffin Maker, and the priest found himself waking from a night of tortured sleep, hurrying across the graveyard towards the side door of All Saints church.

"Coming to get you," said Coffin. "Ready or not."

COFFIN MAKER   MARK L. FOWLER

4: FATHER HENRY

Every seat in the Great Central Aisle was occupied, and the few spaces in the side aisles served as the only indicator that a celebrity wedding was not in progress. It had been like this for so long at All Saints that even the church roof was no longer in need of repair.

The organist, arriving early to be certain of his seat, made his presence felt to any would-be poachers, rupturing the air with improvised chords calculated to jingle the kidneys of young and old alike.

Holding his Bible in one hand and supporting his heart with the other, Father Henry climbed uncomfortably into the pulpit. The burning in his chest had started after supper the previous evening, and he'd suffered an unpleasant night cursing in turn the spare ribs, the fried chicken, the vintage Stilton and the wisdom of such indulgence at so late an hour.

He surveyed the expectant faces of the congregation and wondered how, in his torment, he could deliver the message of hope that only last night had pulsed through his veins and out through his pen with such force that it had seemed dictated by the Holy Ghost. He closed his eyes and prayed the Holy Ghost would see the job through.

The near-anarchic roar from the huge pipes pressed on relentlessly, threatening to tear out chunks of masonry until, raising his eyebrows in the direction of the organ loft, Father Henry ushered in an immediate and deafening silence.

"Friends, I know that it isn't customary to begin our communion with a sermon. Be assured, I have not taken leave of my senses. The placing of this address to you is not the only unorthodox aspect to what lies in store this morning, and I ask for your patience and understanding."

Father Henry closed his eyes, partly from an impulse to devotion, partly to let the physical memory of over-ripe cheese bubble up into a silent belch. "In all the years that I have stood here talking to you, I have never been tempted to stray directly into the political world. Until today, no politician's name has passed my lips from this holy place. But the day has come, my friends, and I feel a duty that presses me beyond the constraints of orthodoxy."

Not a breath stirred among the congregation.

"But before I go any further down this dark road, I would like to thank you all for your kind thoughts and wishes in regard to my late sister. I hope that you will keep a place in your hearts for my nephew, John, for whom the pain of losing his mother has, in so many ways, barely begun.

"No matter how devout our faith, death can catch us all off balance. It takes a long time to restore the equilibrium. Death, my friends, is rarely as easy as we would wish it to be. Death is complex, full of mysteries and ambiguities. It changes every time we reflect upon it, and often, if it doesn't defeat us entirely, it becomes in the end what we choose it to be.

"It is so easy to believe that we have no say in such huge matters, but I don't believe that to be the case. Our beliefs structure the reality of death, and we alone can make it good or bad according to the filters that we keep in our hearts, in our minds, in our souls.

COFFIN MAKER   MARK L. FOWLER

We hold the moral key. Yet in the immediate face of death, it is hard for us not to demonise it; hard for us to find the positives. Often, it seems that the task is downright impossible.

"John is still a child, but his loss has brought him face to face with the deeper realities of life, when he ought to be concerned with its trivialities. God's purpose isn't always easy to comprehend, because we can't see the complete picture. Maybe there is a reason for John's terrible loss - a reason impossible to grasp in this world."

He paused again, said a silent prayer, and swallowed hard against the acid-burn rising up from his belly. "And now we must move on, friends, from the sufferings of one young boy to the sufferings of our world. We live in difficult and troubled times. We live in shadows cast by evil men. Those among you, who should be rejoicing in the fertility that God has granted you, instead hesitate, reluctant to bring new life into such a world as this. We look around at the pristine beauty that has been given to us; we see that beauty laid out before us like a field of virgin snow. And what have we done to that beauty?"

He turned his palms upwards as though awaiting an answer; but once that voice had started there was not a man or woman alive who would wish to hear their own intruding on it - the bishop excepted.

"Look closely. Can you see the ugly footprints everywhere, desecrating what the Lord has given? We live in godless times. No respect, no empathy, no responsibility. We are content with our failings, telling ourselves that this is a changing world, that anything and everything is acceptable. We are considered prudes and old-fashioned tyrants if we complain about moral standards; fascists if we speak out about raising our children to behave with the manners of bison -"

He turned his face into the arm of his cassock and tried to belch away the agonies building up inside him. It felt like a spare rib had wrapped itself around his heart and cheese was dripping into his lungs.

The belch brought little relief, but was executed with profound discretion. Only a handful of choirboys heard it, and most thought it only a poor impersonation of an animal they weren't familiar with, done for dramatic effect and aimed at lampooning their own habits.

"There has never been a time of greater urgency for good people everywhere to turn their backs on the growing tide of evil, and to embrace the Holy Spirit. All around, the signs are abundantly clear: we are moving ever deeper into the clutches of the Evil One. We talk of progress, of learning the lessons, harsh lessons, of the past. But what lessons have we learnt? What evidence is there that we have taken anything from all the pain and sorrow we have inflicted on ourselves as people? I tell you this, friends, we are going backwards. We are going backwards into darkness. We are going backwards into a night so dark that even the Lord himself won't come in to save us. Is that the legacy we want to leave behind? Is that the thanks we want to give to our Creator, our Redeemer?

"We don't have forever, anymore. I promise you this, friends: if we go on the way we're -"

COFFIN MAKER   MARK L. FOWLER

He clutched his chest and the congregation gripped its seats. Not an eye flickered. The drama of Father Henry's sermons had long guaranteed miraculous levels of attention from the congregation, and expectations were rising that a monumental finest hour had arrived.

But the priest, in spite of his agonies, wondered how many of them would understand his words, how many ever understood them. He suspected that many came for the sound rather than the meaning. Yet still he felt nothing but love for them. They were all, in their own unique ways, good people, and not one among them was undeserving of his affection. As imperfect as the Church itself, he thought. Wasn't that why he loved them?

There were two present who *would* understand. For them not a word from the pulpit was ever wasted. Brigadier Browning was one. And there, at the back of the left side-aisle, the nameless Old Man who could recite every sermon Father Henry had ever delivered, along with those of the three priests who'd preceded him.

Fighting against the pain, the priest pulled himself up to his full and humble height, a determined expression bearing down on the open-mouthed multitude.

"There is little time left. Out there a virus is growing. It isn't something that you need a microscope to see. Look around you and see it in the streets, on your televisions; hear it on your radios. I'm not a politician, friends, but it's a politician you should be afraid of. It's a politician who can - and if you let him, who will! - mobilise your hopes and your fears. Who will exploit your hopes and fears and turn you ever more deeply against each other until all mankind is at war with itself and the destruction of your world - God's world - becomes no longer the childish territory of feeble science-fiction, but a *waking nightmare.*

"He may come as a politician, or he may come as a warrior. He has many guises and we have to be vigilant, alert to his deviousness. Beware of this time of peace and prosperity. Yes, I know: it is a strange warning. It would be so much easier to be able to say, 'Beware all the chaos and misery that you see around you, for it is the perfect foundation for Hell on Earth.' So much more prosaic to say, 'Out of all this desperation and heartache, you are all in danger of turning, unknowingly, into the mouth of the dragon.'

"How easy, my friends, that would be. We've been there already, some of us; in our lifetimes we have lived it, watched the film, bought the shirt. I'm talking about war, brutal and bloody. And those among us who are too young to have witnessed it first hand, have nevertheless been shaped by it. Yet the scale that I'm talking about on this beautiful and peaceful, prosperous and heavenly morning - that is something none of us have seen or would want to imagine."

The pain cut loose inside the priest, holding aloft a sharpened scythe, freely playing its merry games inside his bloated body. He started back down the pulpit steps, gasping for breath.

No-one in the congregation moved. Every eye fixed on Father Henry's trembling descent. Feebly he muttered a word, a name. "Gouge." And again,

COFFIN MAKER   MARK L. FOWLER

"*Gouge*...he's coming...he's *coming*..." The Old Man and Brigadier Browning edged forward in their seats. Father Henry's strength had all but deserted him. "God save President Doveman," he gasped. "Church and State...heal together, no foothold cracks...places for evil to hide, grow..."

He fell towards the ground and was dead before he reached it.

Brigadier Browning and the Old Man folded forwards, soul-rich tears breaking through their fingers. They knew what had been lost.

And what was beginning...

The rest of the congregation sat in dazed confusion, the realisation of what had happened dawning slowly behind a clearing mist. They came forward in ones, in twos, in dozens to try to save their beloved priest.

"Gotcha!"

Smiling, and feeling a touch better all round, the Coffin Maker dropped his hammer to the floor and admired the completed coffin. Lovingly he ran his fleshless hands along its fine edges.

"Now that's craftsmanship!"

He turned back to his journal and wrote, *Gotcha,* underlining it for good measure. Underneath he added,

A very tricky customer finally dispatched. Last nail took some hammering. Must have hit a knot in the wood. Almost had to abandon the entire coffin and start from scratch. Some live forever on late night feasting.

COFFIN MAKER   MARK L. FOWLER

He placed his pen down and eased back on his chair. Wasn't it gloriously ironic? The priest writes something that's finally worth reading, and the bishop wants him to burn it. But what does a priest know about obeying orders?

On the rare occasions that they inadvertently hit on something real they call it fantasy. And the Church wants to destroy it. The biggest admirers of the rebel priest's ridiculous book happen to be the next two on my list. No immortality for you by the look of it Father Henry. That kind of baloney will hardly appeal to a thirteen year old boy still grieving for his mother.

The Coffin Maker pressed time forward again. He didn't understand time anymore than he understood the Divine Plan, though he knew he had power over time. At least to some extent. He could slow it down when he was busy and let it speed up a little when business was slack. For that matter he could slow it down, speed it up for whatever reasons took his fancy.

    The bad feeling was crawling back over him. To stay ahead of it he drove the final nails into the second coffin and then whipped time along a little to escape the settling blues.

    It would give the world a little respite from death.

COFFIN MAKER   MARK L. FOWLER

They wouldn't realise it, of course. They realised little of any consequence. More importantly it would allow him to cut straight to the funeral.

Somewhere in Zone Thirty-Nine, an old man was falling from a tree. Coffin, a moment later, was settling down to the formalities.

5: OLD MAN

For years it had been the Old Man's wish that, when his time came, Father Henry would conduct the funeral service. The incomparable priest would say whatever was left to be said.

It wasn't to be.

The last minute replacement, it was generally agreed, lacked not only the oratorical sorcery of Father Henry, but also the extraordinary compassion and the rare gift of convincing practically everyone he met that the repent sinner had nothing to fear in death.

The Old Man had said a few words at Father Henry's funeral, begging the hundreds who turned out to remember what the priest said in the last moments of his life. He'd reminded them of Father Henry's warnings; asked them to be fearful, vigilant, brave in the eye of the coming storm. Then he'd asked them to pray for President Doveman. "A voice of rare honesty rising out of, yet transcending, the sycophantic slag-heaps of political corruption that have for too long riddled this land. This planet. The devil is a politician. His name is not Doveman."

He asked that, in the absence of a leader of greater gifts, the nation rally around the best it had - and, in the present climate, the best it could hope for. He asked also that people pray for Brigadier Browning, whose already fragile health had crumbled in the immediate aftermath of Father Henry's death, "... and whose commitment to fighting oppression and tyranny over half a century proves that a true man of peace can, in any age, proudly wear a soldier's uniform."

COFFIN MAKER   MARK L. FOWLER

Brigadier Browning's deteriorating health caused him not only to miss the formal farewell to the priest, but also to miss the funeral of his other great friend. Robbed him of the chance to dip a final time into the river of stories and tears that had flowed over this one amazing life – across the decades, through every twist of war and peace, as the faithful remembered, recounted, the life of a man who had never been content to leave politics to the politicians, religion to the clergy, education to the teachers.

The Old Man's last days had been spent cultivating an obsession that for many was reason enough to disregard him as a senile old fool. An obsession with a man - if 'man' was the right word - talked of only in whispers. An unshakeable belief that the greatest threat to humanity was already here, walking the globe.

The Old Man died with the name on his lips. Died as he had lived, seeking justice and peace, and falling out of a tree attempting to rescue a neighbour's cat, two days away from his ninety-seventh birthday.

He would have considered it an honourable enough death, though he would have died more peacefully, more happily, if he'd been called from the world in the act of putting a bullet through the brain of *Colonel Gouge*.

Coffin picked up his pen. This bad feeling was taking some shifting. So much for the trick of time.

Cricketing metaphors and dull war stories. Some send off. At least I spared the miserable gathering the torture of a Father Henry eulogy. Not that I expect any thanks. I might have wasted some wood and nails along the way but that last nail was sublime. One soft old fool and one cat up a tree. The Poet has spoken.

Fine words, thought Coffin, though not fine enough. Sneering into the page, he couldn't resist a final flourish.

Maybe this next one will clear my head. This one's been as slippery as the last one. I've hounded him through war and revolution. Thinks he's going to see the birth of his grandchild. Nearly done now. Nearly done.

COFFIN MAKER   MARK L. FOWLER

6: BRIGADIER BROWNING

It was the best Brigadier Browning had felt for a long while. Stirred by the impending birth of his daughter's first child, he asked if he might be taken to the coast, taken along the sea-front for an hour to taste some real air, and blow the last cobwebs of illness out of his strengthening body.

He saw the beam of gratitude break across his son-in-law's face, silently thanking him for breaking up the gloom-clouds that death-carrying sickness had brought, casting its shadows over them all, robbing them of their full quota of happiness. It was a holy joy to see the skies clearing for the coming light of new life.

The wheelchair clattered along the promenade against a fresh wind. The startling sunshine in the midst of winter seemed to symbolise to both men the spirit of renewal and hope. Together they breathed in the rugged and beautiful scene.

An ice-cream van pulled up a few yards ahead of them, and it set off a train of thought. "Not a soul," said the brigadier, "not a solitary soul can be bothered to come to the ocean, to see it at its best, its wildest. They all wait for the lion to lie down. They wait for the queues of summer, the arcades and candy floss sellers, and the promenade littered with beer cans."

He looked again at the ice-cream van. It appeared somehow sad and lonely, miserably out of season; a little like how he felt himself, these days. This wasn't a time for old brigadiers, old men of war. Now the season was for peace only by peaceful means, and damn the cost in human suffering.

A little further on, he asked if they might stop awhile. His son-in-law turned him towards the ocean, and the two watched in awe at the power of the waves, forcing themselves angrily into huge and terrifying shapes.

Brigadier Browning couldn't stop thinking about the ice-cream van. It was absurdly out of place and time. He felt sympathy for it, waiting to serve a time gone by and maybe a time still to come.

"Tell you what," he said, suddenly. "Let's celebrate, let's have a treat. One of those tasteless monsters covered in raspberry sauce. And three flakes."

"Have you gone mad?" asked the younger man. "You hate ice-cream."

"I've hated a lot of things, and let me tell you: life's short. What do you say? I won't tell anyone."

The young man laughed. "Okay by me."

Brigadier Browning pulled a note from his wallet. "The biggest and the sickliest - and tell him to keep the change for making an old man happy."

While the young man headed back towards the waiting van, the brigadier watched the mighty sea batter the wall, and he licked at the salt spray, renewing his faith in the tenacity of life. Maybe the darkest hour was passing and a new dawn breaking over the world. Maybe President Doveman could bring the people to their senses and rip out this cancer before it choked the planet. Maybe President Doveman could break the stranglehold of lethargy that allowed vermin like Colonel Gouge to thrive.

But sombre thoughts soon cast a shadow over his optimism, and a chill passed through him as he remembered the night that Bishop Stones came knocking on his door.

Recruiting for a conference to raise the profile of the Church, Stones had spotted Father Henry's manuscript and asked if he might borrow it. The conference had immediately ceased to have any importance whatsoever, and the bishop had quickly made an exit, with Father Henry's manuscript clutched tightly under his arm.

The guilt, oh, the power of it. He'd meant to tell Father Henry, but events had taken their course. Seeing his friend in such torment at the end, he hadn't been able to shake the fear that he had been at least partly to blame. And then reports of the bishop's curiously lukewarm address at the funeral - hadn't that confirmed it?

Stones, by all accounts, had looked decidedly uncomfortable when the Old Man had made his own address at Father Henry's farewell, commending the priest's honesty "on the page as at the pulpit."

The bishop didn't even bother to attend the Old Man's funeral, and the brigadier couldn't help but see that as a calculated snub, a blatant act of spite, leaving a young and inexperienced cleric to officiate.

Had this chain of events occurred because he had been foolish enough to let Bishop Stones catch sight of Father Henry's manuscript?

The brigadier started to breathe hard as the hammers beat in his chest. He tried to steer his thoughts back to President Doveman, but in vain. All optimism

had fled, deserted him as a single, consuming thought spread like the dark wings of a raven across his mind: that the world had gone too far and learnt to tolerate too much.
That the world had come to deserve Colonel Gouge.
Browning tried to tear the thought away; deny himself the terror of lingering on it, focusing instead on his family's coming joy. As thoughts of his family started to broaden he found himself looking on the cycle of life, like a vast wheel spinning before him. He was overwhelmed by the clarity with which he was seeing the miracle of the world and the infinite richness and value of humanity.

Yet as the wheel spun ever more vividly he recognised that humanity was full of tears and crying out to be saved. With all his strength he prayed that God would grant Doveman the wisdom of the Saints in Heaven and the devil take Colonel Gouge.

The wind was starting to howl, and a tremendous wave exploded against the sea wall. Browning tried to stand, throw his arms around the spinning wheel of mankind, but all of his strength had deserted him and he fell back in the chair. Another huge explosion set up echoes in his mind, carrying him back through the years to the nights of war, rushing forward to nights of happiness in the bed of his marriage, to the birth of their daughter, the death of his wife, and then, in a gigantic arc, he was back at the fireside with his own father and mother, looking at the photograph of his eldest brother who never came home from the sea.

COFFIN MAKER   MARK L. FOWLER

Carrying two giant ice-creams, Brigadier Browning's son-in-law ran back through the lashing storm that had broken from nothing. The rain was beating hard on Brigadier Browning, though his eyes were closed in an attitude of serene peace that stopped the younger man in his tracks and sent the ice-creams hurtling to the ground. Kneeling down, he folded himself around the dead soldier as though he needed protection from the lashing rain.

Coffin raised a triumphant fist. *Now* he felt on top of the bad feeling.
    The jubilation brought with it a transformation in his thinking. He was seeing his apprentices in two very different lights. A halo was developing around Beezle, whilst something closer to a pitchfork was growing in the hand of Hieronymus.
    Coffin turned to a fresh page of his journal.

A poetic ending I think. Only wish I could get young Hieronymous to appreciate the Poetry of Death. Beginning to despair of that young man. He isn't lazy and he has intelligence. But sometimes I'll swear that while I'm working myself inside out getting them into their coffins he's doing his utmost to keep them in their miserable skins. Wish he could be more like Beezle. No second chances with him. If I can harness some of the wilder aspects of young Beezle's enthusiasm then we really might see the growth of a truly magnificent Coffin Maker.

COFFIN MAKER   MARK L. FOWLER

He blinked at what he had written, and then quickly scratched out the word 'magnificent', and lowered the case to 'coffin maker'.

This done he set to completing a smaller coffin. A coffin of just the right size to welcome a new arrival into the world. Busy grinning into the metal face of his hammer, repeating the mantra that he had once picked up from an old play by some idiot by the name of Shakespeare, "Out, out brief candle."

So busy was the Coffin Maker that he failed to notice one of his young apprentices sneaking a hand around the door, and stealing a single nail.

The shock of her father's sudden death threw Brigadier Browning's daughter headlong into labour, bringing his grandchild into the world within hours of his death. Tense minutes passed in the ambulance and in the maternity ward as a life and death struggle ebbed back and forth between its opposite poles.

But the last nail was missing.

The Coffin Maker had never mislaid a nail. Not in uncountable millennia had the Poet of Death mislaid a nail.

He hissed and seethed and cursed and screamed in fury as he searched for its replacement. But it was in his hand a fraction too late, and the proud and exhausted mother, father, and half the maternity wing finally collapsed into a roar of triumph as courage, faith and the instinct of life gave the green light to a new survivor.

Coffin glared down on the scene. His fury inconsolable, he stormed through the Coffin Complex

COFFIN MAKER   MARK L. FOWLER

like a tempest, until his wild skeleton at last resumed some control over its collective parts. The remainder of his anger found expression in furious scribbling as he held his pen with the grip of a strangler.

It was two pages before the vicious scrawl became decipherable.

Confound that nail. My carelessness might cost me three score years and ten of wholly avoidable labours. Hieronymus didn't seem too cut up though he seems to have had a delayed reaction. Caught him wiping tears from his face. Looked embarrassed when he saw me. I reassured him that we can't win every time. Reminded him that at least we got the brigadier. Started blubbing again. I left him to it. It can only be a good sign. Can only mean the escape of the newborn has touched a professional nerve. Gives me hope. Gives me something to work on. Perhaps I've misjudged Hieronymus after all.

Coffin sat back and reflected. It seemed that the bad feeling was going to take some shifting. His mind didn't want to settle, the irritation gnawing again. There was something distinctly different about those last three coffins.

Something unprecedented.

He picked up his pen to let out a little more frustration.

First Beezle and Hieronymus now this. What have I done to deserve it? What sins? Have I been too hard on

COFFIN MAKER   MARK L. FOWLER

the world? Or too soft? Has the world forgotten who I am? Must I remind it?

He lost himself for a while in fruitless thoughts, before putting down his pen and turning to the monitor.

It was time for his Round the World.

At regular intervals, Coffin would engage in his ritual of scanning the Earth, zone by zone. He found zones far better than countries and had long abandoned human place names altogether. They couldn't leave them alone; forever tinkering with them. It was one of the unfortunate side-effects of war.

That and the human tendency to mess constantly and reinvent at every opportunity.

So he'd taken the liberty of carving the world to his own convenience and sticking immovable numbers on the results. A zone was a zone and that was that. There were seven hundred and seventy seven of them. That was how it was and how it would always be. His Round the World started at Zone One and worked through to the end.

He enjoyed them, to a point, though it wasn't as good as writing in his journal and paled completely against making coffins. Yet it wasn't bad, and was an opportunity to assess strategies and maintain an overall balance and perspective, to gauge trends, nipping unfortunate ones in the bud.

Seven hundred and seventy seven zones later, Coffin reached for his journal. He chewed the end of his pen until his teeth were hurting, then wrote,

COFFIN MAKER   MARK L. FOWLER

I don't like it. I don't like it and I don't know why. Spent too much time with those damned apprentices. Whatever's taken seed down there doesn't know the meaning of childhood. I've never known germination like it.

He took a moment to evaluate the appropriateness of the 'seed-germination' image, concluding that it was of the first order. But the poet's joy was momentary.

I missed the signs. I've never missed them before. Perhaps I'm worrying too much over too little. Perhaps I will look back on the Zone Thirty-Nine Affair and tell myself for the last time that there is nothing new that can happen under the sun.

His fingers were trembling.

Perhaps...

COFFIN MAKER   MARK L. FOWLER

7: HIERONYMUS

Coffin swept the monitor over Zone Thirty-Nine until he was ready to scream. He was damned if he could pin it down, whatever it was. It was there, somewhere, but hang it and bathe it in acid if it wasn't the slipperiest customer he'd ever come across.

Or tried to come across.

At last he gave it up and turned his attentions to a different problem.

Hieronymus.

That business with the missing nail was troubling him. No, *Hieronymus* was troubling him.

He didn't add up. An impossible equation. Try the sum this way, that way, the figures refused to compute. But it would take more than a paradox on legs to defeat the mind of the Coffin Maker. He was a professional! A craftsman! An artist! He would rise nobly to the challenge of difficult youth because the Coffin Maker never shirked from a challenge. The big occasion never had and never would find him wanting in the application of his duties. He'd worked like a thing possessed through two world wars in the twentieth century alone. Yes, and he'd done it - alone!

"War," he'd told Hieronymus, in reply to the youngster's impertinent suggestion that all conflict demonstrated a wanton desperation, lack of control and abandonment of professional integrity, "War, young man, is sometimes the only way one has of meeting figures."

He hadn't much cared for the look on the youth's face, casting its naive doubts on the judgement of the

COFFIN MAKER MARK L. FOWLER

master. For that matter, neither was he over-struck with the youngster's appalling freshness and striking good looks. If the Creator, in his *infinite wisdom,* had seen fit to fashion the Coffin Maker with the sour countenance of vanquished youth, why was it necessary to sprinkle every gift of beauty and spring-like promise on this young pretender?

No, he didn't like it, didn't like it one bit; and he'd said so, many times, in the pages of his journal.

Unblemished skin and crystal eyes are not the essential tools of the skilled craftsman. Neither is an absurd preoccupation with old age. This youth knows he will never be old yet he seems determined to bestow the ridiculous qualities of old age on every creature the Creator turns out.

Take last night.

Hours I'd spent coordinating the new flu-virus project. Young Beezle had sweated over hundreds of coffins with an industry that would have worried me if it hadn't brought tears of what humans would no doubt call fatherly joy *to my eyes. And where's Hieronymus in all this? Supposed to be covering so-called Third World hospitals. Supposed to be cutting his teeth on some major league medical incompetence that would have left them piling corpses five high in the streets.*

A clear enough brief! Get in there and take no prisoners!

But instead he secures the arrival of Western Aid taking more time than a senile cabbage to place sentimental brass name plates on the coffins. Seventy

COFFIN MAKER   MARK L. FOWLER

five percent of those coffins ended up going to waste. Brass plates and all!
   Now that should have been enough incompetence for one night. Not enough for young Hieronymous though. Had to borrow Beezle's screwdriver to fix the brass plates. Didn't tell Beezle. Beezle's left charging around like a sunburnt scorpion trying to finish seven hundred coffins before some bright spark at the medical institute can come up with a wonder drug that annihilates the flu-virus!

Coffin had sensed trouble the day Hieronymus arrived. It wasn't enough that the Creator saw fit to bless the youth with encyclopaedic knowledge of world history. More dangerously, he'd twinned that knowledge with something suspiciously close to a moral conscience. Worse - if worse could be imagined - the youth had an unsettling weakness for the philosophical, and was liable at any moment to ask the most outrageous – not to mention downright awkward - questions. Barely had Coffin finished shaking the youth's hand on their first meeting, when he had been asked, "Why *Coffin?*"
   "Why anything?" replied Coffin, with a superior smile. "Why...*Hieronymus?*"
   Coffin had quite enjoyed the little interchange up to that point, amply demonstrating that it would take more than a mere apprentice to put one over on the Coffin Maker.
   What he hadn't liked was the grave and shocking impertinence that had followed.
   "Everything has a purpose, a reason. *Hieronymus*, for example, might seem to imply the

COFFIN MAKER   MARK L. FOWLER

notion of the hero. But what does Coffin signify? Insignificance? Methodical industry, perhaps? The mundanity of death, maybe? Is someone trying to tell you something, Mr. *Coffin*?"

It hadn't been a good start.

Coffin remembered, bitterly, showing his apprentices a poem he had written. How he had anticipated their amazement at the range of his talents. Beezle, granted, had looked suitably impressed - though when pressed on the point said he found poetry too gentle, too mannered, too...pointless. Recognising something more cultured in Hieronymus' manner, Coffin had turned his attention toward the youth, and what a fine time he'd had, revealing in detail every aspect of his poetic technique and sparing no technicality.

"Ever heard of Swinburne?" asked Hieronymus.

"I've heard of everyone. Swinburne you say?"

"The poet."

"I seem to remember him, yes. Was he any better than that fool Shakespeare?"

"He had his moments."

"Name one."

Hieronymus' eyes widened. "As a god self-slain on his own strange altar, Death lies dead."

"That isn't funny."

"It wasn't meant to be."

"There's a great deal of difference between a dead poet and the Poet of Death."

"Is that so? Tell me, what's your creed?"

"Creed?"

"Okay, philosophy, then."

COFFIN MAKER   MARK L. FOWLER

"Philosophy I leave to the mortals. It seems to amuse them."

"I'll put it another way," said Hieronymus. "With only so much space down there, did the Creator need a terminator to ease the congestion?"

"Terminator?"

"Maybe the Creator's grown dissatisfied with his terminator. Hence the arrival of myself and Beezle."

Coffin's mouth had fallen open.

But Hieronymus hadn't finished.

Youth had been about to cut like a razor.

"Perhaps human history has disappointed the Creator."

"That wouldn't surprise me at all," said Coffin, triumphantly, stifling the urge to drive a nail through that pretty alabaster forehead.

"Perhaps," said Hieronymus, "the Creator hoped the world would come to reflect the great imagination he had bestowed on his creations, and not simply represent the warped and immoral practices of your good self."

"And what do you know of the world?" spat Coffin.

"Everything."

A touch phased by this reply, it took a moment to effect some repair work to his thinking, beating the wilder thoughts back into some kind of order.

Then inspiration struck – and struck hard. He had to fight the urge to go rushing back to his journal to write the sentence down before its poetic majesty could evaporate.

COFFIN MAKER   MARK L. FOWLER

Standing his ground he delivered the immortal words right between Hieronymus' ears. Point blank. *Bang*.

"I, young man, *created* world history."

Hieronymus hadn't looked impressed. "I'm talking about the history of life, not death. What fascinates me is their endless striving, their unfathomable resilience and resource. I'm interested in their achievements and in their capacity for good, not just a smooth finish to their coffins."

Coffin had been rendered temporarily speechless.

Hieronymus had not been so afflicted.

"The world degenerated quickly into petty arguments. You, *Mr. Coffin*, with your obsession with figures, introduced the petty argument along with its logical development, the full scale row. You nurtured disagreement and conflict; you worked up jealousies, hammered at the moulds of covetousness and pride. You conjured murder, you showed the way to war. But war was only one of your little ways of keeping up your figures. Because you, *Mr. Coffin*, decided that illness and natural disaster would serve your industry and you gloried in them."

Coffin had regained his powers of speech, though for the moment seemed unsure how to use them. A faint squeak issued from his quivering mouth. He coughed some venom back into his voice. "I make coffins. When a new life is conceived I start work on the coffin. That is not something I choose. That is the way the Creator made things. At every stage of every

COFFIN MAKER   MARK L. FOWLER

life I'm working at the coffin. When it's completed, a journey in the mortal world ends. Do you understand?"

The sudden violence in Coffin's voice threatened to burst the stony Adam's apple clear out of his throat.

Hieronymus grinned. "What you're saying is that you hound every living creature from its cradle to its coffin. Yes, I think I understand."

"I'm the Coffin Maker! What else can I do?"

"Well, I hope that's what I'm here to show you," said Hieronymus.

Coffin, almost in flames, rasped, "Show me? *Show me!* You are the apprentice and it is I who will show you if I have to knock every bone out of your body. I make coffins. How and when they end up in those coffins is up to me. But they all have to end up in one."

Coffin remembered the look on the young apprentice's face. It had unnerved him then and it unnerved him now as he thought back on it.

It had been a look of rebellion. Defiance. Yet missing had been any trace of spite or malice. As though the youth, for all his slanderous impertinence, bore him no ill will.

Coffin flicked back through his journal, to the page he had written soon after the encounter. He scanned the searing fury stamped into paragraph after paragraph, until he came to a curious passage near the bottom of the page. The passage seemed almost as odd as the look itself had been.

COFFIN MAKER   MARK L. FOWLER

It wasn't hate I saw on that face today. It was pity. Because that youth knows or thinks he knows something dangerous. Thinks he knows something that he can't or daren't put into words.

He's hiding his thoughts behind a cheap web of philosophy and a fabricated belief that I'm responsible for the misery of the mortal world. But that youth has an infernal conscience and if he really believed I alone caused all that he accused me of causing then I'd have seen real hate in his eyes. But I didn't see hate. I know what I saw. I saw pity. But I'm damned if I know why. Whatever knowledge is taking seed inside that mind I want to know it.

But I'll let it grow awhile. I'll let it flower and bear fruit.

And then I'll have it out of him.

Coffin stopped reading. The passage had taken off again on the wings of fury, and another fifty lines had been spent cursing and spitting in increasingly indecipherable scribble.

He sat and reflected on the strange words, and the memory of the look on the youth's face. Could it really have been pity? It didn't make any more sense now than then. All his close attention to Hieronymus had yielded nothing but exasperation and muddle.

He thought again of the youth's remarks about his name. What kind of a name was *Coffin*, after all? What had the Creator meant by calling him the Coffin Maker? It had never crossed his mind before. He'd seen a billion names come and go but he'd never given a thought to his own.

COFFIN MAKER   MARK L. FOWLER

And why should he? Until now, who had there been to call him anything? Mortals had long forgotten that a supreme craftsman called the Coffin Maker was responsible for their earthly destinies. And the Creator wasn't exactly one for dropping in to say, "Hello, Coffin, old mate, how are you doing?"

The youth's words echoed in his mind, "*What does Coffin signify? Insignificance? Methodical industry? The mundanity of death? Maybe someone is trying to tell you something...Maybe someone is trying to tell you something...Maybe someone is trying to tell you something, Coffin...Coffin...Coffin...*"

He slammed a fist down heavily, causing an unsightly bruise to appear on the flesh coloured page. Why was he letting a mere apprentice get to him - an apprentice who showed no aptitude whatsoever for his (presumably) chosen occupation? No recognition of the value of death; no respect for his elder and better, and a naive and loathsome pursuit of so-called honesty that held no room for tact and diplomacy.

And the rancorous cherry on the cake: a complete lack of appreciation for fine poetry!

And so it was that Coffin gave himself a talking to; demanding that he pull himself together immediately and concentrate on the business of making coffins.

That and trying to salvage some worth out of that pretty piece of philosophical junk that the Creator, in all his increasingly questionable wisdom, had chosen to send him.

Then he turned his attentions, reminding himself that every coin has two sides.

And thought of Beezle.

8: BEEZLE

How can two creatures made by one Creator be so different? Is this a testament to the greatness of the Creator? Or to his uncertainty? Or the first manifestations of insanity?

Coffin let the ink of this last thought dry before thinking better of the blasphemy and ripping the page into confetti. It seemed a pity to waste such fine words, but blasphemy could be a dangerous business, even for Death's own Poet. He turned over the two-sided enigma until his brain was bursting, and was not a shred wiser for his efforts, which he abandoned, giving his full attention to the flame-haired one.

Industry. Hunger. Imagination. Oodles in every department. His Eastern projects alone were nothing less than breathtaking in their audacity. He enjoys the larger canvass. Multiple work. Loves numbers. Big numbers. A meticulous planner. Not so strong on domestic one-offs. Seems to think they're beneath him. Have to tame this arrogance if I'm to make a craftsman of him. Suspect a malicious streak. If I'm not mistaken there's some ugly resentment at missing the Great Wars. Seems to have it in for the Creator on that score. Yet making excellent progress. Recognises craftsmanship and is not afraid to pay it due respects. Will go far. Will make a big noise one day in the world of coffins.

Something about him though that -

COFFIN MAKER   MARK L. FOWLER

Coffin broke off, his pen hovering indecisively over the page.

Reluctant to commit the thought to paper, he resolved to return to it later, turning instead to the monitor to watch a bubble of excitement rise above all the other bubbles that were constantly bursting over the World.

In Zone Fifty-One there was a deathbed silence that unnerved even the spiders and snakes.

Out of the desert stillness, came the flash of steel and the roar of engines. In seconds the horizon was in flames. The sound of human screams seemed to last forever, outlived only by the smell of burning flesh. Two-hundred and fourteen people had been on board the plane.

Yet what brought the mark of virtuosity to the desert, was the completion of seven-hundred and eleven coffins corresponding to the workforce and families living in the shadows of the oil instillation. To Coffin this, above all, marked extraordinary talent and, quite possibly, genius.

He switched off the monitor, and let out a long breath. The moment begged to be recorded.

Young Beezle is coming of age. His speed. His coordination. Truly breathtaking. I have not a single doubt that Beezle has limitless potential as a maker of coffins. It is my duty to watch his emotional development. Virtuosity has value only in the hands of the sane and the disciplined.

COFFIN MAKER   MARK L. FOWLER

He stopped for a moment to admire the poetry of the phrase, then added, impressively he thought,

Coffin making demands craftsmen not expressionistic banana heads.

Closing his journal, the ragbag assortment of bones in motion moved with remarkable strength and purpose across the Coffin Complex towards the Coffin Dome.

The Coffin Complex was partly the Coffin Maker's inheritance and partly his creation. Accordingly, he both loathed and treasured it.

He inherited the unnatural, unknowable location of the Kingdom of Death, along with its almost infinite emptiness. He inherited also the four buildings - Office, Tower, Vaults and Dome - that alone disturbed its surface, and which he collectively called the Coffin Complex.

The circular building at the centre housed his living quarters and his office. The numerous other rooms lay empty. His living quarters were also unused. He had found very early in his career that a Coffin Maker has no time or inclination for the mortal pursuits of sleep and play. His office was his real home. It was here that he wrote his journal and lavished the best part of his craftsman's skill, making individual coffins at every conceivable pace. The two peculiar attachments that ruined the perfection of the circular construction were the clumsily erected quarters of his apprentices.

On his one and only pre-apprentice visit to the Tower, Coffin had noticed, looking down from that

COFFIN MAKER   MARK L. FOWLER

high place, that the circular construction was a perfect full moon. On subsequent visits he saw how the two lopsided ears blasphemed against the perfect moon, and it saddened him. He had built the extensions himself, placing them at opposite sides in case of a conspiracy against him. It hadn't taken him long to rid himself of that anxiety: Hieronymus and Beezle were too opposed to conspire about anything, except each others' destruction.

Forming a triangle due north of the ruined moon-face stood the Coffin Vaults, the Tower and the Coffin Dome.

The Vaults, to the left, above the ear inhabited by Hieronymus, resembled an immense tunnel and contained every coffin ever made, stored in order of completion, with its earliest occupants farthest back.

The Tower, standing at the tip of the Complex, and looking down mightily with a sardonic grin, was a complete mystery to Coffin. It was a ridiculously tall monstrosity comprising a huge and tortuous staircase with a single room at the top.

He had walked to the top on that first, strange visit, driven upwards by sheer curiosity, and baffled to find a key waiting in the lock. Entering the room cautiously he had been surprised, and not a little relieved, to find it empty. The window at the far end offered an unparalled view of the Coffin Complex, but Coffin had no intention of ever making the journey again; and he'd cursed discreetly at such a waste of materials on the Creator's part. He'd made a swift exit that day, relieved to be safely back in his quarters and

COFFIN MAKER   MARK L. FOWLER

relieved that he could think of not a single reason why he would ever have to venture there again.

Above the right ear invisibly marked 'Beezle', stood the Dome. It was the Dome, above all, that encapsulated Coffin's ambivalence. The power of the place thrilled him while its potential unsettled him. It filled him, every time and in equal measure, with joy and repugnance. Every machine, every conveyor belt had been made by him, and he alone had engineered its devastating unity.

It had started off modestly enough, to cope with the growing numbers. But as the technology of mankind developed, and with it the capacity for death on an ever expanding scale, so Coffin had expanded its capabilities, until the Coffin Dome reached its present, gargantuan proportions. To see and hear those giants clank and grind into action stirred poetry in the Coffin Maker without fail, until the recognition of mass-production would also, without fail, force him to bemoan the fact that the human race had ever grown so large and so capable of fulfilling its own paradoxical will to destruction. And though so much of the Coffin Dome had been his own work, he dimly recognised that its apparently limitless capacity for expansion, suggested pre-ordained growth.

Entering the Dome with his usual ambivalence raging, Coffin was knocked back by the deafening roar of the machines. "What the...?"

Guarding his ears with two bony digits, he hurried past the impressive rows of conveyor belts, all laden heavily with coffins, all groaning beyond capacity. Moving through his vast armies of machinery

COFFIN MAKER   MARK L. FOWLER

he saw that not one of them was idle, not one square foot of his workshop free from the business of making coffins. Had some fault occurred in the system, pressing his precious tools towards destruction, he wondered, following the sound of heavy banging that was breaking through the general cacophony.

He stopped. Took a moment or two to make certain that what he was seeing was not some mental aberration occurring on the inside of his own head.

No. It was real. He was stuck with it.

There, at the centre of the workshop, hammering nails six at a time into coffin after coffin, stood Beezle. A crazed version of Beezle.

Coffin watched in awe at the vitality and fever that was running his workshop at near meltdown.

The speed; the accuracy; the sheer virtuosity.

Astonishing.

Long seconds passed before fear of the damage being done to the tools of his beloved trade crept back over the Coffin Maker, breaking the spell.

Without losing another second he grabbed Beezle's arm as it descended towards another row of perfectly aligned nails, causing the apprentice to spin around. Coffin stepped back, shaken by the savagery in Beezle's dark eyes, the fiery youth's hand still gripping the raised hammer.

The coffins were piling up as the conveyor belts continued relentlessly, yet it still took a considerable effort of will on the part of the Coffin Maker, to tear himself free of the hypnotic fury seething from Beezle's unrelenting stare, and cover the distance to the main

COFFIN MAKER   MARK L. FOWLER

control unit, pulling decisively on the central lever and bringing the workshop to an immediate and silent halt.

Coffin turned to reveal a look of splintered bone. Then walked slowly towards the stunned apprentice. "What the hell do you think you are doing?"

"Making coffins, sir."

Beezle's glare had softened beyond recognition, respect now oozing from dumb eyes. "I only wanted to please you," he whined. "I'm sorry if I have disappointed you."

Coffin felt his bones creaking into a smile. "You haven't disappointed me. I'm impressed by your industry. I was only concerned that you may be working the equipment a little too hard. Repairs take time. Do you understand?"

Beezle nodded, humbly. "It's just that I'm nearing completion of my Eastern Project. I was trying to complete thirty thousand coffins in time for the midnight earthquake, sir."

Coffin gasped. "Thirty thousand? I thought we'd agreed eight."

Beezle closed his eyes, lowered his head and whispered, "Sorry."

Coffin rested his hand on Beezle's head. "You have nothing to be sorry for, other than natural youthful exuberance. Come, we'll work together. Thirty thousand, you say?"

And so, like father and son, the two of them slaved to meet the midnight deadline. The Coffin Dome had never witnessed such a night. Even in the most frenetic days of the Great Wars, days of monumental slaughter when numbers had exceeded the efforts of

COFFIN MAKER   MARK L. FOWLER

this awful double act - even in those merciless days and nights there had at least been a dancing rhythm, a living pulse.

In those ferocious times there had at least been a recognisable *beat*.

Now the feel was different. Now the pulse, the beat, the rhythm of the dance was grotesquely distorted. If this was a dance at all, it was for horned creatures with three-pronged spears and firelighters. It was a dance with *no* rhythm, and what had replaced rhythm was as disturbing as it was indefinable.

Coffin tried to rationalise the oddness of the feeling; tried putting it down to working with another after millennia of working alone. Yet even to him the rationalisation seemed desperate, and in no time at all the need for it was gone. For Beezle's enthusiasm infected Coffin increasingly as the deadline approached, the old craftsman pushing his own machinery close to overload.

The first rumbles of the earthquake were breaking the silence in the valley where thirty thousand people slept. Hammers and nails bombarded the last few timbers and the fate of a few 'lucky ones' hung in the balance. A handful might crawl from a wrecked community hidden from civilisation; might live to tell the world of the horrors of the night that a killer came from the ground and ate seven thousand years of history, and thirty thousand human beings.

The last coffin had the privilege of the two slaves of death pouring nails into it, and felt their final blows at the stroke of midnight, the appointed hour of darkness as thirty thousand, one hundred and seventy-

COFFIN MAKER   MARK L. FOWLER

nine innocent souls disappeared into the night, leaving the world, unnoticed by the world.

Coffin and Beezle collapsed, exhausted and triumphant.

A night to remember.

Later, returning to his quarters full of the urgent need to relieve himself of much poetry, Coffin noticed a light on in the quarters of his other apprentice. So unblemished was his mood following a night of such industry, that he inadvertently found himself touched by a strange yet oddly familiar emotion.

Perhaps he had misjudged Hieronymus. Perhaps the youth needed time to adjust to the job. Not everyone could be blessed with the natural talents of the exceptional Beezle.

A burst of optimism took hold. Could it be that Hieronymus was, even at this late hour, engaging in his profession? What else would keep youth from its sleep?

Coffin peered around the door of the shambolic ragged ear, his heart beating with the anticipated joy of seeing his second son coming of age. Gazing into the room he could see Hieronymus lying on the floor, holding something close to his face.

Then the wayward apprentice started to cry, soft tears falling like drugged acrobats down his smooth cheeks.

Coffin shook his head. It wasn't right that an apprentice should brazenly cry over beauty like some sixth-form mummy's boy.

Unless it was one of his poems?

COFFIN MAKER   MARK L. FOWLER

Now that was a different matter. A different matter altogether.

Hope surged again in the Coffin Maker, yet a few steps into the room quickly dispelled that hope. He could see now that the object was something small, something that glinted in the light. And he could make out a bigger object, there, at the youth's feet. A coffin. Virtually completed. He crept closer, keeping his eyes trained on the object in the youth's hand, watching the tears splashing off it. Could it be...?

It was! He might have guessed!

Coffin stood glaring over the prostrated figure. "It's a nail, Hieronymus. A coffin nail."

"I know," said the youth, heavily. "Isn't it tragic?"

The Coffin Maker exploded. "It helps fasten the lid down on such an article as you have at your feet. In other words, my dull-witted one, a coffin!"

Hieronymus said nothing, his wet eyes fixed sadly on the nail.

"And how long have you been looking at that particular nail?"

No answer.

"Any idea how me and Beezle have been spending the evening?"

Nothing.

"Then let me tell you. We've been making thirty thousand coffins. We've had the workshop the width of a coffin-nail from meltdown. And why have we been pushing ourselves and our tools to such limits? I'll tell you why. To meet a deadline. Because we are professionals. Because we understand the meaning of

COFFIN MAKER   MARK L. FOWLER

hard work. Because we value the sense of satisfaction gained from doing a difficult job well and - and let me underline the word for you - doing it to a DEADLINE!

"And while we've been skinning our hands at the very threshold of endurance, you've been sitting here staring at a nail. Am I getting the picture through - a certain discrepancy between your commitment and the efforts of your fellow apprentice? Do the wooden planks of your philosophical thoughts allow my simple words to form little pictures on the inside of your dunderhead?"

Hieronymus took a deep breath and looked, pathetically, at Coffin. "I'm afraid I have found myself in a dilemma," he said.

"Have you now," said Coffin. "Better tell me about it, and better tell me *now.*"

"I've been working on a coffin for this particular lady, Ethel Mans-"

"Spare me the names," said Coffin, trying to steady his anger.

"Well, it seemed her time had arrived and -"

"Arrived? Over-due, I'd say. She's ninety three, damn it!"

"Anyway, she was disappearing into the night as I worked on the last few nails. But, and please don't take this badly-"

"Just say it, Hieronymus. Just take care of saying it and I'll take care of how I take it."

"Well, I was close to completing the coffin when I heard one of her thoughts. One that I must have overlooked. You see, I had the idea that she was dying

COFFIN MAKER　　　MARK L. FOWLER

fulfilled. Her daughters both have successful careers, even her granddaughters are doing extremely well -"

Coffin put a hand over his face and groaned. "Just come to the point."

"Well, to cut a long story -"

"If you could."

"It's her younger brother, you see. She never had chance to say a proper goodbye to him. They'd once been close, but grown apart. It happens -"

"I know it does," said Coffin. "It's *heartbreaking.*"

"And now he was travelling to see her, to put things right between them before it was too late, and I was holding the final nail in my hand and -"

"Stop! Do you hear me? Do you know what you've done? You've missed the boat - again! Your hesitation has consigned yet another empty coffin to the junkyard. She will have changed - ever so slightly - but changed nonetheless. You've missed the death call and now you will have to start on a new coffin to accommodate the differences. Do you know what else you've done?"

But before Hieronymus had chance to answer, Coffin told him.

"You've proved beyond doubt that you are an incompetent fool who refuses to learn."

"I wouldn't agree with you there," said Hieronymus. "I think that's an unfair summing up."

"Really?"

"Yes, as a matter of fact –"

COFFIN MAKER   MARK L. FOWLER

"Enough. I have nothing more to say to you, but believe me, I'll have plenty to say to the Creator. You would do well to count your days here numbered."

Coffin left a bemused Hieronymus to count his numbered days, and headed back to his office. What was the Creator playing at? Was he trying to ruin the coffin making business completely? And if so, why send such huge potential in the shape of Beezle?

It made no sense.

He sat at his desk and tried consoling himself, repeating, loudly, that he was the Coffin Maker, the Poet of Death, not some mortal that could be replaced by another generation. Not some insignificant servant of death. Dammit he *was* death! And what he didn't know about death wasn't worth knowing and would never be worth knowing.

Needing comfort, he let his thoughts travel back once more to the day the Creator introduced him to the first mortals. How proud he had felt on that glorious morning, shaking hands with those nervous creatures, announcing that work on their coffins was underway and progressing nicely. How proud feeling the warmth of the Creator's presence, hearing the Creator announcing that the Coffin Maker was not to be feared in his work, but to be revered as a great artist, perfectly conceived as the Poet of Death. How fear had melted from those fragile creatures. How they had warmed to the Poet in that stupendous garden. How utterly *dream* like it had all been.

He thought again of his apprentices. How like Hieronymus he had been that day in his sensitivity.

COFFIN MAKER   MARK L. FOWLER

Yes, it was true. And yet at the same time how like Beezle in his professional, clinical precision, and in the vastness of his ambition.

Balance.

That was the key.

Coffin tensed. Felt a shudder sweep the length of his skeleton frame. Suddenly he didn't like the implications of such thoughts. Suddenly he felt unsure of the dangers lurking down in the shadows of such comparisons.

In that chilling moment he made up his mind to do two things. He would, for the first time in the History of Life and Death, request, formally, a meeting with the Creator. Get things ironed out. Demand some clarity. Some answers.

But first there was unfinished business in the pages of his journal. There was a sentence to finish. A sentence about the saner half of this crazy apprenticeship scheme.

A sentence about Beezle.

He opened his journal and looked scornfully at the unfinished line: *Something about him though that -*

"Scares me!" he said, mockingly. "That's what you were going to write, you fool. "

Taking up his pen he scratched heavily into the page, *INSPIRES ME!!!*

Admiring his boldness for a moment, the choice of words still failed to satisfy. Was he really inspired by Beezle? Was there really anything in either apprentice that reminded him of himself?

Didn't he just want his solitude back and be rid of the pair of them?

COFFIN MAKER   MARK L. FOWLER

It wasn't like him to ask so many questions. It wasn't like him to feel so unblessed of knowledge. Yet one thing he did know: the sooner he was face to face with the Creator, getting down to the fundamentals of what in damnation was going on, the better it would be all round.

He was sick of it, all this fooling around, and the Creator was going to know it and answer for it.

In fact, Coffin decided, there and then – it was time to lay his cards squarely on the table. "Either reveal, once and for all, my part – at least – in the Divine Plan, or else start doing your own dirty work."

COFFIN MAKER   MARK L. FOWLER

9: THE CREATOR

When it came to it, Coffin had absolutely no idea how to get in touch with the Creator. Communication had – on the rare occasions that it had occurred at all – always been a strictly one-way affair.

Since that first glorious day in the Earthly garden, the air wild with promise, Coffin's only contact with the Creator had been that wretched note sailing past his window, thanking him for an eternity of loyal service by destroying his solitude.

Oh, he'd raised an angry fist and demanded an explanation. But the only explanation forthcoming had been an intense pain leaving him almost in tears on the floor. At the time it had seemed wiser to let the matter drop.

With this painful memory in mind, Coffin moved cautiously, penning a polite note which he left outside his door. And if his actions resembled a child waiting for Father Christmas or perhaps the Tooth Fairy, then like all faithful children, he was not to be disappointed...

Coffin called an emergency meeting.

The punctuality of Hieronymus and Beezle bore only a superficial resemblance. To arrive at Coffin's office on the stroke of midday had taken two very different kinds of effort. For Beezle it had meant the sacrifice of one hundred and fifty coffins planned around a spectacular rock slide in a remote and unsuspecting village. How narrowly they would escape death. How unfairly they would cheat the Reaper.

COFFIN MAKER   MARK L. FOWLER

And for what? A meeting? A meeting when time was so precious. Killing time. *Killing* time.

For Hieronymus the summons had given rise to fears that his sabotage in Zone Nineteen had gone too far. That after sixteen bloody years and steadily rising death-tolls, the cease-fire would be seen as too characteristic of his moral conscience.

Coffin marched into his office, eyeing the two apprentices keenly. How different they looked, standing there, side by side: one so tall and straight, cretinously beautiful, the other so bent and twisted, charmingly repulsive. Silky black hair and dazzling green eyes against black, starless eyes and jagged orange curls.

It seemed to sum up the Creator: real talent recognised by the mark of ugliness while vain beauty paraded as a thin veil for sloth and incompetence.

Coffin closed the door and opened the meeting. "Gentlemen, I took the liberty of sending a note to the Creator. The content of that note directly concerns you both. I have requested that only one of you remains with me. Also I have tried to establish the purpose of this apprentice-scheme, particularly in terms of where it leaves my good self."

Pleased with the pompous sense of importance he was bringing to the occasion, he almost neglected to bring in a tone of brutal irony.

Almost.

"The Creator, *in his infinite wisdom,* has allowed a note to sail out of Heaven to *grace our little gathering.* It is reminiscent of the one other *correspondence* He *saw fit to send me,* not so long ago. But a word of warning: *Heaven must be out of ink."*

COFFIN MAKER MARK L. FOWLER

Coffin produced a small square of paper on which a mass of coloured lights flickered wildly. He held the paper up so that Hieronymus and Beezle could read the message:

TWO. CONTINUE. END.

Coffin carefully folded the square of dazzling lights and placed it safely in his desk drawer.

"Any questions, gentlemen?"

Beezle, conscious of the quaking anger being held back, thought it best to say little and get back to the business of slaughtering innocents in the pointless battles of the Lower Eastern Zones.

Hieronymus, on the other hand, saw, in polemical discussion, the chance to tie up the time of both Beezle and Coffin, thus saving the lives of thousands. He opened his mouth to speak, but Coffin had already launched into a bitter critique of the Creator's literary technique.

"Doesn't leave much room for discussion, does it? *Two! Continue! End!* What fine words they are. How dripping with meaning. Take the word *Two*, for example. What possible ambiguity? I mean, gentlemen, and correct me if I'm wrong: what can that little word mean, if not that it is both of you that the Creator is referring to. So, I might conclude, *a fine choice of words*, or rather, *word."*

The intermittent snarl of irony was so out of control that Hieronymus had, for the moment, to bow his head in an apparent show of appalled humility. It was either that or send out a suicidal volley of laughter right into Coffin's face.

"Which brings me to its bedfellow: *Continue.* Now there *is* a word for you. Longer than both its flanking bedfellows. Positively generous in its proportions. Eight letters. Three syllables. And what does it mean all those syllables and letters? Let me have a stab at it. *Carry on with this absurd festival of cosmic lunacy, perhaps? Let the farce go on, maybe?*

The irony flickered like a broken bulb not quite ready to die. Hieronymus could bow his head no lower; his chin was already hurting his chest. The bulb flashed relentlessly - on, off - threatening at any moment to explode.

"So let us delve a little into the final part of this *feast of meaning. End.* End of message? End of sentence? End of the world? Note the way that the word *perfectly* balances with the first part of the message. The same number of letters. The same single syllable. Beautiful, isn't it? Such construction is so deceptive because, you see, to the uneducated it looks so easy. Looks as though any idiot could pull it off. *Two. Continue. End.* Those words leave me practically speechless. So please, gentlemen, if you have anything to add, now is the time to enlighten me."

Beezle was the first. "No comment to make at this point in time, sir," he said. "Permission to return to work."

Coffin allowed the fragment of a cockroach smile to crack through the stone wall of his displeasure. But in a second the crack was healed, the insect crushed.

COFFIN MAKER   MARK L. FOWLER

"I have a question," said Hieronymus.

"Go on," said Coffin. "I'm listening."

"Why don't we go on strike?"

Coffin glared with such intensity it seemed he was trying to erase Hieronymus by sheer force of will; erase him and replace him with the re-assuring fire of industry.

"You see, if we went on strike, the Creator would *have* to answer questions. It would give us a voice."

Coffin took one small but menacing step forward. "Let me warn you that I am not in the mood today for impertinence or tomfoolery, understand?"

He had half-turned towards the door when Hieronymus added, "With respect, Mr. Coffin, I'm being serious."

The silence that followed filled the room like an ocean of treacle that no-one seemed keen to navigate. It was left to Hieronymus to set the course forward. "You see, if we stop work, one of two things will happen. Either the Creator will make his feelings more fully known by addressing us - or more likely you - personally. Divine clarification, as it were. Alternatively, and more likely, in my view, the Creator could opt for the preservation of his creations and applaud our inactivity as the true enlightenment of our noble profession. We will be saviours of the world and heir to the real treasures of eternity. Just imagine -"

The speech was cut short as Coffin slammed a fist into his desk. Beezle's grim eyes sparkled for an instant, but he controlled them quickly, retreating skilfully into the perfect manifestation of the obedient.

COFFIN MAKER　　　MARK L. FOWLER

Coffin looked long and hard into Hieronymus' deep, green, exasperating eyes.

"It seems for the present that we are stuck with each other. As two is clearly your lucky number, may I suggest that there are *indeed* two possibilities? Firstly you learn to keep your childish thoughts to yourself and reserve your energies for the advancement of your professional development. Or secondly you find yourself in so much hot water that a subsequent posting to what your earthbound chums call Antarctica will not cool you down ahead of hell freezing over. Understand?"

"I think so," said Hieronymus, scratching his head, puzzled by the confusion of images. He'd meant to ask about Heaven and Hell, but suspecting that the moment was far too delicate for metaphysical discourse, said nothing more.

Satisfied that the ridiculous rebellion had been quashed, Coffin made his final address. "Beezle, carry on as before in the East. You are handling the battlefields with remarkable dexterity. At the same time, however, I want you to concentrate a little more on domestic dispatching. Your natural instincts and imaginative flair will bring you great rewards in that area of work. You are simply too inexperienced to appreciate all the possibilities, but it will come, believe me. It's an area in which we must all commit our best efforts. It is our bread and butter, so to speak."

Coffin placed his hands behind his back and tilted his pointed chin at an impressive angle. "You see, Beezle: though war still has a profoundly important part to play in our profession, global conflict has become,

COFFIN MAKER MARK L. FOWLER

paradoxically, the enemy precisely because the fools are now capable of blowing themselves entirely off the face of the planet. If we destroy life entirely, then we overplay our hand and destroy death too. Death requires life: it's one of the unfortunate rules underlying our existence here."

He paused to let his profound thoughts settle into Beezle's apprentice brain. "Domestic death is infinitely more controllable. Work at it, Beezle. Reap its rewards. Don't underestimate the devastation of the individual death, the personal apocalypse."

Beezle's eyes flashed at the image, and the spark lit something in the Coffin Maker's heart.

Here was a student willing to listen to his teacher; a son willing to drink in his father's words with an insatiable thirst.

Coffin pulled his stooped shoulders as far back as an eternity of poor posture would allow, and let his creaky-bone voice take on a smoother, more dignified tone.

He was on a roll.

"Now, Beezle, I have to say that though your military work is consistently excellent, you do have a tendency to over-use the techniques of natural disaster. I'm afraid you will have to learn to control this in future. Keep a reign on that love affair of yours with the fiercer side of *Mother Nature*."

Beezle frowned but kept his confusions to himself.

The Coffin Maker was an idiot. That was all he needed to know.

COFFIN MAKER   MARK L. FOWLER

"Oh how I love to see such youthful exuberance," said Coffin, switching voices with the confidence of a stage-impressionist on the other side of sanity. It was the turn of his best fatherly tone. "Don't take my words too harshly. I only mean that too many lightning fires and hostile hurricanes, a plethora of earthquakes, volcanoes and unprecedented tidal waves gives too strong an impression of external forces at work. It is not in our interests to bring too much superstition back into the world at a time when science-obsessed mankind believes in its own capacity for destruction."

He turned his attention to Hieronymus, now adopting a clipped tone, as though wishing to deny him the very movement of air that speech required. "A full assessment of Zone Thirty-Nine and the resumption of hostilities in Zone Nineteen by morning. This meeting is closed."

Coffin watched his apprentices troop out of his office, noticing the twinkle in the eye of Beezle and something closer to a tear in the eye of Hieronymus.

He sat down to ponder. Something bothered him. Not simply the diabolical lack of clarification from the Creator, or the absurdity of sending an apprentice as useless as Hieronymus... there was something else.

It is not in our interests to bring too much superstition back into the world at a time when mankind believes in its own capacity for destruction.

The curious sentence echoed around his mind. What the hell had he meant by that?

He put himself through an absurd ritual, trying to think of a hundred sensible reasons why he would say such a thing. But even Coffin could only sustain the fooling of himself for so long. He knew why he'd said it. He'd said it for the effect the words would have on Hieronymus. It was the weapon he'd chosen to punish the youth for his stubbornness, his argumentativeness - damn it, for his misdirected and utterly wasted cleverness. He'd been looking at Beezle, but he'd been aiming at Hieronymus. Aiming at that moral conscience and ridiculously naive love of all creation.

Coffin thought the peculiar sentence over, chewing the words carefully, analysing the weird surge of excitement he'd felt delivering them.

But he hadn't meant it. He had no wish to see the end of mankind. No wish to put himself out of business, out of a job - possibly out of existence, for all he knew. Hadn't he said that the Second World War had been as far as he wanted to go in that direction? And he'd meant it. So why come out with such a statement for the sole purpose of hitting out at an inconsequential numbskull?

Full of the desire for self-chastisement, Coffin wondered whether to burn one of his poems.

It was a foolish thought. Why should literature suffer?

Yet the anger remained. In trying to hurt Hieronymus he'd given the wrong impression of his real nature to both of them. He was no enemy of mankind, rather a highly skilled craftsman with a job to do. How he wished he had left that stupid sentence unformed. What was happening to him? *And where would it end?*

COFFIN MAKER   MARK L. FOWLER

Not through the destruction of fine poetry, but in its creation did Coffin seek consolation.

Am I asking too much? I've not pestered the Creator unduly. One request in the entire History of Life and Death. Is that excessive? And yet all I get is another ridiculous note telling me nothing. Laughing at me in lights. Is one miserable request really too much when some of those humans are down on their knees every five minutes pestering with prayers for this and prayers for that. It's no wonder the Creator allows wars and earthquakes and famines when he has that incessant crying for attention to contend with.

The truth is I'm worried about Zone Thirty-Nine. What's going on down there. I've missed the beginnings of something. It's growing like a tumour. I've given the zone to Hieronymus to assess. Maybe a numbskull's 'philosophical analysis' can illuminate where logic and reason are clearly failing. Time he earned his keep.

Something else to worry about. I'm asking too many questions. I'm becoming. Becoming. Philosophical. Once it was enough that I made coffins. Hieronymus is corrupting me. I must get back to work. Must remain what I am.

Must remind the human race who I am.

10: TROUBLED ZONES

Hieronymus sat in his room, looking sadly down on Zone Nineteen. It might have amused him, relieved his anxieties, to have seen what Coffin was filling his journal with. That *he* was corrupting the Coffin Maker.

Instead he gazed into the monitor, miserably aware that a wonderful opportunity for rejoicing was passing into a time of greater misery, and there wasn't a thing he could do to stop it.

When he'd first trained the monitor over the land it had renewed his sense of purpose to look on so many relieved faces in the streets and in the hillsides of Zone Nineteen. Faces that had become hollowed-out skulls after nine long years of pitiless and pointless suffering were beginning to look human again. All over the land a terrible and prolonged wailing had ceased and no longer were the people covering their nostrils in preparation for the stench of a new day's slaughter. The last fires of barbarism had reduced to harmless columns of smoke, and the unmistakable signs of play were sunning the faces of the children.

It should have been something to celebrate. A triumph of the human spirit to take so much for so long and still find hope among the ashes and statistics. And he'd helped them achieve the seemingly impossible through nothing more than bold inactivity and defiant moral indignation.

But *now* where was that sense of purpose? Now it seemed he had become the cruellest of executioners, giving out hope that he couldn't sustain, and merely drawing out the moment before the hammer fell.

COFFIN MAKER   MARK L. FOWLER

He could hardly bear to look at them. Their smiles, their praises, mocked him, wounded him. They stood so innocently at the edge of a holocaust as though it were a field of dreams stretched out before them. Dreams they had only now dared to embrace. It was pathetic to see them, blind as new-borns to the agonies that fate was holding in store.

But the options cupboard was bare. The Coffin Maker had ordered the restoration of violence and slaughter by morning. It wouldn't take craftsmanship to point the people of Zone Nineteen back to the grindstone of bloodshed - any idiot could accomplish that. Nine years of relentless butchery hadn't left any shortage of exposed and tender buttons to press. One coffin would do it. One coffin would set the thing in motion. One act, one significant death and the fragile peace would come tumbling down, smashing into a million blazing bullets.

Hieronymus trembled over the brutal clarity of the realisation that with a single death, the invisible chains that linked Zone Nineteen to the Kingdom of Death would synchronize in the solemn grind to genocide. What craftsmanship would that involve? An imbecile could do it with a handful of nails and the God-given gift of death.

Hieronymus paced his empty room, the hours rolling under his feet. He threw the problem backwards and forwards, bouncing it off the walls of his mind, trying to find a value in one course of action against another, weighing right and left and finding not a feather between them. And the harder he worked his brain, the less it repaid him until at last, tiring from his

COFFIN MAKER   MARK L. FOWLER

long and fruitless efforts, he sat down and buried his head in his hands, allowing a thick cloud of desolation to engulf him.

So much for his young and noble mind. So much for this friend of mankind, this new-found saviour of the world.

Hours passed and Hieronymus didn't move. Despair covered him like a blanket and he went under it, down and down, hour by lonely hour, falling to the bottom of the pit.

And there, at the bottom, he found it.

Less an idea than a feeling. A stirring inside. Little by little it started to grow, taking form, shape; a wand poking out of a cloud, transforming the sky.

There was a way, a simple way.

Hieronymus laughed, then hopped and skipped, clapping and whistling and twisting around and around until he made himself feel sick. He sat back on the floor, a little groggy but grinning. "You take up your hammer and you set to work on the coffins of both so-called leaders. You make the two coffins simultaneously, plank for plank, nail for nail. You bend and shape the wood so that the two monsters come out of their palaces, not surrounded with the weaponry at the command of their twitching fingers, but with their bare knuckles primed."

He was up on his feet again, hopping, punching at the air. "They leave the people of Zone Nineteen at the foot of Holy Mountain, the one god still shared by both sides. They go to the top of the mountain, right to the top of that last remaining symbol of unity untouched by their divided ideologies, and they fight.

COFFIN MAKER   MARK L. FOWLER

For days they fight, those warlords – animals! - until the victor throws the other from the summit. Then, as agreed at the outset, the victor leads a re-united people into a golden age of peace and prosperity."

Hieronymus stopped the dance. "Brilliant! In a previous incarnation you must have been in the movies." Then he shook his head. "Only one problem, movie-man: it won't work. Two men soaked in evil. Whichever wins, there'll be no golden age of united peace, just more persecution and oppression as the victor celebrates in the time-honoured way."

He groaned, slumped to the floor, placed his head back into his hands and sat unmoving as the night ticked by, turning him into a statue, except for the tireless fingers still drumming on the back of his head.

The hours passed until finally a moment came. The fingers paused. Two eyes snapped open. "Superstition!" He blinked, blinked again. "That's what Coffin said - *Not in our interests to bring too much superstition back into the world.*" Not in whose interests? These people have worshipped Holy Mountain for generations. Countless times that mountain has spoken to them.

He stood up, cautiously. Was youth playing its tricks again? He didn't think so. "I think we're due some old time religion."

Back on his feet, the dawn had ousted the night, and the way forward flew like an angel around his head. "While those two devils are up on the plateau, beating each other senseless, the people will hear a voice that sends shivers, scaring them witless, but saving every one of their precious skins.

COFFIN MAKER   MARK L. FOWLER

"Can you imitate a holy mountain? Coffin's done it a zillion times. It pays to know your history. Pays to read that journal he's forever scribbling into - if you can put up with the bullshit and the lousy excuse for poetry. The mountain will announce a special sacrifice, one that will satisfy what remains of the need for bloodshed. It will command that this sacrifice is a sign Zone Nineteen is moving into a new age. Then, with a hammer in each hand and the final nails in place, I will bring my hands down together as those two demons fall in symmetry from the mountain.

"How do you like that, Coffin? Not bad for an apprentice, eh? It could restore peace in Zone Nineteen for generations.

"Let hostilities commence."

Hieronymus looked down now on Zone Nineteen with a breathless sense of anticipation. Now they had hope. The nation was about to become re-acquainted with an old and trusted god.

He thought of the Creator, and felt a rush of confidence in whatever or whoever had set the world of life and death in motion. Yet so many questions remained unanswered; so many questions still seemed barely comprehensible. Why was he here? Why had he been sent at all? Why was he so different to Beezle? There had to be reasons. It couldn't just happen.

The gravity of the questions let a solitary bubble of certainty rise up through the opaque soup: that he had been sent to this land of shadow to accomplish great things for mankind.

The thought set his heart racing and he grasped at the precious bubble like it was a ball of solid rubber bobbing on a hostile sea.

And the bubble exploded. He was the saviour. Sent by the Creator.

But then why send Beezle?

What could Beezle offer mankind? What had he and Beezle in common apart from their Creator and trade? Was that enough, somehow? And how could he ever hope to find out what else they might have in common when they never spoke to each other? And why was that? Why had they been cast in mutual loathing? Brothers formed with the primary objective of destroying the other.

Cosmic sibling rivalry.

It was all infinitely more complicated than the relatively small-scale headache of saving Zone Nineteen from the resumption of genocide.

Hieronymus made no more headway that night than Coffin himself, who sat in his own quarters, pondering hopelessly over the same matters, stopping only to throw wild and occasional thoughts into the pages of his journal.

If the Creator in his infernal wisdom -

He put a line through the sentence and obliterated completely the word 'infernal.'

If the Creator wants his creations to live longer why doesn't he send me a letter to that effect? Why doesn't

COFFIN MAKER   MARK L. FOWLER

he tell me? Why send a strange youth full of strange ideas to put me through this torment?

And if it's greater longevity He wants for His creatures then why send Beezle who given half a chance would see the extinction of the species and spend the rest of eternity with his feet up content to gloat over happy memories?

It makes less sense the longer it goes on. All men are mortal! *That was my brief. That was the extent of my apprenticeship! And* three score years and ten *as a rough working guide.*

How can two anything's be as different as Hieronymus and Beezle?

Coffin noticed a faint light opening up the sky. Another dawn breaking. He wondered what it would bring. What torments. What revelations.

It had better bring the resumption of hostilities in Zone Nineteen and some illumination into the problem of Zone Thirty-Nine.

Hieronymus left the problem of his existence and turned his attentions to Zone Thirty-Nine. He'd thought a few minutes would be enough to come up with some half-baked ideas, enough to keep Coffin off his back while he formulated plans to limit the death toll. But the first light of day, breaking the anguished frustration of the night so wholesomely over Zone Nineteen, was breaking no ground over Zone Thirty-Nine.

Gloom fell around him once more as he tried to fathom the enigma. Whatever it was that was growing down there, he doubted two coffins and a holy mountain would sort it.

In his frustration he took the most unusual of measures, and carried out his duties to the letter, detailing everything he had seen down in Zone Thirty-Nine and compiling it into a report. He would leave it to Coffin to interpret the facts, and judge by the Coffin Maker's reaction whether he was right to be so concerned about Zone Thirty-Nine.

And by the rise of Colonel Gouge.

11: EXPERIMENTS

Thousands of miles across the water from Zone Thirty-Nine, strange things were happening.

On the islands making up Zone Five Hundred and Three, death was developing a taste for the bizarre. In a single week almost a third of the population had been killed, and the remainder seriously traumatised, by a series of horrific visitations.

First came the stones.

At around midday on the Sunday, peculiar clouds had drifted across the southern half of the zone. Without warning a vicious storm had broken, and what emptied out of the sky for more than two hours that day defied the explanation of scientists the world over. Stones the size of fists had rained down leaving a land trembling under a deluge of death and destruction.

Just after two in the afternoon, the stones stopped falling and a bright sunshine laughed over the pock-marked land. It was days before the living ventured out of what shelters remained, and everywhere people were jumping out of their skins at any sound that might herald another downpour of the killing stones.

By Friday people were surveying their broken towns and ruined lives; what remained of the churches and temples were filled with terrified men, women and children, blessed and cursed with the knowledge that a wrathful, vengeful god had woken to greet them. Ministers of all creeds, thankful that divine intervention had rescued dwindling congregations, responded with long and powerful addresses to the people the length and breadth of the stricken land. It was an unmissable

COFFIN MAKER   MARK L. FOWLER

opportunity. God was out of the wilderness. If He had ever been dead at all, the grieving was over and the resurrection tipped to be the party to end all parties.

But fortunes were not stable in the south of Zone Five Hundred and Three during that strange week, and late on Friday afternoon hordes of petrified grievers scrambled back out of the churches and temples as the buildings began to shake and crumble. Once again the devastation obeyed to the yard the boundaries of the southern half, yet now the destruction focused exclusively on places of religious worship. By early evening not one sacred structure of any creed or denomination was standing.

The early hours of Saturday morning saw events turn once more, the course of blood changing direction, running into the northern regions. Now the violence had a human face.

A group of self-proclaimed fanatics had broken ranks with the military and were rampaging through the land, killing anything that moved. Their trademark was a single bullet through the left eye, regardless of colour, race, sex, age or the intensity of the cries for mercy. Dogs lay next to babies, all as one with the mark of this madness blown into the left side of their faces. Once it became clear what was happening, the military set out to search and destroy. Thirty-six hours later saw the execution of the last of the Left Eye Battalion.

Thankfully for the sanity of the people of the stricken zone, the military commander had a sense of humour. Those fanatics who hadn't acted quickly enough in committing suicide by shooting out their left eyes, were rounded up and dispatched with a bullet to

COFFIN MAKER   MARK L. FOWLER

the right eye. The irony of the method restored a sense of justice to the terrorised people and restored calm as the region huddled itself together and tried to come to terms with what it had witnessed.

The final instalment of the week's catalogue of events occurred in the late hours of Sunday evening, and brought the whole of Zone Five Hundred and Three together in one final savage act of suffering.

A fine dust had blown across the land, settling into the lungs of everything that lived and breathed. The old and the young fell like flies. The zone coughed its collective guts into an incurable knot, until the stroke of midnight finally brought a terrible hush.

The hour of silence hung over the stricken land and even the ground was trembling. Then, deafening and inconsolable, the silence gave way, falling like a fortress wall and shattering into a roar of grief.

Fresh from the Coffin Dome, Beezle sat unsatisfied and restless in his quarters. He was like a reptile that had survived on starvation rations and now wanted to gorge itself on every insect that had ever beaten its wings.

He set off back towards the Coffin Dome, his orange hair like a torch against the bottomless sky, and in minutes the machinery, still hot from the previous hours of excess, was grinding back towards meltdown. A week of systemised experimentation confined to Zone Five Hundred and Three was about to be succeeded by random experiments dotted throughout the world.

In Zone Eleven an epidemic of suicide smashed into the teenage population, flirted briefly (but

COFFIN MAKER   MARK L. FOWLER

impressively) with the very old, before descending full throttle on the juniors, at last petering out over the bones of infants.

In Zone Three Hundred and Ninety, a thousand people died from spontaneous combustion. In Zone Two Hundred and Eighty Five, seventy people died when, for no apparent reason, their heads exploded off their shoulders.

And the night wore on in a relentless series of atrocities until the light of dawn brought Coffin across to the Dome to brush up on a few old techniques.

His night had not been spent idly. In every corner of the world he'd stalked the living in a busier than usual schedule of humdrum disease, accident and murder. But now he felt inspired; fancied something juicier.

Time for a little indulgence; an overdue treat.

He had a hankering to start up that old volcano in Zone Five Hundred and Three. It had lain dormant in idle sleep for centuries in a land that had known peace for too many generations. He was thinking on a grand scale, and that meant the machinery of the Coffin Dome, to handle the weight of work he had in mind. They'd been having it easy in Zone Five Hundred and Three, and it was time for a little reminder that they were living on an unpredictable globe spinning around a crazy star.

Coffin stood at the threshold of the Dome, his thin mouth hanging dangerously as he watched his metal Goliaths being driven like galley slaves. Watched the aftermath of insanity still unfolding on the monitors positioned throughout the Dome.

COFFIN MAKER MARK L. FOWLER

"What? Again? So soon?"

Gathering his bones into the formation of the focused warrior, he stormed through the building, knocking back a battalion of levers, bringing the Dome to a halt. He walked right up to the jagged-haired apprentice, and thundered, "Explain yourself!"

Beezle closed his eyes for a moment, allowing the violent light in them to seep down to a safe place, out of sight of the Coffin Maker. When he opened them again, a moment later, it was to reveal a calm, subservient humility pouring through them. "I enjoy my work so much, sir. I may have got a little...carried away, perhaps. Please forgive me – I only wish to please you."

Coffin felt his marrow soften, his rage diminish. "I know you enjoy your work," he said, "and it brings me nothing but joy to see it so." Beezle measured out a perfect frown, sufficient to show puzzlement, but falling safely short of insubordination. Coffin went on. "If you could ease up a little bit, tame some of your wild enthusiasm - after all, what's the hurry? Our job can never be finished, not entirely..."

Something dangerous flickered in Beezle's eye, but he covered it with a subservient nod.

"It's like this," said Coffin. "I don't want to blunt your zeal, far from it. You're young and eager, but sometimes we need to, well, curtail our eagerness."

Beezle continued to nod, even sneaking in an inspired ghost of a frown, keeping the need for explanation in the court of the Coffin Maker.

COFFIN MAKER   MARK L. FOWLER

For almost an hour Beezle kept Coffin stumbling over his words, using nothing more than finely judged facial movements.

"Don't take this the wrong way," said Coffin, working up to the climax of the reprimand. "You must learn, as we all must, to ease up on the inexplicable. As long as you give their scientists something on which to cobble together some inane hypothesis, fine. I think we'll leave it at that for today."

Coffin sauntered back from the Dome, all enthusiasm for the old volcano dampened down. He sat at his desk, scanned over the aftermath in the places where Beezle's fury had played out. At last he reached for his pen.

Rocks from the sky! Exploding heads! Left Eye Battalions! Saints preserve us. And yet such talent. He loves his work so much and throws himself into it so whole-heartedly that I haven't it in me to chastise him. I wonder what he is capable of.

His thoughts scurried through his head like blinded mice, and he chewed the end of his pen until his best tooth ached. The pain helped. It cut into the confusion. Aided by his pain, Coffin gathered back some of his wits, and wrote,

Superstition! Friend or foe? The world has changed down there. Science has made mankind more afraid of themselves than of unknown forces. They don't think about external evil like they used to. Now it's the evil within that terrifies them. Did I teach them that?

COFFIN MAKER   MARK L. FOWLER

He chewed at his pen until another tooth was aching. Preferring poetry to pain, he wrote some more.

Beezle was clever the way he used the dust. It'll give the scientists plenty to think about. Left Eye nonsense showed imagination if a rather peculiar sense of humour. Not something I would associate with Beezle. No doubt the scientists will rationalise the falling stones. Could be interesting watching them squeeze the facts into their frail little theories. No doubt someone will pick up a doctorate. The destruction of holy buildings? Too bizarre. Even the scientists will have a job convincing anybody of a rational explanation there. Lays the thing open to end-of-the-world superstitious clap-trap. And I draw the line at exploding heads. Childish. Immature. Makes a mockery of the whole business of death. Or am I becoming too conservative?

Coffin chewed at his pen, and this time he didn't stop until every tooth in his head was aching.

Time to review Hieronymus. Can't believe that the Creator would send me an apprentice devoid of redeeming qualities. Perhaps I will find them in the resumption of hostilities in Zone Nineteen. And in his analysis of Zone Thirty-Nine.

I better had.

For his sake...

12: PUNISHMENT AND LAUGHTER

"Explain yourself!"

Hieronymus looked as though he would love to explain himself, but simply lacked the tools to do so. He hadn't the foggiest idea what it was that Coffin wanted explaining. He'd tripped dutifully along to the office with a strategy for Zone Nineteen, and a report on Zone Thirty-Nine. What was there to explain?

"Let me make it easier for you. Why have hostilities not resumed in Zone Nineteen?" Coffin's eyes bubbled like cauldrons of molten metal, threatening to spill over and consume his apprentice at any second.

"I have not been idle in Zone Nineteen," said Hieronymus. "I've set up the deaths of the two leaders of the warring factions. As we speak, they are fighting to the death on Holy Mountain, and the fight will end in the completion of two extremely significant coffins."

The temperature in Coffin's glare rose, no doubt breaking another law of the physical world.

"Two coffins? You did say...*two*?"

"I did indeed."

"And am I supposed to celebrate by asking you to dance?"

Hieronymus tried not to laugh at the unexpected image. "A kind of *danse macabre,* you mean?"

It was a mistake. Humour seemed anathema to the Coffin Maker. In a mood as black as this, flippancy might burn hearts, human or otherwise, to cinders.

The youth instinctively edged back towards the door, as Coffin edged forward, toward him.

COFFIN MAKER   MARK L. FOWLER

"Never underestimate my temper, Hieronymus, and never underestimate my capacity for retribution on those who provoke that temper. You were given a clear brief and you have failed not only to carry it out, but to treat it with any sense of responsibility. I am sorely tempted to punish you now."

He paused for a moment, his eye settling like a vulture's on the retreating youth.

"I will, however, hold my fire. Two reasons. Firstly, I want you to witness the outcomes of your *in*actions in Zone Nineteen; outcomes that, had you intended them, might have earned you my unqualified respect. I'll say no more on that matter for the moment as I don't wish to ruin the lesson."

His emphasis on the word 'lesson' was not subtle, and he noted the stirrings of anxious curiosity twitching on Hieronymus' brow. He had raised a question in the youth's mind; and was content to leave it there for the time being.

"Secondly, as I've yet to look at your report on Zone Thirty-Nine, your future hangs in the balance. In other words, that report had better be good."

Hieronymus handed the report to Coffin and waited as the old bone man engrossed himself in its pages.

When Coffin had finished reading, and pacing up and down the room, hands behind his back, occasionally stopping to flick back through the pages before resuming his thoughtful pacing, he at last delivered his verdict. "Brilliant."

"Really?" said Hieronymus, somewhat stunned.

"Brilliant utterly and brilliant absolutely."

COFFIN MAKER   MARK L. FOWLER

Hieronymus scanned every last echo of Coffin's words. Was that a tinge of irony around the edge or was Coffin in earnest?

"Brilliant."

It didn't sound sarcastic.

"How can such an imbecile produce such quality?"

The danger light flickered. This could go either way. Hieronymus crossed his fingers that the question was rhetorical.

It was.

"What you have produced here is comprehensive and detailed. It is written with clarity and insight. You astound me."

Hieronymus felt some of the tension start to drain away.

"However."

The tension drained back.

"However, even the 'however' is not a major 'however.'"

The tension pooled into limbo.

"The report fails to interpret and conclude. You and Beezle will report back tomorrow to give verbal interpretations of the situation in Zone Thirty-Nine, giving your recommendations based on potential.

"And potential means numbers. It doesn't always mean numbers, because the craftsman is neither so crude nor so obvious. But the time I have given to training you both has caused something of a log jam down there. It is getting rather crowded on the beach, so to speak. And whilst I don't intend any further ventures down the pathway of World War – not immediately,

COFFIN MAKER   MARK L. FOWLER

anyway, due to certain long-term side-effects, but that's another matter - I do intend to see some major industry, and soon. When I've heard from you both I will lighten your darkness, if, after such reflection, any darkness remains."

Coffin allowed himself a little inward smile.

So he had missed the weird seed growing in Zone Thirty-Nine. So what? He was using his new skills as delegator to let fresh eyes take the strain; using his cunning to let their eyes battle with darkness, to penetrate the mystery.

And let the best pair of eyes take the prize. Who would know that the Coffin Maker's eyes had been less than perfect - except possibly the Creator? But these days, that seemed neither here nor there.

"Directly after tomorrow's meeting we will look again at Zone Nineteen and, dependent on how certain matters interact with my humour, we may once more need to broach the matter of punishment. But then again, we may decide that Zone Nineteen is punishment enough."

"I'm not following you –"

"Good. Dismissed."

Coffin sat down exhausted. It had been quite a speech from one not given to making them; from one who had spent uncountable millennia never having to even *think* about making speeches. He had to admit it, though: he'd handled the matter well. No, he'd handled it *very* well. And he'd sensed a little respect at last from the youth. No philosophical meanderings, no stubborn arguments or quips about his name. And as for that report on Thirty-Nine - it really was quite brilliant.

COFFIN MAKER   MARK L. FOWLER

Feeling sure that he was on the eve of getting the full measure of Zone Thirty-Nine, his spirits bloomed. He'd soon be back in full command of the situation, missing no tricks, lacking no knowledge.

He picked up his pen and this time didn't stop to chew.

Hieronymus has shown remarkable potential in the field of analysis. Tomorrow I will introduce competition. I will set his wits against Beezle and let vanity run its course. It promises to be an interesting battle. As for Zone Nineteen. It will teach Hieronymus an important lesson.

His eyes flashing like mean daggers, he added,

Zone Nineteen will teach Hieronymus a lesson he will never forget.

Laying down his pen, Coffin felt a strange sensation moving through his body. Most peculiar it was, like a fish had got inside him and was swimming up and down the length and breadth of his bones, tickling them. His shoulders started to shake up and down, and his stomach and facial muscles felt ready to burst open. Then a sound roared out of his mouth. He tried putting a hand up to stop it, but was too late.

"*Danse macabre*," he roared. "That really is very good."

It was some time before the laughter completely subsided, and it left him feeling both worn out and revitalised. Quite wonderful in fact. The best he'd felt

COFFIN MAKER   MARK L. FOWLER

since the Second World War, and at least three times better than at any stage since his solitude had been broken by the scourge of apprenticeship. He thought again of the lesson awaiting Hieronymus, and in a moment was re-entering the uncharted waters of laughter.

This time the Coffin Maker laughed until he found himself beating his fists on the desk in a helpless plea for mercy. When he finally stopped, breathless and weak, he wondered if someone hadn't taken out his bones and left only an uncontrollable, if miserly, wobble of flesh.

The image was almost enough to start him off again.

Wiping his eyes, it struck him how everything felt different. As though he had been shaken from head to toe. His mind rinsed through, cleansing his thoughts. Even the quality of light, within and without, was somehow changed. A purer light, he thought.

Perhaps things were about to take a turn for the better.

Perhaps it was all going to work itself out.

Perhaps, in the Kingdom of Death at least, they were all going to live happily ever after.

13: TWO REPORTS

The next day brought Hieronymus and Beezle to Coffin's office early. Coffin breezed in with an expression of gleeful anticipation. "Ah, gentlemen. Yesterday I talked too much. Today is your turn. Let us to Zone Thirty-Nine."

The apprentices turned to face one another, both gesturing to the other to go first. This display of apparent politeness brought proceedings to a premature halt, and earned them both a wilting glare from Coffin.

"When you're ready!" he thundered.

Beezle was first to respond. "Zone Thirty-Nine has the greatest potential on the entire planet at this time. Elimination of President Doveman is imperative for progress. Colonel Gouge holds the future."

Beezle snapped his report shut.

"Is that it?" asked Coffin.

"In essence, yes. The rest is mere detail."

"Then let's have some detail," said Coffin. "Or are you modelling yourself on the Creator and pursuing brevity as your religion?"

A murderous look shot across Beezle's face, startling both Coffin and Hieronymus. Yet in an instant Beezle had re-modelled his features to the practiced look of benign professionalism, and was answering the charge of brevity with anything but. "President Doveman is extremely dangerous. He has somehow managed to hold more than a dozen hostile factions in a state of extended peace. He has the diabolical distinction of easing tensions between tribes that have been steadily butchering each other for generations. He

COFFIN MAKER   MARK L. FOWLER

has invested massively in health, subsistence and education, and shows no remorse on any count. He has said publicly that his middle name is 'peace.' His coffin should be marked 'urgent.'"

"And this...*Gouge?*" said Coffin. "What about him?"

"Colonel Gouge has vision that flesh and blood will never compromise."

"Vision?" interrupted Coffin. "What kind of vision?"

"Vision that extends far beyond Zone Thirty-Nine," returned Beezle, cryptically.

Coffin turned to Hieronymus. "And are you a subscriber to the Gouge fan-club?"

Hieronymus took a breath and opened his report. "The mortality rates in Thirty-Nine are only marginally below birth rates."

Coffin blinked. "Are you about to deliver a lecture on birth control?"

"I make the point," said Hieronymus, "to illustrate that, though the political situation is complicated, minimal intervention is necessary. That is, with a single exception."

"I know why you made the point," said Coffin. "Exception, you say?"

"Colonel Gouge."

"My, my – our Mr. Gouge seems to be a key figure this morning."

"Gouge is a virus. His potential for destruction goes beyond anything a craftsman of your stature could ever embrace."

COFFIN MAKER MARK L. FOWLER

Coffin smiled at the compliment. This young man was learning the art of diplomacy at last.

"But I wouldn't call it vision," continued Hieronymus. "I wouldn't say that a virus has vision. Gouge is evil and he wants the world. He'd have the Coffin Dome in flames coping with the slaughter and leave us all twiddling our thumbs through eternity."

"What exactly do you mean?" asked Coffin, intrigued.

"Isn't it obvious?"

"It might be. Let's see."

"Well," said Hieronymus, "it seems to me that mankind has never had a greater threat in its midst. It's only the existence of a leader of the calibre of President Doveman preventing me from fearing the worst."

"The end of all life?"

"Very probably."

Coffin thought for a moment, then asked the two apprentices if they had anything to add before he read their reports.

Hieronymus spoke first. "To use Beezle's turn of phrase, if to rather different purpose: mark Colonel Gouge's coffin 'urgent.'"

Coffin looked at Beezle, who shook his head slowly and silently, his startling orange hair looking fiercer and more explosive than ever.

"Right then. Best report gets Zone Thirty-Nine. Return here in an hour. Prompt."

He sat down with the two reports and ploughed them meticulously, searching every line for meaning, trying to wring the last drop of insight from the observations and interpretations of two fresh minds.

COFFIN MAKER — MARK L. FOWLER

How different in style and content they were. How impossible at times to believe that they were writing about the same situation. Only the names sounded a common note. Those two names that haunted both reports:

Doveman and Gouge.

Though it was the latter that most intrigued Coffin, and he reduced the reports to tatters in his eagerness to devour every last crumb of insight into this dark character.

Until there was little doubt left.

Gouge was the very thing that he had missed.

It had been his duty to notice each coming of death's raw material into the world. Each new life. And that meant being aware of every birth. It was in his remit to be at work on every mortal's coffin every step along life's way, from the first drawing of breath and even before. If he didn't know about a new entry into the world, or impending entry, how could he ensure an exit?

Controversial figures had come and gone with tedium. Claims of *Saviour of mankind; Greatest Leader of the Age; Spiritual Leader of Nations* - all had many times bored the Coffin Maker. And these reports weren't saying anything about Doveman that Coffin hadn't seen for himself a thousand times already. He'd seen Doveman come into the world and he'd see him out of it.

Gouge though was different.

Evil, Hieronymus had said. Well, claims of evil were nothing new, either. But there was something here that was new.

COFFIN MAKER   MARK L. FOWLER

In the mind of the Coffin Maker, the last of a number of precariously balanced coins dropped heavily, echoing for minutes around the haunted chambers that directed death. *Gouge was the thing he had missed. Gouge entering the world.*

How had he missed it?

Like a simple cloud, the answer drifted into focus; an uncomplicated raindrop splashing dead centre of his clammed-tight face: *he'd missed Gouge entering the world because he'd never entered it.* He'd always been there - like evil itself.

Evil: that most paradoxical of concepts. Something else that the Creator seemed unable or unwilling to explain. Another fathomless pit of confusion.

Of course he'd known evil pass the baton before; one manifestation dies and hands over the crown to the next incarnation, for whatever ultimate purpose. But he'd always seen it, because it had always gone through the ridiculous ceremony of birth. It had always arrived in the Kingdom of Death in-tray, stamped, approved, marked 'to be dealt with in due course'.

Gouge, though, belonged to another realm entirely. There had been no handing over of batons here. No pretence at innocence, with heads dipped in fonts while ladies with brand new hats cried and took endless photographs.

Gouge simply hadn't been born.

Coffin groaned. Such thoughts could only lead in one direction. An old chestnut was back and roasting on the metaphorical fire.

COFFIN MAKER MARK L. FOWLER

Evil was baffling enough, but this was a billion times worse. The devil was always worse. The 'devil' left no get-out that humanity was to blame. The devil came with all the metaphysical trappings that had haunted the Coffin Maker's darkest and most ancient hours. The devil was the apotheosis of the superstitious mind. Yet the devil, if he did exist, was even less visible than the Creator himself!

Not one whiff of sulphur; not a single beat of a cloven hoof.

Coffin shook his head. "If there was a devil I would know. There's me and the Creator and that's it. The rest is merely mortal.

"Whatever Gouge is, he is not the devil."

Taking up his pen, the Coffin Maker filled an entire page with repetitions of a single sentence.

Gouge is not the devil!

Yet with each repetition the Coffin Maker became a little less convinced.

COFFIN MAKER   MARK L. FOWLER

14: THE LESSON

Hieronymus and Beezle entered the room together, looking the most alike that they would ever look. The grim determination to win the prize of Zone Thirty-Nine, albeit for very different reasons, had, it seemed, temporarily united them in the unhappiness of unflinching ambition.

"Looks like you've both come back from a funeral," said Coffin.

He had to admit - he was quite getting the hang of this humour business.

"Look at you both. Your lives don't depend on who gets Zone Thirty-Nine - though that might be a thought. I'll make a note of it."

But humour was far from the hearts of his apprentices. For them, and in equal measure, the stakes were higher than Coffin could imagine.

As he looked into two pairs of eyes, he saw nothing of the battle between war and peace, love and hate, pain and pleasure; none of the pride, vanity and disgust at the sufferings of human-kind that was raging inside those young heads. All he could see was the yearning for victory, and it tickled him.

"I'll put you out of your respective miseries," he said, watching them tensing up another notch. "Hieronymus: you opened a substantial gap by sheer quality and depth of insight. Beezle: you closed the gap a little in the clarity of your objectives and conclusions. Hieronymus: you lack just about everything when it comes to making a decision. However, the gap was too large to be closed by conclusions and objectives alone, and I therefore have no hesitation in giving Zone Thirty-Nine to you."

"I object!" said Beezle. "Objectives are everything. Doveman must be disposed of immediately."

Coffin looked sternly at the reptile ugliness that hissed beneath jagged orange curls. "It's a pity you didn't channel some of that enthusiasm and passion into your report."

"Reports? While I was wasting time on that *report* I could have done the job. I could have nailed Doveman and ripped the insides out of Zone Thirty-Nine."

"Beezle, you are dismissed."

Spitting with fury, he slithered out of Coffin's office, leaving a stunned Hieronymus to contemplate a strange victory. As the sounds of Beezle's exit echoed in the distance, Hieronymus looked at the Coffin Maker. "Why did I win?"

"You wrote the better report."

"Did I?"

"You hesitated at the end, but made it clear that minor practical measures would produce satisfactory figures. That Gouge is a malignant force that must at all costs be destroyed. Unfortunately, I have one condition in offering the zone to you."

Hieronymus sensed the worst; Coffin confirmed it.

"So fascinating was your profile of Colonel Gouge, that I'm going to take steps that you would not normally expect of the Coffin Maker. Understand this: I am temporarily declaring his life sacrosanct."

COFFIN MAKER   MARK L. FOWLER

"You're saying –"

"I'm saying n*o coffin for the colonel."*

He raised a hand, warning Hieronymus against reply. "I know you expected Beezle to win, because you think I favour him. You thought I would want the killing of Doveman because it would pave the way to slaughter. You both have many lessons to learn. You are about to learn a very important one."

He pointed to the monitor and focused into Zone Nineteen.

Multitudes were gathered around the base of Holy Mountain as the two leaders fought out a battle to the death on the high slopes. The two maniacs were practically indistinguishable, their faces battered and bloodied beyond recognition. Fist, elbow, knee and foot drove relentlessly into groin, temple, kidney and throat. Bones cracked, precious life fluids trickled out into the thin air, but still neither would die. Neither would fall defeated from the mountain.

Far below, more were gathering. Men, women, children - the life-blood of Zone Nineteen - assembled on the narrow rim of peace, waiting for the gift from Holy Mountain. Ears straining to catch the splinter of bone and the ripping of flesh from high above, catching only a low growl like the sound of demons arguing. Perhaps the mountain was signalling its displeasure at the savage ritual acted out on its slopes. Or perhaps something other than a deity was stirring from the bowels of the earth.

The growl grew louder; the ground starting to shake. Terrified faces looked from one to another. Then a violent roar erupted from deep within the mountain,

COFFIN MAKER　　　　MARK L. FOWLER

freezing the faces of the gathering into statues of fear. The smell of sulphur choked the air, and it seemed likely that at any moment Beelzebub, the prince of demons, might descend from the sky or rise up from the ground.

Someone shouted, pointing up at the side of the mountain. Two figures scrambling downwards; running, sliding, *falling*. Close behind, a thick river of fire chasing them. One figure back on his feet, then crashing down again as the other tumbled into him. The river of fire picking up speed, becoming an unquenchable dragon-snake, licking its lips, setting alight the hair of the two masters of war.

The people were screaming, transfixed by the horror. The leaders back on their feet, their fists beating frantically against their own heads, trying to put out the flames. Then the river was on them, their screams lost forever in the gigantic rumble of the cascading dragon-snake of fire.

The tyranny was over, killed and buried by Holy Mountain. Yet the dragon-snake was still hungry, rolling its eyes as it prepared its belly for the feast of thousands standing below.

The multitude turned to run, turned its back on Holy Mountain. Bodies fell and the air became rich with the smell of burning, the demons of slaughter euphoric with the heady cocktail of sulphur and flesh. The ground shook violently causing more of the fleeing to fall; drowning, burning, choking in their last agonies. The air crackled like an incinerator feeding on insects. Fire was raining from the sky and sticking to the backs of the few still outrunning the molten river...

COFFIN MAKER   MARK L. FOWLER

Hieromymus turned from the screen, weeping. Coffin placed a bony, almost fatherly arm around him. "Now you see the dangers of inaction. Your naivety has wiped out an entire people. Unlikely Pied Piper that you are, you've led them to their mountain - enchanted by your childish little tunes - to be burnt alive by their own deity."

"You've slaughtered them to punish me?"

Coffin shook his head. "I've been sitting here with you."

Hieronymus buried his head in his hands. He didn't need to go over to the Coffin Dome to see the sweat still pouring off Beezle as he hammered the last few nails into the final coffins of a nation. This was Beezle's anger at losing Zone Thirty-Nine. This was for not getting a crack at Doveman.

Hieronymus felt the thin weight of Coffin's arm leaving him.

A hard lesson for Hieronymus but a valuable one. He has the intellect to outwit Beezle but not the brutality to stay ahead. If I didn't think he was worth it I wouldn't bother to put him through such suffering. Or maybe I would. I think this will be the making of him.

I do not intend to reprimand Beezle over the affair. He too has learnt a difficult lesson. He has learnt that virtuoso slaughter has its place in the world but will never alone guarantee favour with the Coffin Maker. Beezle expected that the promise of genocide in Zone Thirty-Nine would secure permission to do just that. He was wrong. But he's had his genocidal pleasures all the same.

COFFIN MAKER — MARK L. FOWLER

Holy Mountain isn't as dangerous as Gouge. All three of us can see that. We can all see who the real Pied Piper is.

Hieronymus will not give Gouge an inch. He will be tireless in that. More importantly he will think twice before disobeying me in future.

Coffin felt gloriously in control. To celebrate he let out an inch or two of honesty.

I have overlooked something of unspeakable significance in the world. It is not evil that I've overlooked. I've always known about evil. But what I have missed appals me. Is this why the Creator sent apprentices? I'm not sure. I'm not sure of anything. What does he expect them to do that I couldn't?

Coffin smashed his hand down on the writing desk. Another fine mood ruined.

Why can't I get some answers? Why not a note? I don't mind the flashing lights.

Aware that the last such venting of spleen had merely resulted in more suffering for himself, Coffin closed his journal. Then, checking over his shoulder to make sure that no-one had witnessed the outburst, he let out a long release of bottled up air.

He sat for a while, suffering the centuries-old produce of ill-humour that his insides had been fermenting on his behalf, inhaling every last drop in a weird act of penance.

Then, like a schoolboy wishing to keep untrustworthy class-mates from stealing precious answers, he opened the *History of Death* just enough to get his pen inside.

Okay. I admit it. If this is what you want I'll make my confession. I don't know what to do.

COFFIN MAKER   MARK L. FOWLER

15: THE QUIET REVOLUTION OF DEATH

Here and there, all over the world, events were taking a turn. Death was still trundling on, but the ride seemed gentler. Life and Death were developing a rapport; asking each other for the occasional dance. There was an unmistakable balance and harmony, joining the hands of the living with the hands of the dead.

People were dying at the right time; the right time for *them*. If they needed, wanted the chance to put things in order, put things right, they got it. If three months was long enough to see a grandson born, attend a wedding, or take that trip of a lifetime, then three months it was. Sometimes a day was enough. Even an hour.

Sudden death seemed to suit some people, and they were the ones who were dying suddenly. Some had no reason to endure another two months of pointless suffering; had no inclination for it. They were packed and ready, looking forward to chatting over old times with lost loved ones. And so it was, for them. Death was beginning to smile a little, show flexibility, a touch of concern. Death was starting to take account of the *individual*.

It wasn't happening everywhere, all the time, but it was happening somewhere every minute of every day. And it was a start.

In this way Hieronymus began slowly to recover from the harsh lesson of Zone Nineteen. He worked hard, kept his figures high enough to keep Coffin off his back, and day by day he pushed the revolution forward.

COFFIN MAKER   MARK L. FOWLER

It had been the night after the lesson, looking down on Holy Mountain in the aftermath. It had changed him. Seeing the embers of an entire culture had burnt away all traces of ivory-tower idealism, and sown the seeds of pragmatism. It had hit him like a hammer across the temples: the way forward. A revolution in death. A quiet revolution. A revolution that wouldn't bring Coffin screaming for genocide or set Beezle to the task like a tortured animal straining at its master's leash. This way there would be no complaint from above or below. Coffin would get his figures and the world, or at least parts of it, could get on with the job of living.

It was the way it had once been. Hieronymus, with his gifts of historical insight (along with the odd peek into Coffin's journal) had looked back into the fog of time and seen the way Coffin had once operated. Then, all that time ago, Coffin had truly been a Poet of Death; and for now, Hieronymus was assuming that mantle. One day he would show Coffin what he was doing, remind him of the way it had once been and could be again. One day, when he understood the Coffin Maker better, when he had earned his credibility, the time would be right to give the king back his crown.

But not while the old fool was acting like a buffoon.

Hieronymus learnt quickly after Coffin's lesson, and one thing he learnt was not to cry every time the last nail was driven home. Time was too precious to spend weeping and too precious for philosophical sojourns on the essential wrongness of death. Such pretension

COFFIN MAKER MARK L. FOWLER

wouldn't benefit the world because what the world needed was action. He had to be as industrious, in his own way, as Beezle was in his. Hold the balance. Show Coffin a better way.

A new way.

The old way.

He could never succeed by telling Coffin, reminding the master of the craftsmanship he had once achieved and might achieve again - that would accomplish nothing, and risk bringing out more of his bile. He had to be sharper than that to earn his right to change the course of death in the world. He would succeed best, not by standing against death, but by giving dignity to it and to those its shadows crossed.

This new conviction brought about its own revolution in the heart of Hieronymus. A revolution that caused him even to venture over the threshold, to the land of multiple deaths. To enter the Coffin Dome. A revolution that caused him to bring tense skirmishes to the fruition of brutal conflict. To sometimes, as the lesser of two evils, let the hatred and frustration of the world boil over into the exchanges of battle, rather than see the slow festering of old wounds claim even more lives with even greater obscenity.

One day, Hieronymus looked down on a churchyard in the heart of Zone Thirty-Nine. A huge crowd was gathering outside the main entrance of the impressive gothic structure that was *All Saints Multi-Denominational Church of the Living God.*

While Hieronymus watched through the monitor, the crowd swelled as the faithful spilled out of the church and into the sunshine, to stand beneath the

COFFIN MAKER   MARK L. FOWLER

magnificent spire. With the final ferocious chords from the mighty organ blazing behind the assembled, Bishop Stones began the ceremony that was to culminate in the unveiling of a statue.

Standing alongside the still-veiled mystery, the bishop read to the hushed crowd, reliving the birth of the Church through carefully selected extracts from the Acts of the Apostles, followed by a few verses from the great convert, St. Paul. Another hymn, a few prayers, and the moment of unveiling was at hand.

Gasps of wonder filled the churchyard. Another hymn, another reading from Paul, and another silence followed as the faithful gazed on the stone representation of an unidentified holy-man kneeling in prayer. It was never intended that the statue should represent Father Henry directly, certainly not by Bishop Stones; but to the congregation of All Saints, it would never fail to evoke his memory. He was already their saint, and, they had no doubt, he would guide them when they needed him most.

After the unveiling the bishop said a few words. "We have cause today to be both joyous and sad. Joyous because this fine statue will forever remind the people of this parish of the life of a man of God; sad because he is no longer among us to continue his ministry. But we also have cause to be more than a little afraid."

Mutterings rose from the gathering, but petered out as the bishop cast an assertive eye over them. "When Father Henry died, he left words reverberating around this fine church. Words that we would do well to remember. Words that we ought to find difficult to

COFFIN MAKER MARK L. FOWLER

forget. A terrible danger, a dreadful force, has come into the world. A force bearing seed close to our own community. A night that we are headed back into. A night so black and pitiless that even God will not venture in to save us. A virus, an evil virus. Not something for men in white coats to study under microscopes. One we can see by simply opening our eyes. A man. Flesh and blood. Yet far more than that. And I think that most amongst us heard the name of that man, that curse, that *abomination* for the first time from the dying lips of our departed friend."

Mutterings arose once more among the assembled. That Bishop Stones was losing it. That he had once forbidden the priests in his charge to talk the way that *he* was talking now.

But Stones was a man who could stomach his own hypocrisy over and above the merest hint of subterfuge from mere flock, and with a glare he silenced them.

"I feel awkward - no, *absurd* when I suggest such a thing as the devil visiting the world in human form. I know that sort of talk feeds scorn and pours ridicule on the Church. But the fear of saying such things has long hung over the world like a witch's curse. The devil works best through ridicule, and even better through the fear of ridicule. I want to tell you something that isn't easy to say. Yes, I fell out with Father Henry over a book he was writing. A book written to comfort a grief-stricken relative. I made him burn the book because I believed it was inappropriate and superstitious. I regret that now. I didn't realise what a visionary we had in our midst. I wish that I had listened closer to the words of Father Henry. I'm glad that he defied me when he delivered his last sermon and spoke out that forbidden name."

A pin falling onto grass would have been deafening in the pause that followed.

"Father Henry died for a reason. His death has driven the message into our hearts more forcefully than any amount of preaching could have done, even from one so gifted. This monument is a symbol to us all of the united strength we have as a people; we must use that strength to do battle against the virus that is amongst us now. We must stand together until Satan is slain. I know, with more certainty than anything that I have ever known, that someone up there is watching over us and that we will win the fight."

Fight the Good Fight blasted out, and Hieronymus turned away from the monitor. How could his quiet revolution of death succeed whilst the growth of the world's nemesis remained unchecked?

Paranoia was building in Zone Thirty-Nine. But people were people, and a few rays of sunshine distracted them. The paradox of the human condition: combat fear with indifference; know the beast but never name it, and confront it with apathy.

Yet the name had been spoken.

And even the Church was speaking it.

Realising that belief in a devil in human form – or in any form, come to that - was good business for an ailing institution.

Without Father Henry, the nameless Old Man, Brigadier Browning - without the courage of such rare

COFFIN MAKER   MARK L. FOWLER

souls, lethargy on a suicidal scale was only a parting of the clouds away. There was a call to arms needed amongst all good people, and perhaps there would be no shortage of them once the battle began.

Hieronymus knew his history, though: knew that blind courage would leave behind only a land of martyrs. That once the killing started it would never stop.

Yet could humans alone destroy Gouge?
Was Gouge himself human?
Was Gouge of the devil - or was *Gouge the devil?*

If so, what effect could they have, when all was said and done, on a fallen angel? They could live in such a way that their goodness might touch the heart of the Coffin Maker. Make him spend more time *loving them and less time hating them.*

Or else they could make the conditions right for Beezle. They were not helpless in this. It made no sense that they could ever be bystanders in a cosmic battle between good and evil. It was surely in their power to either bolster the strength of Gouge, or weaken him. Make his coffin that bit easier, or...

Hieronymus caught a glimpse of hell.

He was forbidden to complete a coffin for Colonel Gouge because through his own stupidity he had made his profile too fascinating. He, Hieronymus, saviour and friend to all mankind, had given the human race's greatest enemy immunity from death.

How long would this insanity go on? What would it take to convince Coffin that the beast had to be destroyed? That Death wasn't the deity that humanity needed and that appeasing Death was not the Meaning of Life. There had to be more to life than that. Death, for reasons mysterious, had been made a condition of life and mortals were stuck with it. Moral choices had no jurisdiction over it.

Death and evil were not the same thing.
The clock was ticking.
Why was it all so complex?
Unknowable?

Father Henry had opened up a minefield. Or at least posted directions to it.

Hieronymus looked back at the monitor, at the figures kneeling in prayer outside the vast structure of All Saints, preparing to fight against something they didn't understand and willing to sacrifice everything.

How easy it would be for Beezle to slip into the Coffin Dome and destroy this dreaming, hymn-singing band of resistance standing huddled around the church. How easy to bring this splendid new monument, this great symbol of hope, crashing down onto that fat and hypocritical oaf Bishop Stones, who had changed his tune because of an edict from above. Not even guilt. The Church, at its highest level of authority, recognised that Father Henry had become aware of something that nobody else had seen. Something that could no longer be kept quiet.

The hierarchy wanted – no, demanded - to see the book that the bishop had the priest destroy.

Bishop Stones, under considerable pressure, had even stooped so low as to visit the priest's now doubly bereaved nephew, John, in the hope that another copy of the book existed. Thankfully the boy had been too

COFFIN MAKER   MARK L. FOWLER

clever for the bishop, and a credit to Father Henry. Bishop Stones had left empty handed and the boy had started reading his uncle's manuscript even before the pompous fool had even made it down the garden path.

And now a copy was on a flight to the other side of the globe, to Zone Six Hundred and Sixty Six, the place where John and his father hoped to begin a new life.

Hieronymus smiled. *Beezle is not allowed in Zone Thirty-Nine.*

Beezle is no more allowed to meddle in this affair, than I am to hammer nails into Gouge's coffin. At least, that's how it stands for the moment.

He switched off the monitor. There was supposed to be a revolution underway and Zone Thirty-Nine would not miss out. Gouge might have immunity from death, but his closest would soon be feeling the anger of an indignant moral conscience.

The youth headed for the Dome. There was an underground meeting planned in the isolated northern hills. Every major figure in Gouge's twisted party would be there. Gouge was travelling to meet them, to deliver important orders. To begin manoeuvres. He would arrive to find himself the sole survivor of his own satanic army.

If, that night, Coffin had stood with his ear pressed against the door of the Coffin Dome and listened to the incessant hammering and the fevered wail of machinery, he would have guessed that Beezle was reaching new heights of passion, even approaching the zenith of his desire for slaughter. Yet inside the Dome a

COFFIN MAKER   MARK L. FOWLER

stranger to its vast armoury of dispatch, was acquainting himself with its secrets, and discovering the extent of its power.

Hieronymus left a single nail poking out of each coffin, then waited, his eyes trained on the monitor. He wanted Gouge to smell the incineration of his army. He wanted Gouge to feel the torn limbs raining down on him as he mounted the secret hillside.

It frightened Hieronymus that he felt like this, as though the crusade to bludgeon evil bred its own insanity. But when he looked hard into the future of a world under the spell of Colonel Gouge, he knew that inaction was the worst kind of evil.

With split second precision he brought the hammer down.

Colonel Gouge dived to the ground as the hillside exploded. It was like a human volcano erupting.

Gouge lay still as the sky filled with bleeding chunks, gravity missing a breath, holding the screaming debris suspended for a slow-motion instant before the human jigsaw was finally released to bombard the blood-soaked ground. Only when the storm had spewed out its last morsels did he crawl through the debris of scattered flesh and bones (some cooked, some raw) until even that inhuman constitution started to heave on the carnage, his stomach giving way to deep spasms, setting up its own series of explosions as he emptied his insides over the remains of the chosen.

Moving on his own wave of nausea, Hieronymus ran out of the Coffin Dome, running until even the bulking

COFFIN MAKER   MARK L. FOWLER

shadow of the foreboding Tower was obliterated in the swamp of darkness that grew like a black stain behind him.

This place, the Graveyard of Death itself, was beyond the territory of the Coffin Maker. It was the outer edge of a mythical land - a land that the Coffin Maker believed he would one day walk, when his work in the Kingdom of Death was finished. Where, at the very end, Death itself would follow Life deep into the soil, and where the bones of the Eternal would at last find rest to await the final call to whatever glory was waiting.

Here, far beyond earshot of the Coffin Complex, Hieronymus fell to his knees and roared out his soul to the dark night, raging in fury and disgust until, wretched and exhausted, he whispered into the dirt, "What is this quiet revolution of death? Do I *out-Beezle* Beezle? - fighting fire with fire until the world is burnt to ash?"

He looked up at the starless sky. "These men were evil; corrupted cells multiplying with a single objective: to help Gouge turn the world the colour of cancer. Yet they were people once, God-made and mother-born. Who am I to judge them? Who am I to decide who lives and who dies? Who am I to go killing in the name of whatever I happen to believe in?"

He looked up from the dirt, into the cold darkness above. "Whatever it is out there, creating me to serve my time in this place - I beg you, have mercy. Whoever you are, whatever you want - spare me this unwanted existence."

COFFIN MAKER   MARK L. FOWLER

It was some time before Hieronymus found the strength to drag himself back to his feet. A ghostly moon had crept under the dome of night, lightly bathing him as he prepared again to address the empty sky.

Looking hard into the eye of the silent night he asked the questions that he knew could not be answered. *How much torture and misery is going on in the world in this single night at the hands of Beezle and Coffin? How many lives are ending, tonight, as brutally as the lives of Gouge's madmen? - and for no reason other than to satisfy the ambitions of Beezle, and the pathological sense of duty of Coffin.*

"Why me?" he shouted in what he believed might be the direction of Heaven. "Why have I been brought here? To put things right? It's too much to ask of anybody. The burden's too great. You've chosen badly. I can't go on."

The tears came down like they might last forever. Tears for the world and tears of self-pity. There was nothing to distinguish them from mortal tears.

When at last they stopped falling, he gathered himself. "What choice do I have?" he said. "The revolution is everything. It must go on."

It did.

Coffin had been more than a little impressed with Hieronymus' exploding hillside, but less than impressed with just about everything else. Everywhere that Beezle's terror didn't reign, the mark of Hieronymus was falling over the world like a gentle blanket of warm snow. Human beings seemed to be in

COFFIN MAKER   MARK L. FOWLER

control of death. Death seemed predictable and sensitive, a goodnight kiss at the end of a long day.

And there was something oddly familiar in the gentleness of death in those areas governed by Hieronymus, though the familiarity was vague, like an old dream or a long forgotten or abandoned thought.

He watched the world under the shaping hands of his two apprentices and tried to make sense of it. Watched the world dividing more deeply into two: the places where powerlessness and primal fear etched savagely into the faces of every breathing creature, running scared with nowhere safe to hide; and the places where life was shaking hands with death in a mutual agreement of negotiation and trust.

Both apprentices were moving too far towards the edge, and Coffin thought of appealing once more to the Creator. He even wrote the memo, before ripping it into confetti and cursing himself for his continued idiotic faith in the face of clear desertion.

Desperate to find some outlet for the feelings welling inside, he wrote,

This is getting beyond a joke.

He spent an age wondering what else to write. It came to him slowly.

Need to move them back to the centre. Both at once or one at a time? Who first? No good speeding up Hieronymus. That will press Beezle on to dizzier heights. So it must be Beezle first. How do I halt a

rampaging bull? Show it a mirror. That's how. Show it a mirror.

With an intoxicating mixture of excitement and pride blossoming within, Coffin turned to a fresh page.

New mission for Beezle. Urgent assignment. Colonel Gouge's coffin.

Coffin's shoulders were shaking again, though with some effort of will he held back. He wanted to admire, without distraction, the full brilliance of his idea. For what better way to slow down Beezle than to put him into a quandary over how to keep one man alive. It was better than brilliant, infinitely better.

When Coffin had examined his infinitely-better-than-brilliant idea from every conceivable angle, gorging himself on it until he was full to the brim with it, he granted licence to his new found friend, and allowed laughter back. And when it came, rushing through him like a cleansing storm, he wasn't at all willing to let it go.

Like a hysterical schoolboy, he wrote, repeatedly,

Beezle to get Gouge. Beezle to get Gouge.

He laughed harder and louder every time he wrote it, until at last the page was filled and his body was aching. As the laughter finally drained from the Coffin Maker, he spoke softly to himself, as though addressing a very old and very dear friend.

"Of course he'll never do it. He'll wriggle and he'll squirm and he'll get out of doing it. And I want him to get out of doing it.

"Because I want to see how Gouge responds to the annihilation of his organisation. I want to know what Gouge is. I want the measure of him. And I want the measure of his number one fan. Young Beezle. I want to see a little of the character beneath that brutal professionalism. *What makes him tick?*

"Hieronymus played a clever hand with that exploding hillside. I want to see what Beezle's going to do about it.

"Who said the Coffin Maker couldn't be allowed a little fun once in a while? And it has been a while. Now we're starting to get somewhere."

Beaming with post-laughter pride, he wrote,

Now we're getting somewhere.

16: COLONEL GOUGE

From under the smoking ruins of his mutilated army, Colonel Gouge stirred. He pulled himself to his feet and surveyed the human debris. "Amateurs!"

The brief moment of nausea had passed, leaving only a hungry rumble to ricochet around his lead-lined gut. He kicked an orphaned head down the hillside. "You spineless little pigs got what you deserved. Gutless bastards." He picked up a half-cooked arm and tossed it down the hill. "If Doveman's creeps hadn't done this, I'd have done it."

He lashed out at a few more of the human remains, then came across the upper torso of his second-in-command. The man he had trusted and valued too highly. "You wanted to rule the world but you hadn't the faintest notion of what ambition means."

The head still sat intact on the neck, the features practically undamaged. Only in the severing from the waist could the extent of the man's ordeal be imagined.

Gouge licked his lips. "Gouge by name, Gouge by nature."

In a moment the eyes were out of the sockets, the colonel chewing voraciously. "Something to settle the stomach." He let out a volley of sewer laughter, already wondering whether an ear or a nose would make the finer dessert. In the event he made a pig of himself and ate the entire face.

Beezle turned off the monitor and headed to the Coffin Dome to vent spleen. On behalf of Colonel Gouge and for the injustice dealt him, ten thousand people were about to lose their lives. First the earthquake, then the tidal wave. Zone Thirteen was about to earn its title of the Unlucky Island.

He had no doubts that Hieronymus had been responsible. He could smell the odious morality. It was only right and proper that Zone Thirteen pick up the tab. After all, it was small enough to be wiped out of existence, and that was the kind of statement he was looking to make.

Of course he credited Hieronymus with a good deal more than an exploding hillside. He was sure he was behind Coffin's about-turn, ordering Gouge's death. It had that same reek of moral irony.

As Beezle saw it, his opposite number was running up one hell of a bill, and Zone Thirteen would make a good instalment.

It was this thought that fuelled a night of hungry slaughter as Zone Thirteen all but disappeared beneath the ocean. In the aftermath, Beezle's appetite was even stronger, as though eating was merely a way of getting the gastric juices flowing. Ten thousand people had become hors-d'oeuvres, and in the middle of the plate was Hieronymus, with an orange sticking out of his arse.

Gouge was lying on the ground, resting after his meal. A single breath of wind reached over and tugged lightly at his tunic, making him sit up.

He pressed an ear into the silence. A voice, sensed not heard, yet at the same time distinct, solid. A somehow silent voice promising everything. A kindred voice, outside of reality yet more real than death itself,

COFFIN MAKER   MARK L. FOWLER

coming at him from all directions, bringing him closer to power.

"Believe," breathed Beezle into the monitor. "*Believe*."

He left Colonel Gouge to the transcendental stillness and flicked the monitor to see how Hieronymus was spending the night. To see how death was revealing itself in the rest of Zone Thirty-Nine.

Hieronymus was in full swing, his revolution soaring towards a personally fashioned utopia. Death had learnt, again, to shake the mortal hand and work it out together. And the handshakes were getting longer and the gentleness of the black shadow beginning to cast doubt over the reality of life itself.

The balance breaking, the hand overstretching, moving too far and too fast.

A young woman, swimming in the dangerous waters off Zone Four Hundred and Eighty, found herself staring into the eyes of a hungry shark. She had thought her dream would never come true.

For years she had lived in the eye of every conceivable danger, moving around the monster's mouth, waiting for it to happen. She was tired of the impossible miracles that persistently spared her.

Her coffin was all but done; a single nail would finish it.

Hieronymus hesitated. A part of him wanted to let the tragedy of her life end here. But something was missing.

Love was missing.

COFFIN MAKER   MARK L. FOWLER

This young girl had never known love. Not one experience of it in twenty nine years of life. Just deeply trodden paths of sorrow. Death had let her come to the threshold again and again, believing that, with each escape, the value of her life would dawn. Yet every time she craved for the 'better place', reached for it, life intervened to save her.

Her ambition hardened into a desire to die a savage death. To purge the pain of life with the agony of a brutal final scene. Her own twisted preparation for eternity.

As the shark widened its mouth to take her legs, Hieronymus looked under the skin of her death-wish and he knew that this young life was not ready to end. What kind of revolution would let death steal one last chance of love?

And so, as in a dream, she hung suspended above the shark's crashing teeth, until a gorgeous tremor of breeze gathered her and carried her beyond the dangerous waters, not letting her down until it found the warm soil of dry land where, as in all her favourite fairy tales of childhood, a handsome prince would come to find his long-searched-for lover.

Hieronymus let out a rapturous sigh and watched the shark move away, back into deeper waters. He watched the young woman for a while, and a strange sensation came over him. He suddenly longed to be mortal. To enter that world. To fall from this place of eternal death and be with her.

Denying the tear forming in his eye, Hieronymus left the woman to her privacy, burying his feelings back into the revolution.

COFFIN MAKER   MARK L. FOWLER

He knew her fate. Knew that in the face of his impotence, she would, finally, step back into the waters...to embrace her razor-toothed lover.

Beezle stood transfixed, gasping in disbelief as men, women and children floated out of the jaws of death in a hundred unnatural ways, as bullets swerved harmlessly, or else spluttered to the floor; explosions froze until the streets had cleared of people; cancers devoured themselves and belched away into thin air; murderers fell down and begged forgiveness from intended victims; plummeting airliners kissed the tops of mountains and slid harmlessly to the rescue of heroic villagers...
If it could be imagined, Hieronymus was making it happen. What could never be was happening openly and shamelessly.
And yet in the blinking of an eye, Beezle's horror turned to happiness.
He flicked the monitor back to the grim hillside where Colonel Gouge was still in the thrall of mystical knowledge. "Believe," he breathed, grinning into the monitor. "*Believe, believe, believe.*"

Coffin was busy with his journal, wrestling big issues and great thoughts, his pen ploughing a furious course across the pages. He hadn't the faintest idea that Beezle was marching to see him with revelations that would blow such thoughts out of his head and rip a gaping hole through his new found faith.
At the top of a fresh page he wrote in his best hand,

COFFIN MAKER   MARK L. FOWLER

Thoughts on Creation.

He underlined it and continued in a rampant spirit of pomposity.

It has long puzzled me why mortals seem to need to do things like 'Philosophy.' Asking questions about why the world was created and why things exist. It has always been enough for me just to get on with my job. I still had the likes of Plato and Aristotle in their coffins for all their supposed brain power. Thinking didn't give them an escape from their mortal destinies. St. Augustine got his head in a tangle trying to fathom Time. Didn't stop it running out on him. And all of them asking the same stupid questions. What good did it do them? Did they stop believing in the Creator? Did they start believing? What do they know about Him? Less than I do! But they waste more ink. Did thinking about freedom make them free? Did it chain them? As for their futile speculations about death. What can the living possibly know about that? They've never experienced it. Though they will. Every last one of them.

    Hieronymus thinks about these things. It's got me thinking too. It can't be merely the perversity of the human spirit that brings it on.

    The day he asked why I was called Coffin. That got me thinking. Why should I be called anything when there's only one of me?

    Not likely to get myself mixed up am I?

    This kind of thinking's contagious. Before I know it I'm questioning the Creator's purpose in setting

COFFIN MAKER   MARK L. FOWLER

all this in motion. Not just why he sent two apprentices but why he created life and then shoved death in its face. And the funny thing is that the more I think of these things the more questions arise. I'm not getting nearer to any answers but I'm having the devil of a time stopping asking the questions.

Coffin stopped, scratched his head with his pen, and read over what he'd written.

"What nonsense! I was better off content to be a great poet instead of a great philosopher. Better when I got on with it instead of thinking about it. Trouble is, I can't stop thinking about it."

His new friend laughter came out to play as he swept a wild pen stroke through the idle thoughts lying there on the page. He could afford a little childish indulgence, surely. Beezle's wings had been clipped and Hieronymus - well, a different light was shining on that young man now. Exploding hillsides! It got better the more he thought of it. Perhaps the Philosopher and the Poet of Death had a future after all.

With a peculiarly paternal feeling, he wrote,

Hieronymus has moved on from the arrogant wastrel that first came here smelling of violets. He's learned the hard way but learned all the same. I want to help him. I think he will let me. I think I can learn from him -

Coffin broke off. *Learn from an apprentice?* He flicked his eyes around the empty room, engulfed by a wave of paranoia. Yet it was true. Why deny it? Was he afraid

COFFIN MAKER   MARK L. FOWLER

to show weakness, afraid to admit to his mistakes? He'd show who was afraid!

Hieronymus has caused a revolution inside me.

It felt good, his pen finding difficulty keeping up with his thoughts.

Hieronymus reminds me of a part of myself. A long time ago. I was never young like him but I once used to think for myself. I once tried to be fair. I admitted my mistakes and I strived to change my ways. I cared. And it's taken a fresh-faced apprentice to show me what I am. What I've become. A proud fool trying to top the purple patches of his dark-age excesses.

The lid was off. No going back now. Holding his breath, he wrote,

And the so-called pre-history years. The thirstiest and most malignant spirits were born from those strange centuries. Experiment and wilful abandon replaced the principles of true craftsmanship on which I built my early reputation. I corrupted death and it's taken a gentle youth who can cry over a single coffin to teach me some compassion.

A loud knock at the door made Coffin jump to his feet, knocking his journal off the desk in the process. The huge tome hit the floor with a crash, setting up echoes so monumental that he had to wait a full minute before it was quiet enough to answer.

COFFIN MAKER   MARK L. FOWLER

"Yes?"

Beezle's face appeared around the door. "I hope I haven't called at an inconvenient moment," he said, watching Coffin struggling to retrieve his precious journal from the dusty floor.

"Well you *have* chosen an inconvenient moment," said Coffin, mauling the *History of Death* back onto his desk. "But now the damage has been done, so I suppose you'd better come in and tell me about it."

Beezle might have been startled by the coldness of the welcome if it had occurred a few days earlier. But he'd seen the way the old bastard had been edging towards Hieronymus; the way the sun had started to shine out of the philosophical dimwit's darkest orifice.

Beezle closed the door behind him and strutted up to Coffin's desk. He was going to enjoy the next few minutes.

Restoring his writing set, Coffin sat himself down and peered deeply into the young apprentice's eyes. "No doubt you've come to inform me that Colonel Gouge is safely inside his coffin."

Beezle shook his head.

"No," said Coffin. "I thought not. So before you tell me why you've come, I want to know how you can stand there with that cocksure look and tell me you've disobeyed my orders."

Beezle didn't even blink. The cards he was holding were just too good. "I've not come here to discuss Colonel Gouge, but since you mention him, let's just say that I know you don't really want him in a coffin. At least not yet."

"Who told you such a thing?"

"You just did."

"What?"

"Gouge is too interesting, isn't he? You wanted to slow me down. Shame about Zone Thirteen, don't you think?"

"How dare you talk to me like that?"

Beezle's cards were getting itchy in his hand, but he held on to them.

"I may sound impertinent; I may sound brash, bloodthirsty..."

"Come to the point!"

"The point is: if my youthful exuberance sometimes leads me to get a little carried away..."

"Don't take me for a fool, Beezle. Your actions have nothing to do with youthful anythings. I'm beginning to see in you, not the hand of a craftsman, but a barbarian."

So Hieronymus really had got under Coffin's skin. A long way under, by the look of things. Time, thought Beezle, to set the table straight for the big hand.

"Gouge has ambition, and I don't doubt that he'll shed rivers of blood to attain his ends. But the world has more to fear from stupidity, and if you want to look on stupidity incarnate, then look no further than President Doveman. Except that stupidity can often be a fence for evil."

"Doveman?" said Coffin. "You can't be serious."

"Can't I? In Doveman you have the seeds of real destruction. The World Wars were a playground squabble compared with what's on the other side of the door that the good president holds the key to. Are you really so easily deceived?"

Coffin noticed that the fluorescence of Beezle's orange hair had intensified, taking on the unstable quality of a badly wired reactor.

Coffin narrowed his eyes. "Doveman is a man of peace."

"Exactly so."

"Beezle, you are severely trying my patience. If you have a point, please come to it."

"We're talking apocalypse. We're talking of the devil himself down there, rolling that sad globe under his feet all the way to hell and damnation."

"Devil on Earth?" said Coffin. "You *are* talking about Doveman?"

"Do you really think the devil would come in the guise of a man like Gouge? Doesn't it seem a little too obvious? Doveman is the enemy of us all: you, me, mankind...the Creator. Gouge alone can stem the evil waiting to ambush the whole shooting match. Gouge is the saviour; our saviour, their saviour."

On the face of it Coffin didn't believe a word. Yet things did seem to be turning upside down and inside out, and generally getting stranger by the hour. It was hard to be certain of anything anymore – and that damned philosophy wasn't helping, obscuring his thoughts like it did.

Was Beezle serious, though? Talk of the devil was one thing - though as far as he was concerned, the devil was a disputed and abstract unlikelihood of which no direct evidence had ever been manifest.

COFFIN MAKER MARK L. FOWLER

Yet to suggest that this metaphysical bundle of improbability was President Doveman!

Beezle grinned at the turmoil he had clearly caused in the Coffin Maker's mind. The fog he'd generated was practically blowing out of the old fool's bony ears.

Now the table was well and truly laid.

Now it was time to let those itching hands play the big beautiful cards.

"I can see that I've left you with a lot to think about, and I'm sorry I've given you the wrong impression about me. I don't want to take up any more of your valuable time," said Beezle, casting a sarcastic eye towards the journal on Coffin's desk, "but there's something I have to show you. I think you should look at the monitor. I'm really very concerned about what Hieronymus is doing and I think you will be, too."

Beezle walked over to the monitor, Coffin's personal monitor, mounted beneath the window. "May I?" he asked, with exaggerated politeness.

Coffin stood up, his mouth hanging open already. Slowly, as though in a trance, he placed one foot in front of the other until he was standing at Beezle's side, watching scenes from the quiet revolution of death unfolding on the screen, Beezle flicking from zone to zone, revealing the same unbelievable scenes in every corner of the globe.

Everywhere, human beings were defying the natural laws in glorious escapes from death.

Beezle waited until Coffin's eyes were practically popping out of his head, before revealing a final image. With the grin of Armageddon bursting over

COFFIN MAKER — MARK L. FOWLER

his face, he took Coffin to Zone Five Hundred and Ninety-Nine.

To a cemetery.

At first there was nothing but stillness and silence. Then it started to happen. All over the cemetery the dust of the earth was beginning to move. Sounds from beneath the earth breaking the night open.

Coffin swallowed hard, his eyes welded to the monitor.

The sounds grew, the movements becoming unmistakable.

Somewhere in the Coffin Complex Hieronymus was at work.

Not with a hammer - but with pliers.

Ripping the lids off coffins.

All over the cemetery, death was moving backwards into life.

"Now," said Beezle. "What do you think about that?"

COFFIN MAKER   MARK L. FOWLER

17: THE TOWER

Coffin turned off the monitor in disbelief, then switched it back on again in deeper disbelief. The graveyard was alive. "My God," he said, his vocabulary slipping. "Where else is this happening?"

Beezle flicked the monitor eagerly over burial grounds around the globe.

"My God," said Coffin again. *"My God."*

"I'm afraid he's a very sick young man," said Beezle.

Coffin turned off the monitor, and this time he left it off. An ancient question had been answered. Now he understood what the Tower was for.

"Beezle, you must excuse me. I have some business to attend to."

He left the room with an urgent sense of purpose, not stopping even to usher the ugly apprentice out of this most private place, and not even closing his journal.

Beezle was already taking on the look of a fox in a chicken house, licking his lips as the farmer left town.

The Dome was going to be busy.

Coffin found Hieronymus in the Vaults, that immense structure containing the coffins of every soul that had once breathed Earth's sweet air. The Vaults held the history of mankind in its endless rooms, and to walk through them was to take a trip back through time, from death's recent trophies to its oldest prizes.

COFFIN MAKER   MARK L. FOWLER

It had always seemed a curious state of affairs to Coffin that the Vaults never ran out of rooms. The first time that the outer room had been filled to capacity, he'd panicked, only to find the room empty on his next visit, as though an additional one had secretly been added at the back, yet not visibly so, and all the coffins shunted one room on. This had happened so many times over the centuries that he stopped noticing it, and the mystery ceased to be a mystery in the same way that a mortal might cease, most days, to find mystery in the breathing of air.

Coffin was spared the endless walk through the immense tunnel. Didn't have to walk beyond the first station, where he found Hieronymus squatting on the floor, pulling backwards, hard, with sweat-beaded pliers, ripping nails out of a recently completed coffin.

"What are you doing?" asked Coffin, softly, as though in the presence of great suffering.

Hieronymus put the pliers behind his back in a feeble attempt at deceit. For a moment he held a desperate look of innocence, but quickly recognising its futility, he gave it up.

The revolution was over.

He sighed, deeply, and sought bitter consolation in an ancient philosophy. At least he'd given some life back to the world by emptying a few coffins. He could have done more, would dearly have loved to have done more, but it simply wasn't to be.

The stoicism creaked, giving way to an eruption of outrage.

He hadn't done anything here that hadn't been done many times before. He'd merely borrowed the idea

COFFIN MAKER   MARK L. FOWLER

from the *History of Death*, written in Coffin's own fair hand. Coffin was nothing more than...

Battling against the sense of injustice, he loaned out the benefit of the doubt and looked into the gunmetal eyes of the Coffin Maker, searching for recognition, pride, even embarrassment at seeing old practices given new life. Finding none of these, he thought it wise still to leave the past alone awhile. Self proclaimed poets were notoriously reluctant to acknowledge early compositions – or even to be reminded of them. Known to get tetchy when the buried 'treasure' of bold but embarrassing experiment was unearthed and shoved under their noses. Likely to go nuclear at the merest hint of accusation that their own *hypocrisy* was in the air.

He would wait for Coffin to raise the subject. There was nothing to be gained here by wit. Humanity was too precious for more to be thrown away through the temptations of the hasty, well-turned phrase, albeit aimed with the finest intentions at the glorious bulls-eye of Coffin's outrageous double standards.

So he waited for the gravity of the situation to reveal itself, a small part of him clinging to the hope that seeing the restoration of such ancient and once-beloved techniques might bring a sense of nostalgia to the Coffin Maker and jolt him to his senses. But the longer he looked into those dead eyes, the more diluted became that hope, and he started to fear the worst.

"Did you think that I wouldn't find out? Have you any idea what you have done? Any idea what this means?"

COFFIN MAKER   MARK L. FOWLER

Hieronymus caught a flicker of sympathy crossing Coffin's face. Yet the flicker was already an uncertain memory that he couldn't trust. "You wouldn't understand."

"Oh, spare me, please," said Coffin. "I thought it was only mortals that had to endure the stupidity of adolescence. Youth proclaims to be different, unique, woefully disconnected to what's gone before; always believing that the old never had the same thoughts, the same feelings."

"Are you saying that I'm not the first?"

"I'm saying," said Coffin, "that today isn't the first time a lid has been taken off a coffin. And as we're clearly not talking about Beezle, I'll leave it to you to draw your own conclusions."

Hieronymus started to speak, but Coffin raised a hand to stop him.

"I'm afraid that I have to carry out a duty that I find as sorrowful to administer as you will to receive. From this very moment you are suspended from all activity in the Coffin Complex. I will escort you to your new quarters now."

"New quarters?"

"You will accompany me to the Tower."

"I'm to be a prisoner in the tower? Like in some medieval melodrama? Are you mad?"

"Someone is."

What would become of mankind with only a sad old fool and the psychotic Beezle to rule its destiny? "What have I done?" said Hieronymus. "My God, *what have I done?*"

COFFIN MAKER MARK L. FOWLER

Coffin took hold of his arm, pulling the youth to his feet. "Mind your language. Come on, the Tower's waiting."

Hieronymus shook his arm free. "What right do you have to do this? Why should you dictate the rules? You have no procedures set out by the Creator. How can you say that what I've done is wrong? It might be the will of the Creator; it might be why he sent me. All I've done is put some hope back into the world - hope that you stole from it."

Two forces stood at the point of war inside Hieronymus: Fury at the injustice; and responsibility for the world. There was no certainty which course the battle might take. One good outburst might set the record straight.

Might commit the world to flames.

In the event Hieronymus never had to make a decision. Before he could utter another word, he found himself hoisted off the ground with a force he had never imagined, as though the glimmer of metal in Coffin's eyes had been, all along, a warning that he had a body, not of bone, but iron. A moment later he was heading out of the Vaults under the Coffin Maker's arm.

The Tower gazed down on the scene with an expression of unkind welcome. Though it was built from the same materials as every other structure in the Coffin Complex, its fairy-tale architecture appeared the most animated, to the point where it seemed capable of its own thoughts and pleasures.

At the foot of the Tower, Coffin restored Hieronymus to his feet, and let him walk the last few steps unaided to the gothic-arched entrance. The archway seemed, from a distance, to come straight out of a medieval romance. As Hieronymus approached he noticed that the underside sparkled with a startling rainbow mosaic.

He stopped under the arch, to examine the unexpected rampage of colour, until Coffin pushed him forwards into the dim coldness that lay on the other side.

On the dark side of the arch the youth found himself at the foot of an immense winding staircase made of black stone. Mounting the first step felt like falling upwards, powerlessly drawn by a strange gravity, propelling him towards the room at the top.

"What is this place?" he asked, as they approached the summit of the endless staircase. In reply Coffin merely breathed a putrid excuse for air onto the back of his already chilled neck.

When the steps at last ran out, Hieronymus found that he was standing before an imposing wooden door that looked down on him with impatience. Coffin pulled out a suitably large key and placed it in the lock. The key turned easily, but the snapping back of the metal bolt smashed into the nervous silence with such violence, that entering the room with the aid of a canon might have been the quieter approach.

From the size of the door, Hieronymus thought he was about to enter a giant's palace. But when the door finally creaked open, the room was of modest size. And entirely empty. The same austerity that marked the living quarters was evident, though far less inviting.

COFFIN MAKER   MARK L. FOWLER

Coffin ushered him into the room with a wave of his hand, then the door was pulled shut, the key turning decisively in the lock.

He could hear the muffled sounds of the Coffin Maker descending the staircase.

Hieronymus walked cautiously across the room, to the small window that looked out over the Coffin Complex. He watched Coffin emerge from the bottom of the Tower and head towards his office, no doubt eager to waste a few pompous hours scribbling in his book. A moment later Beezle came into view, heading into the Coffin Dome.

What had he done that was so wrong? Coffin had done the same thing a million times, and made no secret of it. It was there in his journal. There was a good side to the Coffin Maker, despite everything. It wasn't as straightforward as 'Death at all costs'. He was more complex than that.

Or more deeply insane.

The *History of Death* was testament to his absolute ambivalence towards the human race, summed up in the echoing line, *'I love them I hate them'*. And there *had* been a flicker of sympathy on Coffin's face, back in the Vaults.

Why? Because he'd been down the same road himself? If so then what was really at issue here? What had Coffin discovered down that road that scared him so much? What had he seen that he couldn't even commit to the page? After all, he committed pretty much everything else!

A light still burned in the Coffin Dome, and Hieronymus gazed out towards it, lost in labyrinths of speculation. Was it left in the hands of Doveman alone now to save the world? Was mortal flesh and blood capable of doing that?

The sound of footsteps coming up the staircase jerked him back to the present. As the key turned in the door he wondered if Doveman was strong enough and clever enough to save the world from the night that was closing in.

18: PRESIDENT DOVEMAN

In towns and cities, remote farmlands and forgotten hollows, people were turning on their televisions. The buzz of excitement had built up over the week. Not an office block, village shop, street corner or hillside tavern had been free from talk of what the president had in store on Friday, three o'clock, live.

The nation had become united in anticipation. Those who could remember spoke of parallel days in 1939. No-one could recall anything like it since.

By two-thirty the streets were deserted. Schools and colleges closed, and industries priding themselves on uninterrupted productivity ensured, on demand, radio contact for the skeleton staff. Uncertainty and doubt stained the air. Zone Thirty-Nine had wandered into a time when politicians could no longer be idly discussed and summarily dismissed in the casual gossip of daily life.

Something was going wrong and nobody seemed sure what it was, why it was, or who it was.

There was a line of speculation doing the rounds, focusing on an evil virus in the form of a man: a man by the name of Gouge. A name brought to public attention by Father Henry in his now infamous sermon. Under normal circumstances the nation would doubtless have disregarded the Sunday morning ramblings of the local witchdoctor, but the dramatic death of the holy man had provoked media interest, and at least one national newspaper featured unabridged transcriptions of Father Henry's immortal swansong.

COFFIN MAKER   MARK L. FOWLER

The story had its day, then largely faded from the public mind until President Doveman returned from his tour of the East and headed unannounced to Sunday communion at All Saints. It was the sort of naive gesture that Doveman's opponents took every opportunity to exploit. It was what they liked to call his "political immaturity," and it was what many believed would one day see him out of office.

The embers of the story roared back into flame, and the name Gouge was once again on the nation's lips. What had seemed nothing more than melodramatic words from a paranoid priest became the hottest of political potatoes. If Doveman was to survive the week, questions had to be answered: Who was Gouge and why was he to be feared and what was being done about it?

It was Doveman's chance to secure a nation's faith in its leader, or to let slip power, possibly forever. He was dealing with something that could spiral into hysteria, and tomorrow's headlines would broadcast his obituary or deification.

When the hour struck, every television channel united. Private satellite stations, specialising in the provision of the nation's pornographic needs, interrupted otherwise sacred slots, so that nationwide a single face filled *every* available screen.

A face of youthful wisdom. A face of warmth and energy. A face light years from the world of politics. Mesmeric green eyes smiling their way into homes and public halls, and with them the calm voice of reassurance, breaking over his people like a mythical sunrise.

COFFIN MAKER   MARK L. FOWLER

The voice made friends and broke its way gently through the first lines of resistance, pulling out fear by the roots under a balm of natural anaesthetic. It worked in perfect partnership with the hypnotising green eyes, leading its children towards the multi-coloured fields of policy.

Dark clouds rolled back like a carpet, and a vision of peace shone sublimely through the electronic nation. It was magical. The country was danced through beautiful gardens of mounting prosperity, security and longevity. Esoteric issues tripped out into the new sunshine to hold hands with economic and social policies - policies that would build on the solid foundations of the past twelve months of unequivocal success.

Yet still one cloud was eclipsing a chunk of the sun: Gouge. The name was left unspoken, as far as possible. Names had power. Its sound might tear a hole through the grand illusion, breaking the trance, creating a vacuum that could suck out the faith invested by the nation in its three-o-clock president.

Doveman was too practiced a magician to let one ill-chosen word ruin the trick. What he had built so carefully would not be squandered easily. He spoke carefully of whispers, asking what power an unseen, unknown lunatic could exert if the nation came together to support its leader. Humanitarian policies would soon be uniting the people, sealing the footholds that some "rogue chancer" might otherwise find to scale the good city walls. "Evil," said Doveman, "only thrives where unrest and discontent exists. Evil looks for divisions. It festers in the cracks between people."

COFFIN MAKER   MARK L. FOWLER

The cameras rolled on, and the rallying cries of unification, faith and the triumph of goodness, were punched into the air in the final words of the presidential address. Then a nation was on its feet, applause ringing through the land.

There would be no obituary for Doveman, only for Gouge, beneath naming, laid to rest and mourned by nobody.

Hieronymus watched the door open and the cautious head of the Coffin Maker appear around it. "It's alright," he said. "I'm not waiting to hit you over the head with anything."

Coffin smiled awkwardly before clothing his clear embarrassment with a transparent and absurdly long-winded attempt to clear a non-existent frog from his throat.

"Swallowed a coffin-nail?" asked Hieronymus.

"Not lost your sense of humour then," returned Coffin.

"Should I have? Should removal of my liberty - particularly when that removal endangers the entire human race - prevent me from enjoying the look of naked guilt on the face of my misguided gaoler?"

Coffin locked the door and walked over to the window where Hieronymus stood. "Incarceration has been known to wipe smiles off faces, if that's what you mean."

The youth opened his mouth to reply, but Coffin was holding up a finger of caution. "Before you tell me it's not what you meant, let me tell you this: setting

COFFIN MAKER   MARK L. FOWLER

yourself up as saviour of the human race is an absurdity that both angers and worries me."

Again Hieronymus opened his mouth, and again the finger was raised. The two looked at each other until a tacit truce had been declared. Then the finger lowered and the two sat down on the hard wooden floorboards.

"How long do I have to stay here?"

"I can't answer that."

Hieronymus was about to ask for permission for writing materials and a stamp so that he could put the same question to the Sultan of Zone Seven Hundred and Twenty Nine, but trapped the words on his lips and let the thought slither harmlessly back from whence it came. Coffin didn't appreciate sarcasm any more than he appreciated human names for places when numbers were so much more durable. The annihilation of Zones One, Two, and Three didn't have quite the same ring of genocide as the annihilation of Egypt, Libya and the Sudan.

Coffin saw the flicker in Hieronymus' eyes and knew that a reprehensible impertinence had been withheld. Progress, he thought. But then hadn't Hieronymus shown signs of progress before? And to what end? So that he could build trust only to slink off to the Coffin Vaults and rip nails out of coffins, raising the dead!

"What did you hope to accomplish, Hieronymus? I don't mean in the short term. I'm not talking about inflated ideals of giving back life where death seemed too hard to bear. What did you think would be the ultimate consequences of your actions? If you brought twenty, fifty, a thousand people back to life, then why not a million? And why stop there? How about an entire generation? How about everybody who ever lived? How about tearing every nail out of every coffin in the Vaults and letting the uncountable billions roam the Earth? Is that what you intended - what you still intend?"

"I would like to know how long I have to stay here?"

Coffin stood up. "Then neither of us is getting any answers today. Perhaps I should try again tomorrow." Looking out of the window, he said, "Looks like Beezle's in a hurry. Heading for the Dome like a man on a mission."

Hieronymus resisted the bait, keeping his head lowered and his eyes fixed to the floorboards. Coffin turned from the window. "I wonder what bizarre enterprise is about to be unleashed on the world. Does make you wonder, doesn't it? What such a mind is capable of. Or perhaps you no longer care what happens to the world. Perhaps loss of liberty is more important to you now."

Without raising his head, Hieronymus asked, quietly, "How long must I stay here?"

Coffin grinned. "So that's the burning question. Not what atrocities are being committed."

Hieronymus was on his feet. "So you agree that Beezle commits atrocities? Yet you let him carry on - and lock me in this tower. What kind of sadist are you?"

Coffin exploded into laughter, indulging the convulsions to the full. The sound was not pleasant.

COFFIN MAKER   MARK L. FOWLER

Hieronymus sat miserably back down. Wiping the tears of laughter from his eyes, Coffin said, "I didn't come to mock you, but things seem to have a habit lately of not going to plan. What do you say to beginning again? Two simple questions and two simple answers - what do you say to that?"

Hieronymus said nothing.

"Okay," said Coffin, "one each, then. You tell me what you intended, what this *Quiet Revolution of Death* hoped, ultimately, to achieve; where bringing the dead back to life was finally going to lead. You tell me that, and I'll tell you how long you're checked in. Deal?"

Coffin waited. Knew the type. Incapable of lying. Mortals had them too. Would face torture and death but never flinch from what they believed was right. The type troubled him just as the trio at All Saints had troubled him.

Hieronymus couldn't lie.

And he didn't.

He told how death could be. How dignity and fulfilment could walk hand in hand with mortality. How Coffin didn't have to be afraid to own up to his mistakes and put them right. Where death has intervened too soon death must be reversed. He spoke of revolutionising death, not replacing it with unconditional immortality. That was the domain of the Creator, not death. A little sensitivity was all he was asking for. Mercy. Compassion.

Coffin listened, intently, though he kept his face turned towards the window.

COFFIN MAKER   MARK L. FOWLER

Had he not thought all this himself, long ago? And practiced it? Wasn't Hieronymus echoing a part of his own past, down the centuries? How it had been once. How, according to Hieronymus, it might be again.

The room fell silent. It was a bleak and questioning silence, clinging to Coffin like feathers to tar.

Able to endure it no longer he hurried to the door.

Yet the youth was looking far from desolate. He had caught sight of a tear in the Coffin Maker's eye, there was no mistaking it. He'd seen enough tears to recognise them even when they glistened in the steel-eye of Death itself.

In that single tear he saw hope alive and kicking. It was enough. For now.

He looked out of the window, waiting for Coffin to emerge from the entrance to the Tower, Death transforming from hard skin and bone into a singing bird of peace that might fly up to the window to rescue him and save mankind.

He smiled at the story-book image. It seemed that naivety had been his birthright and perhaps it was beyond him to ever rise above it.

Coffin hadn't played his part of the bargain. Hadn't said how long this sentence was to go on.

And yet in a sense he had. In that single tear an answer had dripped out. The days or even hours of Beezle's ascendency were numbered, Hieronymus felt sure of it.

The light still burned across in the Coffin Dome. Hieronymus tried not to dwell on what evil projects

COFFIN MAKER   MARK L. FOWLER

Beezle might be executing. Yet it was a losing battle, and so lost in dark thoughts did he become, that he never did see the Coffin Maker leave the Tower.

Zone Thirty-Nine was plastered with testaments to the great victory that President Doveman had secured in putting at ease the collective mind of the population. It had been one of the greatest political speeches anyone could recall. Gouge had shrunk in the public consciousness like a tumour blasted with radiation.

And yet at the same time Gouge had gone viral. Sermons all over the land praised God for the wisdom of the president in not uttering the name 'Gouge'. Children wearing DOVEMAN MAN OF PEACE tee-shirts jabbed a million pins into an industry of Gouge effigies.

Doveman himself was seen publicly holding up such a doll and at the same time brandishing a large needle, proclaiming that as nobody seemed sure exactly what this *nameless* monster looked like, it could hardly be called voodoo.

"I'll tell you what it is: Harmless good fun for all the family. If you think the enemy is fat, buy a fat one. If you think he has unsightly moles covering his face, then buy the Ugly Mother model. And if you think he would plead for mercy, buy one that cries - 'Please don't hurt me, I was a disenfranchised only child.' You decide on the face and you decide where to stick the pins."

It seemed President Doveman couldn't fail. Every word had become a word of wisdom, and every sentence the poetry of a saint. The Church was a little perturbed by the symbolism of Black Magic, but then

COFFIN MAKER   MARK L. FOWLER

every great politician had to expect a little falling out with the Holy Fathers and Mothers.

It came as a shock to the people of Zone Thirty-Nine to learn, as adulation was bubbling up into a frenzy of almost fundamentalist proportions, that Doveman had collapsed.

The word from the hospital was 'exhaustion'.

At first shocked disbelief reigned, swiftly followed by a hope born of desperation: that one so gifted and wholesome could not leave his people this way.

Yet as the hours rolled and no news came, fear again started to wrap its icy tentacles around the nation's heart, the realisation coming home that the beloved president *really might die*.

It promised to be a long and sleepless night for the people of Zone Thirty-Nine.

Early the next morning Hieronymus was looking out over the Coffin Complex. He had a feeling Coffin would be making his way over to see him. He'd spent the night thinking about the strange exit.

What had he seen in those eyes beside a tear?

Remorse?

Guilt?

The pain of remembering how it might have been, *how it had been*, once upon a time?

From his lonely window he saw Coffin dart out of the Dome. He was holding something small in his hand, and whatever it was, he was looking at it very carefully indeed.

COFFIN MAKER   MARK L. FOWLER

Coffin shot a nervous glance up at the Tower, and Hieronymus shrunk out of sight, peering carefully back down at the curious scene unfolding below. Coffin seemed to be grinning at whatever he was holding in his hand.

Stroking it.

Speaking to it.

The peculiar ceremony lasted for some minutes, and Hieronymus watched in amazement as Coffin started to kiss the object. Then he was massaging his shoulder, swinging his arm around like he was preparing to launch a javelin. Then pulling back his arm, taking one more look at the object in his hand before throwing it high into the air. For an instant it glinted in the sun, and then was lost.

Coffin gave a decisive nod to no-one before moving business-like towards the Tower, looking extremely pleased with himself.

In Zone Thirty-Nine, a huge crowd had gathered around the hospital where President Doveman had been admitted. Thousands kept an all-night vigil outside, and millions more kept the candle of hope burning in homes throughout the land.

The dawn brought whispers of recovery and by mid-day there was word that a statement was imminent.

To a roar of deafening approval, President Doveman was wheeled onto the balcony to address the gathering. Holding up a hand, he ushered in an immediate silence. "My doctors advise me that I have to make this a brief one. I want you all to know that I'm okay. A few days rest and I'll be back at the office."

COFFIN MAKER   MARK L. FOWLER

The crowd let out a stupendous cheer. Doveman again raised a hand and a hush descended instantly. "Somebody up there," he said, "must be looking out for me." Smiling, he pulled his hand into a fist and raised it into the air.

The fist of victory brought new levels of pandemonium from the crowd, and then he was gone, wheeled back inside.

The effort had taken its toll.

Inside the building the scene ignited in a dazzle of white coats, as medical science's finest descended upon the premier.

When the pains in Doveman's chest were brought finally under control, he turned to the white-coated guards of the presidential heart, and said, "Maybe I was wrong. Maybe someone up there doesn't like me after all."

COFFIN MAKER MARK L. FOWLER

19: THE RESPONSIBILITIES OF FATHERHOOD

That evening Coffin strolled back to his quarters, digesting the many courses of a long and protracted discussion with Hieronymus. He took up his pen.

Strange day. I upset Beezle over that coffin nail. A curious feeling. I felt like a thief. A thief! All I stole was my own property. I couldn't resist it. Wouldn't have resisted it for the world. How badly Beezle wants Doveman.

We watched Beezle from the Tower. Me and Hieronymus together. We stood at the window like father and son. A moment of joy passed between us.

How we laughed at Beezle on his hands and knees searching for that wretched nail. Wouldn't give up. Searched for hours. And he found it.

Hieronymus screamed when Beezle held up the nail and turned back towards the Dome. Wouldn't listen when I told him it was too late. That too much time had lapsed. That Beezle's frantic hammerings of a thousand nails couldn't secure Doveman's death on that day though it might cause some discomfort. He wouldn't listen though. Insisted on torturing himself with unnecessary fears. In the end I had to go and fetch a monitor to show that Doveman was alive. I even offered to let him keep the monitor to pass the time. Of course he declined. Said he couldn't bear watching the world suffer while he remained unable to intervene.

A knock at the door interrupted Coffin's scribbling.

COFFIN MAKER   MARK L. FOWLER

"Now that will either be Hieronymus, fresh from a daring and spectacular escape from the Tower, or Beezle come to complain about my little game. Enter, whoever you are."

The door opened to reveal a seething stare crowned with the glow of violent orange.

"Been having trouble with Doveman?" asked Coffin.

Beezle's eyes dripped acid. "A little favour for Hieronymus?"

Coffin shook his head. "He's in no position to ask favours."

Beezle raised his eyebrows. It was like two slimy caterpillars vomiting.

"Look at me how you will. It was for *your* benefit. I asked you to make Gouge your priority and you defied me, trying to dispatch Doveman. Defy me again and you'll find yourself competing with Hieronymus for a window view."

Without further discussion, Beezle was dismissed with a brief detailing precise death counts expected over the next few days and forbidding every one of his favourite methods of mass disposal.

As the sour apprentice left the room, Coffin threw a teaser: the death of Colonel Gouge would result in immediate lifting of all restrictions and a free hand for an unspecified period.

I have no doubt that Beezle will re-evaluate the new price on Gouge's head very carefully. Equally I have no doubt that Gouge will find himself in no immediate danger. Such is the situation that we find ourselves in. I

COFFIN MAKER   MARK L. FOWLER

have only myself to blame. I never saw Gouge arrive. Whatever the truth and the purpose and the meaning behind all this I never saw his coming.

Coffin wrote the last sentences with a schoolboy sense of duty, as though writing out lines to the effect that he will never again fail to pay attention in Maths. And like a schoolboy meditating deliciously on how to spend an unshackled evening once the last line of his labour was completed, he bit into his pen with the thought of returning once more to the Tower.

First though there was a page to be filled. Without further hesitation he set down the rest of the thoughts that Beezle had so rudely interrupted.

Today I did something that I cannot account for. Not content to throw the nail that would have secured the last breath of Doveman. An act akin to cutting off my nose to spite Beezle's face. But then I marched straight to the Tower and apologised. What could I possibly have to apologise for? The sole appointed Coffin Maker to the world of living things apologising to an apprentice bent on undoing his master's work! Yet I walked straight into that room and told him I was sorry.

Said he hadn't a clue what I was talking about and asked why I had left the Dome with something "suspiciously like a coffin nail" in my hand. Why I had thrown that coffin nail high into the air and if that had anything to do with why Beezle was on his hands and knees searching for some "lost and clearly significant object."

COFFIN MAKER   MARK L. FOWLER

I have already documented the scene of joy and the moments of high drama that we enjoyed together as we looked down from that window. But imagine this. Once I had finally assured him that Doveman was safe he told me his fate. Told me! He said that he had seen compassion in me and knew that he would regain his liberty when the time was right. That he knew matters were in hand. Trusted me. Believed I had "seen the light" as he put it and that I could now see through Beezle. That I understood the significance of Doveman. That I had finally come to recognise the nature of Gouge.

Imagine what it was like to hear such things. But the truth is that I'm not certain of any of it.

Because I'm unsure of the nature of Hieronymus.

I have a fondness for him that is compulsive. He knows that. But he may still prove to be no more than an arch manipulator. He may yet prove to be the enemy. The ultimate deceiver. I am still seeking answers. His fate remains undecided.

Coffin stopped writing, and began chewing his pen so hard that he winced. Rubbing his complaining tooth until the ache subsided he put the pen back into his mouth and did the same thing again.

Eager to complete the entry before causing permanent damage to his mouth, he added,

Hieronymus trusts me. He has seen a tear in my eye and heard the sounds of compassion from my lips. Those things were real though may yet prove to be misplaced.

COFFIN MAKER   MARK L. FOWLER

For the moment Beezle is at bay. The time has come to find out the truth about Hieronymus. The barriers between us are down. There will never be a better time.

With melodramatic gusto Coffin was on his feet, swinging the journal shut, and making his way towards the Tower. He felt like a loving father visiting a faithful son falsely imprisoned. And that was the way he was going to play it.

To convince Hieronymus he would first have to convince himself. Hieronymus had an eye for the untruth. Could smell deceit. *Perhaps that is the mark of the truly great deceiver.*

Coffin tried forcing out all negative thoughts about Hieronymus, and letting the doting father take full command of his inner stage. He was a professional. He had a job to do. By God he'd do it!

The next time he walked out of that Tower, Hieronymus would have a clean bill of health and walk out with him.

Or else be preparing for eternal occupancy.

On his way to the Tower, Coffin stopped at the Dome to check on his other wayward son. He peered cautiously inside. Beezle should have been pouring his energies into the demise of a small village.

Coffin could see the glow of orange on the far side of the workshop, and under the furious sounds of industry, sneaked inside, placing himself behind one of his own killing machines, to secretly observe the working practices of the fluorescent dark-half.

COFFIN MAKER   MARK L. FOWLER

As Coffin looked on, he thought, for the hundredth time, how this orange-haired fireball contrasted with the mild mannered prisoner in the Tower. He was yet to find a single thing that they shared, except, perhaps that they could both do with a good father.

The increasing violence of the sounds snatched Coffin from his ponderings. By the look of things, there was more than a small village at stake.

Beezle seemed to be connecting up a series of isolated communities, and from the frenetic movements of the fireball, it looked like the totals were going to be impressive. Indeed, he couldn't see how Beezle was going to pull it off. There was scale here. And it took a master's hand to control scale. It was surely beyond a mere apprentice.

Unless...

No, thought Coffin. Enough is enough. Not that old fault line again. Perhaps I ought to leave them both to rot in the Tower and to hell with the Creator's meddlings!

He slid from behind his machine and prepared to move forward at a gallop.

Then froze.

Trembling at his own thoughts, he stood rigormortis still, eyes clenched, trying to erase the blasphemy from his brain.

He opened a single eye; tilted it upward. Believing that the Creator would consider the contents of a whisper more significant than the mere contents of a thought, he whispered, "Only kidding."

COFFIN MAKER   MARK L. FOWLER

He waited a moment. There was no pain; he was still standing. Either the blasphemy had gone unnoticed or else forgiveness had been unqualified.

In thankfulness, another rumble of anarchy was already swelling up in the Coffin Maker's brain:

Who cares a jot what the Creator thinks!

He sends two apprentices without any explanation, allows something called Colonel Gouge to enter the world in the most absurdly mysterious manner, with no indication of whether this thing intends to save the world or destroy it! Why should I tread carefully when He seems to stamp about over everybody's plans and do just as He damned-well pleases! Why should I give a hoot *what* He thinks? I don't know who to trust anymore. Perhaps I should vote for Doveman! Good - Evil - Indifferent - Who knows and who cares! Maybe they're all of them to be trusted - maybe I'm the dangerous one. Maybe I'm insane.

Or the Creator is...

The last thought seemed to require a bit more than a whisper, and Coffin shouted out before he could get a hand to his mouth, "Forgive me. I love you."

Beezle spun around to catch sight of a figure dropping down behind one of the machines.

The Dome was instantly silenced.

Coffin stayed down, crouched out of sight as the slow footsteps of Beezle approached.

The footsteps stopped.

The orange-haired apprentice peered over the machine to find Coffin kneeling with hands held at a devotional angle.

COFFIN MAKER   MARK L. FOWLER

In that moment Beezle's repulsive features came the closest they would ever come to folding into a genuine smile.

"Beezle!" said Coffin, trying to sound surprised.

"What are you doing?" asked the apprentice.

"Oh, well, you see, devotion can strike at any time, young Beezle, any place, and without warning."

"So it seems."

"Working on anything special?" asked Coffin, eager to change the subject.

"Everything in the name of my profession is special. And I would have thought that you above all would know that."

"Good answer," said Coffin. "Better let you get back to it, then."

Coffin left the Dome, his spirits shattered. Was there no-one he could look in the face without lowering his eyes in shame? If he looked up to the invisible face of the Creator, his thoughts might bring the Coffin Complex crashing down in punishment for his blasphemy. If he looked again at Beezle, his blushes would only confirm in that perverse, ugly, orange-haired, demon-mind that deformity had found a secret admirer.

As for Hieronymus...

Coffin stood outside the Dome, looking up at the Tower. At the single high window. He was about to play the part of benign father, but wasn't there a chance - and a good chance - that before this day was out, he might become judge and executioner?

COFFIN MAKER   MARK L. FOWLER

And what of the human race? Would he, one day, have to look into the faces of countless billions and account for his actions? And could he account for them, when the time finally came?

And why was he thinking like this? He shouldn't be looking into any faces. He should be alone. Getting on with his work and getting on with it in solitude. Some state of affairs this was turning into.

It was enough to make his poor, bony head thump and rattle. He couldn't go on like this, carrying this weight, this uncertainty. It was ill treatment of a master craftsman who ought to be revered in every crevice of existence. He'd received no warnings, no reprimands, yet found himself at the centre of Hell's own farce. Had any heart ever had so much to bear? Was ever animated flesh and bone given a heavier burden to carry? It was time for answers. By God if it wasn't time for answers.

Coffin moved quickly towards the Tower, aware that two perceptive eyes were watching and that behind those eyes a keen mind was already asking the most difficult questions of all.

20: THE TRIAL BEGINS

Suspicion was awake, dressed and feeding heartily as Hieronymus looked out from his window and watched Coffin approach the Tower. The Coffin Maker was moving with the speed of a hungry dog, though without the honesty of purpose. His face as animated as so much bone ever could be, shooting nervous glances poorly disguised as architectural evaluation.

Within seconds of Coffin's key turning in the lock, suspicion was bloated. Coffin had deception stamped into every crack and wrinkle. This great deceiver was clearly not used to looking into the eyes of those he was deceiving.

"Doveman's made a splendid recovery, then," said Coffin, by way of a greeting.

"I wouldn't know," said Hieronymus.

"Of course, no monitor. But if you change your mind -"

Hieronymus shook his head. "While I'm powerless to defend the world against Beezle, I'd rather not watch it suffering under his hammer."

"Defend the world against Beezle, eh? Strong words," said Coffin, turning to the window.

He could feel the youth's glare, crawling over the back of his neck. His capacity for guilt, such as it was, had been breached, and a cold trickle of sweat spilled out over his paltry rations of skin. He felt like a thief in a house filled with light.

Think like a father, he thought, as he stared over towards the Dome, dimly wondering what bizarre

COFFIN MAKER   MARK L. FOWLER

games the orange-haired youth was playing. *Think like a father come to save a son, a favourite son.*

But what if that son isn't willing to help himself?

You have to meet him halfway, like a good father, like a real father. You want to get at the truth, you have to trade with a bit of truth. He's no fool. He's got that look in his eye. He'll know you're faking.

"Confession is good for the soul," said Coffin. "Isn't that what mortals reckon?"

"Some," said Hieronymus.

"Well, *some* may be right. Let's give them the benefit of the doubt, eh?"

The youth stole up behind Coffin. "I don't know what you're talking about," he said, "but something interesting must be happening out there."

Detecting the breath of sarcasm on the back of his neck, Coffin turned around sharply. "You're fond of history, aren't you?" He fixed his line of vision a good inch above the youth's questing eyes, and prepared to sail more dangerously into the venomous wind. "I think it's time you learnt something of your ancestry, so to speak."

"I'm listening."

Coffin tried a genial smile, but couldn't meet the blistering glare leaking through into his peripheral vision. "I have trodden some curious paths in my time, and I think you might learn a great deal about your own feelings by listening to some of my experiences - damn it, will you stop staring at me like that!"

Walking back to the middle of the room he sat down, beckoning Hieronymus, who squatted down a

COFFIN MAKER   MARK L. FOWLER

few floorboards from him. "I'll come to the point," said Coffin. "When you ripped the nails out of those coffins, you weren't doing anything that hadn't been done before."

Coffin smiled. He was building up nicely to the matter in hand. *Just like a good father talking to his son.* "Well, let's call today your birthday, shall we? Today you come of age. Find out a little about your...shall we say...*Master's* past. You see, I, too, have ripped nails out of coffins."

"Really?" yawned Hieronymus.

"Long, long ago I made a dreadful mistake."

"Surely not."

"And what's more, I tried to rectify that mistake by making one many times worse."

"You amaze me."

"It was back in the dark ancestry of mankind, and it gave birth to beliefs and superstitions that have haunted the world ever since. You see, I took away a life at the wrong moment and regretted what I had done. It wasn't anybody of particular significance – at least not as far as Earthly history is concerned - though for me it was the darkest moment. It blew a hole through me and I knew that I had to put right the terrible wrong that I had done. I started to rip apart the coffin I had completed. I didn't even know, at that point, that death could be reversed. I just had to let out my feelings by doing something destructive. Do you understand what I'm saying?"

Hieronymus nodded. "I think so."

Coffin, pleased that his apprentice was keeping up with him, went on.

COFFIN MAKER MARK L. FOWLER

"I was so busy pulling that coffin to pieces that I didn't even look at the monitor. It was fixed on the dead man and his mourning relatives. What stopped me in my tracks was the sound of hysterical screaming. I tell you, when I looked at the monitor and saw that man get out of the ground and kiss his loved ones, I nearly joined in the screaming.

"Then I looked at the violated coffin down at my own feet, and it dawned on me. What I had done. At first I was mortified, just like the mortals gathered around the walking dead man; then a strange intoxication came over me. Not only did I have power over death, but, to a point, over life as well. And I dabbled with that power, Hieronymus. Over centuries I dabbled. And there was no warning from the Creator. I was left to dabble until belief in victory over death was so deeply implanted in the mortal psyche that I doubt it will ever be entirely vanquished. And I have only myself to blame for that."

Coffin eyed the silent youth for signs of admiration or repugnance but found only restrained curiosity. He went on, "Sometimes I became so disenchanted with my craft that I would raise whole communities. I would give that *prayed for second chance* by the thousand, only to see the same lives led, the same mistakes made, and the same inevitable endings.

"Sometimes I experimented by giving a dozen chances to the same soul, and they disappointed me every time. Oh, Hieronymus, they disappointed me so badly. In that, and in that alone, they never failed. And one day the truth dawned: That what I was doing was

COFFIN MAKER MARK L. FOWLER

the most destructive thing of all. The most unholy. I was violating death and causing the greatest misery the world has ever known. Everywhere the living were walking in fear of the dead, and all the dead wanted was the peace of eternal rest."

His eyes were beginning to bubble, but not, this time, like baths of molten metal. This time the liquid was temperate.

"You see, Hieronymus, death can only be good. It is a holy and a precious gift to every living thing. It is the Sabbath of Life, to use that manner of speaking, and it should be embraced."

Hieronymus stood up. "Then why isn't it?"

Coffin's jaw-bone dropped with a clunk.

"Why is it universally feared and dreaded? Why is the Grim Reaper so hated in the world? Why are you so hated by every living thing?"

Coffin's jaw found a lower notch, but Hieronymus hadn't finished. "Tell me this: Do you look forward to a time when *you* no longer exist? Do you look forward to *your... Sabbath*? You who've seen the Creator and know that He exists - can you tell me that you don't peer into the emptiness of oblivion and shake with fear?"

Coffin chose his words carefully. "That's different."

It was like a flaming arrow hitting a mountain of ice, and Hieronymus' anger came melting down in a flood of laughter. "Well, what a surprise. Death afraid of its own medicine."

Coffin recognised the impulse of a father to beat out the brains of his son. He'd come to conduct a fair trial, a trial that he was trying to spare Hieronymus the anxiety of knowing anything about. He was giving away his deepest and darkest secrets and being repaid with ridicule. Perhaps it was time to lock the door and throw away the key.

Giving Hieronymus his best look of fatherly disappointment, he walked silently to the window, closed his eyes and let his mind ramble wildly over uncertain thoughts. Perhaps the best way forward - the only way forward - was to take this sorrowful apprentice by the throat and beat his head against the wall until he told –

- Told what?
The truth?
Was there a secret truth still hiding in there?
Unknown to the Coffin Maker?

Did this errant youth really know anything that wasn't already known? Did he understand any better than the Coffin Maker why he had come here, to the Kingdom of Death? What purpose, what plan?

He glanced back to see Hieronymus settling back down onto the wooden boards. Not looking victorious, or sanctimonious. Not in any way trying to look superior.

Coffin turned again to the window, and his thoughts turned with him. The youth was infuriating, yes; but wasn't the most infuriating thing the fact that there was something about him that was, dammit, *endearing*?

And he'd shown insight - of sorts. Even some of the ridiculous things he came out with had worked a peculiar kind of magic; had made him think differently about things.

There was no denying it, Hieronymus had qualities that he was a coffin nail away from...*admiring.*

Coffin cleared his throat. "As I was saying. I too have violated the Temple of Death. I did it for what I thought, at the time, to be honourable reasons. As it's turned out, I've succeeded only in generating a legacy of fear and superstition. Perhaps now you can see why I bark so loudly at the idea of encouraging such...*activities* again. Why I had to take drastic measures to stop you from opening any more coffins."

Behind the Coffin Maker silence reigned.

"Death was once welcomed as the gateway to eternal life. In those days I was the hero, the saviour, and I stood next to the Creator. But then came along the notion of humanism. Suddenly human potential was all the rage; suddenly it was mankind that was exalted."

He glanced back to see Hieronymus frowning.

"Is there a problem?" asked Coffin.

"Actually, yes, there is. First you tell me that you created superstition, and that was the enemy. Then you tell me that mankind created humanism, and that was the enemy. Forgive me, but I haven't a clue what you're talking about. If you'd told me that you'd woken the dead to scare the living shit out of the humanists, I might have seen your point, though I would still have fallen out with your methods."

Coffin fought hard against the urge to turn away and look blankly through the window. The truth was, he *didn't* have a clue what he was talking about.

COFFIN MAKER   MARK L. FOWLER

Or which way to go next. *Keep talking*, said the voice of instinct. *Keep talking and try to get back on track.* "You see, Hieronymus, death hasn't really changed much at all - it's mortals that have changed. Their ridiculous notions of advancement. Science! What has it done for them really? I'll tell you: it's taught them new ways to fear death."

Hieronymus shook his head. "No, you've taught them that."

"And philosophy! What has that done except bring home the reality of death?"

Coffin's voice was rising. Control slipping.

Hieronymus kept his composure, shaking his head slowly, assertively.

Awaiting revelations.

A moment was coming.

On the crest of Coffin's rage, something was coming.

"One day they'll worship death again, Hieronymus," said Coffin, slowly, marking each word. "When they've finished worshipping their petty intellectual vanities, and their *pretty little mushroom clouds...*"

An eerie silence broke over the room, haunted by inaudible echoes of Coffin's words.

In that moment a bond was formed - formed in the knowledge that a precious thing – a gift - was in grave danger. Then the purity of the moment milked over as the agendas of pride and mistrust stole back, and in the reverberating silence, Hieronymus climbed to his feet, joining the Coffin Maker at the window, the two of them looking down on the Dome.

In both hearts, fear and sadness were beating as hard as the incessant rain of hammers in the fists of Beezle.

21: A SWATTABLE FLY

Colonel Gouge was grinning. Far below, beneath the clouds, lay the Promised Land. Or, more precisely, the land he had promised for himself. The land that would play host to the orchestras of doom that would drown the whole world in a final demonic dance of destruction.

Behind him raged the bloody revolutions of Zones Fourteen, Seventeen, Twenty-Eight, Seventy-Eight, One hundred and Fourteen, and One Hundred and Ninety-One, and fresh wars in fifteen other zones and the acceleration of a dozen more.

Satisfying as these campaigns had been, none had succeeded in bringing a grin to his elusive features. For in all the far-flung battlefields where he'd raised the flag of death and misery above the crushed skulls of the defeated, he had been the man behind the mask, the unseen catalyst of fire and damnation.

He had moved invisibly and silently, in and out of nations, as unheralded as the first arrival of a tumour. For Gouge had learnt that a violent cancer cannot do its work by announcing its presence too soon. That way leads to the bloody surgeons' knife, tearing it out before its roots have sunk beyond redemption.

But here, beneath these pale clouds, he was the man of a thousand faces. Here he was the bogeyman, his infamy and legend haunting each and every street corner. Every child had a Colonel Gouge doll, and no day passed here without a thousand needles and as many taunts and curses to his name.

COFFIN MAKER   MARK L. FOWLER

It would be from here that the world would know that one man was responsible for the bloody and unprecedented escalations of conflict globally, and here that the real face of evil would reveal itself to the world.

Pandora, his private plane, illustrated with history's most brutal scenes of carnage, sailed the calm clouds with its hand-picked cargo of lunatics, the crème de la crème of psychotic terrorists, united in a common evil by the one living thing they feared.

Gouge called them together in the airborne lounge. It was time to "toast President Doveman." For Doveman had served him best, raising his status to the proportions of the devil himself. For the price of political capital, Doveman had heaped the problems of the nation at the feet of one; and when the final battle began, the people of that pride-stricken country would truly believe in the supernatural powers of a one-hundred and one percent bad-to-the-bone bogeyman.

"Thank you, Mr. President, from the bottom of my overflowing shit-pipe."

There was a second toast: to complacency. A fine quality in a president. Letting the world down badly by letting the myth remain: that a few words from a politician disarms the deadliest weapons. In honour of this fine work, Gouge proposed a new campaign slogan for the good president: "Trust Doveman today and fry with your loved ones tonight."

When the tossing back of glasses had been completed, Gouge made a brief address.

"Doveman set up two stools. He will fall between them and die grotesquely as a result. It's like this: on the one hand I was dismissed, and on the other

COFFIN MAKER   MARK L. FOWLER

demonised. So not only am I in possession of mythical powers that will immobilise armies, I am also unexpected. You may rightly judge from this state of affairs that I am indebted to President Doveman. You would be wrong if you took that as an indication that I will show him the slightest mercy. Within a matter of hours Doveman will be dead. Now: any questions?"

He scanned the subordinate eyes of his right hand men, detecting not a flicker of uncertainty from any. This time he had chosen more carefully. "Then I suggest that you sleep while you may. This little touring circus of ours has finished with the country fairs. To use the ludicrous vernacular that Doveman is fond of: Gentleman, the show is about to hit town."

President Doveman had found religion. And where better to find it than in a reserved front row pew at All Saints, a few feet from the now historic pulpit where the late Father Henry had delivered his dramatic swansong.

"Heart disease changes a man," he said in response to a question about his five hundred percent improved church attendance. "If we all spent a little more of the day counting our blessings we could make this world a better place. I first came to All Saints out of curiosity. I was looking for the ghost of the extraordinary Father Henry. But my curiosity grows deeper by the day and I've found an even more extraordinary ghost to seek. I'm sure if Father Henry's listening he won't be too offended by the comparison."

On a *Live Audience With The President*, a little girl asked whether he prayed that Colonel Gouge would die. Doveman smiled back at the little girl and praised her mother for bringing such a little cutesy into the world, before replying that, as Gouge had already been killed and buried by the new spirit of solidarity in the country, there was little need for such lack of charity.

"God provides, little girl, and He provides for everyone."

"Does He provide for Colonel Gouge?" asked the girl, earning a sharp slap from her mother.

"Don't chastise the girl for demonstrating an inquisitive mind," said Doveman, then invited the little girl to sit on his knee. The crowd squealed with delight. Anybody this good with children clearly had their vote. "What's your name?"

"Theresa."

"Well, Theresa, as I said, God provides for everyone. But He provides in different ways. Now some people get sick -"

"Did Colonel Gouge get sick?"

"He got very sick. He got so sick -"

"Did he get so sick that God made him die?"

"It's getting kind of hard to get a word in edgeways here," said the president, and the applause brought the house down. The girl hadn't finished though.

"But you got sick and God didn't make you die, Mr. President, sir."

The whoops and whistles that followed threatened to see the night out, and it took a wave of the presidential hand to bring the commotion under control.

"Not being God, and only a president, I'm afraid I can't answer all your questions, Theresa. But think

COFFIN MAKER   MARK L. FOWLER

about this: in our own ways, we all prayed that Colonel Gouge would leave us alone, whoever, whatever he is. And he did. And when good people come together, well, the bad people eventually get squeezed out. Maybe we should feel sorry for people like Colonel Gouge, because nobody loves them, and they end up with no friends in the whole world."

Doveman smiled at the girl and gave her back to her mother. Yet the girl still hadn't finished. "Does that mean," she said, "that I can stop sticking those needles into his eyes, Mr. Doveman?"

The audience seemed to halt mid clap. A flicker of embarrassment passed across the president's face. For one television moment the sun disappeared behind a cloud, causing untold breaths to be held.

Then the quick-thinking president unleashed a sunshine smile the like of which few had ever been so privileged to witness. "Theresa, you're wonderful. Truly a girl in a million. Yes, you can stop sticking pins into dolls and start mending your socks with them."

The following day saw a dramatic fall in the sale of Gouge dolls. Doveman was declared, across the nation, to be the most remarkable of leaders. A man with the inexhaustible gift of bringing people together. A politician, at last, with God truly on his side.

As a wildly illustrated private jet cut still unseen through the clouds, directly below President Doveman was leading the procession of Sunday morning worshippers out through the impressive doors of All Saints, and into the makings of a fine summer day.

COFFIN MAKER — MARK L. FOWLER

The congregation paraded towards the newly unveiled statue of the praying saint, and the president and the bishop, in a joint and moving address, sealed the new era of peace and reconciliation in the land, offering hope for a true and meaningful union between the ancient enemies of Church and State.

Doveman suggested that an inscription might be added to the statue.

"Prayer: Take it three times a day, *everyday*."

Bishop Stones, politely acknowledging the idea, thought that St. Paul's - 'The last enemy to be defeated is Death', might also be worth considering.

Doveman was unsure, thought it morbid, somewhat downbeat.

Respect for theological superiority won the day. "What the hell," said President Doveman, "Order those chisels and let's get the party started."

Against the enormity of the occasion and the splendour of the mighty gothic spire, the descending plane - its bloody illustrations receding at the flick of a clever switch - appeared as nothing more than a swattable fly, humming harmlessly in the distance.

22: THE TRIAL ENDS

Beezle licked his lips as the humming fly descended on Zone Thirty-Nine. If his arms were aching and his back nearly broken with the efforts of his labours, his heart was singing, his soul rejoicing.

He wondered how much longer before Coffin returned to what remained of his senses and picked up that rusting old hammer. One thing was certain: the Coffin Maker was in for some treat when he finally got around to leaving the philosophical fool to rot in the Tower and looked out on a changing world.

For Beezle had done the job of a dozen Coffin Makers. Stoking old fires, lighting fresh ones. The map of the world was growing blacker with the raging flames of war as the humming fly cast its shadow in ever widening circles. It wouldn't be long before the big fuse was ready for lighting, and Hell's Incinerator wired up for the Burning.

Beezle watched the humming fly make its unannounced landing before switching off the machinery in the Coffin Dome, to protect its precious circuitry. Walking out of the Dome on spring-loaded heels, he gazed up at the Tower, guessing the long-winded methods of Coffin's bumbling investigations, and the clever but fruitless ways in which Hieronymus would be dancing around his inquisitor.

Yet despite his fermenting contempt for the Coffin Maker's loathsome weakness and detestable tendency to compromise, he had no doubt that ultimately Coffin's fear of the so-called *quiet revolution* would emerge victorious.

COFFIN MAKER   MARK L. FOWLER

For what Coffin feared most of all was the death of Death.

In the Tower, two minds were racing over the debris of the newly formed and newly shattered bond. The vision of global destruction that had risen up in them had brought the two within a whisper of reconciliation.

Until fear had broken the heart of the whisper.

While Coffin regained his composure with his silent mantra, *Like a father, like a father,* Hieronymus watched freedom slipping away as patience began to lose its grip.

"I think it's time for you to do some talking," said Coffin, at last.

"On any particular subject?"

Coffin let the comment pass with nothing more than a vicious glance. "I'm sure that confinement has given ample time to let your mind loose on the important questions. Like why you were sent to me in the first place."

"Oh, that," said Hieronymus with a shrug. "That's easy. If Gouge isn't stopped, the answer to why we were sent here is simple: To help you cope with the numbers. If Gouge isn't stopped, then your precious Second World War is going to seem like a spring clear out."

Coffin's eyes narrowed. "*We* control numbers, not some mortal."

"Who said anything about Gouge being mortal? Did you see him born? He's Beezle without orange hair."

COFFIN MAKER   MARK L. FOWLER

Coffin digested the implications, or at least tried to. "Are you suggesting that Gouge and Beezle are one and the same?"

"I wasn't," said Hieronymus, "but it's a thought."

"Then I suppose that *you* are President Doveman."

"I see. And you? Hitler? Frankenstein? Lucifer?"

Coffin was at last looking like a father; a father ready to wash his hands of his son. "I came here to try and help you," he said.

"Really?"

"Yes, Hieronymus. Really."

"So tell me: what if the devil sent Beezle? What if that note announcing our arrival came, not from the Creator, but the Nasty One himself...if there's anything nastier than Beezle? What if I'm the devil's distraction, keeping you from watching Beezle?"

Coffin, whilst not wanting to give such ludicrous, immature speculations the remotest respect, found himself edging back towards the window, craning to peer down towards the Coffin Dome.

Just in time to catch a fleeting glimpse of orange disappearing back inside the Dome.

Turning back to Hieronymus he said, "We're getting nowhere slowly and my time is precious. You don't intend to co-operate, so I will ask you three questions."

"A bit late for a quiz, don't you think?"

"Question one: will you promise never again to raise the dead?"

Hieronymus didn't answer.

COFFIN MAKER   MARK L. FOWLER

"Question two: will you renounce the *Quiet Revolution of Death* and act only on my instructions?"

Again Hieronymus kept his silence.

With something that might have been a tear in the corner of his eye, the Coffin Maker asked his final question. "Do you understand that you can never leave the Tower?"

Still Hieronymus kept his silence.

Coffin lifted up the door key with weighty ceremony, looking again at his doomed apprentice, hoping that even at this late stage he might say something to save himself. When the youth still failed to speak the Coffin Maker walked to the door. Opened it.

Then Hieronymus spoke at last. "Stop Beezle. Destroy Gouge. If you have any genuine compassion for the human race, show it before it's too late. But don't stand around wittering about things you don't understand."

"Don't understand? Me? Like, for example?"

"Humanism."

"So you want to know about humanism?"

"Not particularly."

"I'll tell you about humanism," said Coffin. "It leads to vanity. So there it is. And it leaves them Godless. Encourages them to abandon their Creator."

"You hypocrite! You've seen the Creator and even you talk of being abandoned by Him."

"What? Never!"

"Don't you feel for them when they look up and fail to see the Divine? Would you punish them for

COFFIN MAKER   MARK L. FOWLER

feeling abandoned? For feeling what you yourself have felt?"

Coffin's eyes narrowed. "Have you been reading my journal?"

"They can't win with you: you curse them for believing in the supernatural and you curse them for believing in themselves. You're no craftsman, you're just a bone machine. Yes, I've read your precious journal, and no doubt so has Beezle."

Hieronymus turned away, shaking with rage, indignation, pity. "If you have it in you, show them some mercy."

As the door closed and the key turned in the lock, Hieronymus shouted after the Coffin Maker, "It's already decided."

The key stopped turning, then turned in the opposite direction. The door opened, and a puzzled Coffin poked his head back into the room. "What is already decided?"

"Everything. Pre-ordained. Didn't anybody think to tell you? You have no more choice in the outcome than I do. This Tower has always been here, yet it's never been used until now. So what was its purpose? I'll tell you: somebody's had the whole thing planned since the beginning. Me and Beezle – we were always going to arrive here. I was always going to start the *Quiet Revolution* and end up a prisoner in this Tower. Whatever is to happen, it was decided at the outset, and not even you can stop it. There's no freewill. Not for them, not for us, not for *you*."

Coffin let his outrage flood the room before slamming the door and turning the key decisively.

COFFIN MAKER MARK L. FOWLER

No freewill? He'd show freewill. It was time to re-assert some authority – and, yes, that included Beezle. He'd a good mind to take his hammer to the coffin of this infernal Gouge straight away - throw in Doveman for good measure. After all, he didn't want to leave Beezle any opportunities to throw accusations of pandering to Hieronymus.

It was high time the Kingdom was reclaimed and damn the lot of them.

Hieronymus looked down from the Tower and watched Coffin striding towards the Dome. In a strange way it felt like victory. If Beezle's insatiable arrogance and Coffin's new found will to prove his own significance could collide with force enough, it might engulf Colonel Gouge and win the day after all.

With nothing to do but wait, he set his mind to figuring out why the Tower really did exist. But one thought quickly led to another and soon he was back to questioning everything. Perhaps his outburst had some truth in it after all. Was it really down to a pre-ordained game plan? It was as likely as anything else in this business!

And perhaps it didn't matter.

Results mattered; consequences mattered; stirring up Coffin and saving the world mattered. But the metaphysics running the universe - maybe that much was unknowable; maybe true wisdom, if it existed at all, lay in understanding that the whole wretched shooting-match was ultimately and profoundly *unknowable.*

COFFIN MAKER — MARK L. FOWLER

Hieronymus closed his eyes and waited for events to take their course. In the waiting he found himself praying that if it really did come down to a pre-established plan that could never be influenced or altered in any way; a plan already written down in detail, with every event documented ahead of its time, and every hair, as it were, numbered, and all conclusions sealed in prophesy - if all this was really the case and ticking towards its culmination, he prayed that it was a benign being that had set the thing in motion.

COFFIN MAKER   MARK L. FOWLER

23: TWO COFFINS

If Coffin could have watched himself storming into the Dome, riding high on the crest of his new found sense of purpose, he would have been impressed. It would have taken him to new heights of poetic expression, patting himself heartily on the back, bone on bone, and for good measure fixing the mortal world with one humdinger of an immortal stare, defying it to blame him. Yet majestic as his entrance was, the gusto proved short-lived.

Inside the Dome stood Beezle, two hammers in each hand. He'd seen Beezle working at fever pitch before; it was nothing new to see the inflamed youth hammering away to the brink of exhaustion. But he'd never seen anything like this.

Swinging the hammers in a lazy, almost drunken fashion, Beezle was punctuating the rhythm with unhinged hoots of delight. And slobbering.

Coffin looked on, unsure what to make of it. Even to him the term 'unholy' would not have been inappropriate. It was almost as though Beezle had been around strong drink. Yet such a state of affairs was impossible: alcohol was the curse of one race only.

Fearing what revelations might be in store, he followed Beezle's wild line of vision, the bulbous eyes appearing to be locked greedily onto the Dome monitor, not even wavering to look at the nails being driven home by the jazz-beat of the hammers. Coffin couldn't see from his position what was happening on the screen, but from the look on Beezle's face, it was significant.

COFFIN MAKER   MARK L. FOWLER

With an act of will he mobilised his rooting skeleton, edging it around the machinery, wanting and not wanting to see what feast Beezle was gorging himself on.

"Good God!"

The monitor revealed a helicopter hovering a few feet above the ground. In front of it was a trampoline. A procession of men, women and children were being led up to the trampoline, their hands tied behind their backs; men with automatic weapons were prodding the captives forward. The queue for the trampoline stretched out of sight.

In the eyes of each prisoner was the unmistakable bulge of terror. They had all seen what was to become of them, and of their friends, family, and children. And they would all die knowing what obscene imagination was responsible for their fate, for emblazoned on the side of the helicopter was a portrait that once seen could never be forgotten.

Beneath the most sinister of painted smiles ran the legend:

Colonel Gouge Enterprises At Your Service.

To gaze for more than an instant into that sadistic smile - it would become your friend. It would wink at you, and a hand stretch out to you. Then you would see darkness grow like a black rose, and see your own face, hear your own name and smell your own terror. You would know that the blood that dripped from the broken remains of the smile...*was your own.* And then the master of ceremonies, 'at your service', would reveal his true appearance and beam out at you.

COFFIN MAKER　　　MARK L. FOWLER

Coffin watched as the first four prisoners were hoisted onto the trampoline and forced at gunpoint to bounce, ever higher, until the first head caught the whirring blades of the helicopter. At once the armed men bellowed their approval above the screams of the condemned.

Beezle's hammers bounced, four at a time across the assembled timbers, his shrieks of hysterical joy outdoing Gouge's men until Coffin, sickened by such a display of wilful unprofessionalism, slammed down the central control lever.

Beezle swung to face Coffin, a look of rage buried too deeply in his face to be switched for the lie of humble servitude. "What do you think you're doing?"

Coffin didn't much like the way he was being looked at any more than he liked the way he was being spoken to, and the hammers in Beezle's hands were a little too raised for comfort. Marching right up to the raging apprentice, he snatched the hammers.

Beezle's expression was cooling, and the first manifestations of appropriate servitude gathering below the orange mop. "Just having some fun," said Beezle. "Variations on this kind of thing go back to the dawn of civilisation. They didn't have helicopters, of course -"

"Enough!" said Coffin. "I have never seen anything like this...."

"Yes, a nice little idea, the trampoline, don't you think?"

"I was referring to the total lack of decorum. Death is a serious profession. It is in the realm of poetry. It is not a game to be played by bloodthirsty imbeciles."

COFFIN MAKER   MARK L. FOWLER

The hardness returned to Beezle's eyes. "So those lovely days of the Great Wars, for instance, were okay because you conducted them with a serious expression and the pretence that you weren't really enjoying yourself?"

Coffin had suffered enough insolence for one day. "I do not have to, and I do not intend to, explain my professional methods to the likes of you."

Beezle caught a new toughness in Coffin's tone and a glimpse of iron in Coffin's eyes. It was time to humour the old fool. "I'm not criticising you, I'm applauding you. I believe that you have shown incredible genius over the millennia, and I'm the first, believe me, to applaud your fathomless creativity in finding ever more inventive methods of dispatch. All I could ever hope to do is build on some of your sublime techniques. You are still, and always will be, the *Master*."

The patting of Coffin's ego almost made him forget that he had entered a new era of assertiveness, and he smiled at the compliment. Then, catching himself mid-smile, he manoeuvred his face back into a suitably stern shape, and addressed Beezle in sombre tones.

"I have an important assignment for you. It will take immediate priority. And that means *all* other projects cease until this one is completed. Understood?"

"Understood. May I be so bold as to ask, what assignment?"

"I want two coffins out of you. Two very significant coffins."

"So what's Hieronymus up to these days?"

COFFIN MAKER MARK L. FOWLER

"That's irrelevant."

"Is it?"

"Meaning?"

"Meaning that though he remains in the Tower - or at least I assume he does - he still seems, by the look of things, to hold some influence."

Coffin held his anger in check and said, quietly, "You had better explain those words."

"My pleasure. It's like this: you want two coffins - Gouge and Doveman, am I right? Hieronymus has talked you into demanding Gouge's coffin, and you've thrown in Doveman to make it look like you're not acting on behalf of an idiot philosopher locked up in a Tower. Can't you see that you're making a terrible mistake?"

Coffin shook his head. "The only mistake being made at the moment is your failure to grasp what I am saying. I have not come to argue with you, I am ordering you. I want Gouge and I want Doveman. You have the rest of the day or else you had better start looking forward to spending a long time listening to philosophical argument at very close quarters. *Now* do you understand?"

Coffin walked out of the Dome feeling like a captain who had just regained the wheel of his ship, all mutiny quashed, all fine and correct and the weather ahead set fair. It was a good feeling.

Back in his quarters, he took up his pen and filled a dozen pages of his journal with reflections on the past hours. He wrote of how he had played the father sublimely to get the truth out of Hieronymus; how philosophy had lost the unequal battle against the wisdom of a craftsman and a poet; how he had revealed his master stroke to Beezle, and how he had restored leadership.

And the more he wrote, the less he believed any of it. And the less he believed it, the faster he wrote it, as though battling to deny the spirits of truth a chance to gain space in his head.

He could see that the battle was a fruitless one, and at last stopped writing, letting the eager spirits invade completely. And when he had finished listening to them he sat for so long without moving that it seemed the things the eager spirits had told him had proved too much for his bony heart.

Was this the beginning of the end?

Defiantly he stirred, crossing out every self-deceiving word. Then, calmly and very deliberately, he wrote,

Hieronymus knew. My past. He knows everything. I sat up in the Tower fooling myself. The Quiet Revolution *is nothing more than I have already done. And the Tower itself. What is it there for and why have I never questioned its existence? Perhaps it* is *all pre-ordained. Perhaps there* is *no choice. No freewill. And now I'm thinking like Hieronymus. And I have left him locked in the Tower. Why? Because I don't know what else to do. Is he under lock and key because I fear him? Or because I envy his intellect? Or do I love him and want to give him protection? Protection from who and against what? Beezle?*

COFFIN MAKER   MARK L. FOWLER

Coffin broke off to read what he had written. He couldn't argue with any of it.

Beezle was right. I want Gouge dead because Hieronymus has convinced me. And I have given Doveman as a sacrifice to pacify Beezle. But if it all hinges on those two. If it all hinges on Gouge and Doveman then surely their deaths will restore balance and let me get back to doing my work. Hieronymus would accept the death of Doveman in the light of Gouge's death. I don't feel that Beezle will accept Gouge's death in any light. But Beezle will do as he's told or face the Tower. I will have my two coffins out of him. I will forfeit full knowledge of Gouge to see an end to this farce. I can only take so much. I have taken it.

Coffin took a brisk walk back to the Dome, his eager legs cracking along like starting pistols. It was time to get some numbers rolling while Hieronymus was languishing in the Tower and Beezle was busy on his labours of love and hate.

He found the Dome empty, and on finding it so he allowed himself a smile. So the fire-headed youth was elsewhere, carrying out his new orders and abandoning his bizarre enterprises - or at least postponing them. It was a start, and a good one.

He imagined Beezle assembling his materials, wrestling with the dilemma, trying to work out the compromise solution. Of course he would be wasting his efforts, because there would be no compromise acceptable. And what sweet distress *that* would cause inside that disturbed orange head.

COFFIN MAKER   MARK L. FOWLER

He would give Beezle a few hours to sweat on it before seeking him out and forcing his hand.

Bringing matters to a close.

For this was one day that was going to end *his* way.

Yet despite the Coffin Maker's conviction that all rebellion had been dealt with, it seemed that Beezle had other business to attend to that day. Business that had never crossed Coffin's mind, or even come within an ocean's width of it.

As Coffin swung the machinery of the Dome into action to put some poetry back into the world, Beezle was standing at the top of the winding staircase, outside the door that held Hieronymus prisoner.

Through the keyhole he was telling Hieronymus a story.

It was a story about the future, the present, and the past.

It was a curious story that told everything that there was to tell.

The truth, the purpose, *the ending...*

24: BEEZLE'S STORY

Hieronymus had been pondering. The usual suspects: Death, time, good and evil, God, the devil, freewill, pre-ordination...his thoughts flying in circles around his brain, covering the same ground, and each time landing on the spot marked *Gouge*.

The arrival of himself and Beezle had to be connected to the conflict rising like a hurricane from hell in Zone Thirty-Nine. Yet the questions piled up:

What or who was the Creator's real opposite?

Not Coffin: far too stupid to be evil. And Coffin had a good side. A reasonable side, though it was buried beneath a multitude of ridiculous charades.

So was Gouge the devil?

It didn't seem likely. Gouge was vulnerable. Could be destroyed by the same coffin nails that signposted the end of the road for humans. The devil, if he existed at all, could not be at the mercy of the Coffin Maker.

If any logic could be applied to such speculative matters, then it had to be the case that only the Creator Himself could destroy the devil - that is, if the devil existed as a separate and external entity, and not simply as a representation of the evil side of human nature. But then the 'evil side of human nature' didn't seem to adequately cover it either; because Gouge was not a part of the human race.

He was never born; he was never innocent. There was no Fall.

And no Fallen Angel, either.

COFFIN MAKER — MARK L. FOWLER

So what did that make Gouge? If he was neither human nor devil, then what was he? What was left to describe him?

One of the devil's legion?

Satan, if he existed at all, sending a mere foot-soldier to destroy the world? To do his dirty work? Where was the glory in that? Within the same mythology of metaphysical fisty-cuffs between good and evil, hadn't God entered the world Himself? Bloodied his own hands – or had them bloodied? Finishing off what He had started? Wouldn't the devil enter the arena for the final battle? The showdown?

Hieronymus groaned. "I don't know what *I* am. Fat chance I can solve the rest of it."

Was this humanity's burden? To come into the world without a brief? Without an explanation? To become attached to the world in the dawning realisation that the only certainty is that you won't be staying beyond your undetermined span. Your allocation of years – or perhaps months, or weeks, hours...minutes.

Mortal minds – the greatest philosophers – had asked the same questions – had kept returning to the same questions – century on century. The whole thing going round and round like a grotesque carnival ride.

How could you not feel for them?

How could you ever wish to make things worse?

Closing his eyes, he conjured visions of Doveman saving the world. Of Coffin coming to his senses, nailing Gouge. It was tough going.

The sounds of feet clicking up the staircase stole into his fantasies. Footsteps that didn't have the usual stumbling uncertainty and frailty of purpose.

COFFIN MAKER MARK L. FOWLER

No hesitancy in these footsteps. And no guilt either.

Hieronymus felt a shiver play like a xylophone hammer down his spine. Then it came. The voice of a stranger. It was like he was hearing Beezle for the first time. All imitation of humility gone, exposing the raw gristle of seething hatred beneath.

The voice coming through the door was like a saw cutting through bone.

"Prisoner...? Prisoner...? I've come to tell you a story, Prisoner. Want to hear about your old friend Gouge?"

Hieronymus could hear a scratching sound outside the door, and imagined Beezle's face pressed against it, trying to discern the sounds and smells of dread inside.

"Are you sweating for all humanity, Prisoner? You soon will be. The good Colonel has sunk fine roots into the heart of Thirty-Nine and has dear old Doveman in his sights. The president's found religion, and when the going gets rough, in a few hours from now, the colonel is going to find a nation already on its knees."

Hieronymus crept to the door. Two ears pressed against opposite sides of the same thick wood, though the balance of pleasure and pain was in no way even.

"Come up with any answers to the questions yet, Prisoner? Any flashes of insight? Any...solutions?" The chuckle rose like a psychopathic vulture. "You must be worn out with all that thinking in there. Let me tell you a little story to help your poor thoughts rest more easily. Ready? Then I'll begin.

COFFIN MAKER   MARK L. FOWLER

"Once upon a time there was God. Now God decided to have some fun, wanted to be creative. So He made a world. Trouble was, inanimate objects soon bored Him to tears. So came Life. But God, well, He'd never tried anything like this before and was keen to hedge His bets. So He set up a get-out clause. What do you think He called it, Prisoner?"

Beezle's eyes were wild and his nose and ears twitched furiously, desperate to know what thoughts were racing on the other side of the door. Hearing, seeing, smelling nothing, he went on. "That's right, He called it Death. Enter Coffin. And because God likes to work in symbols, he decided that whether Death is accompanied by fire, burial at sea, or simply rotting in the street, a coffin is the perfect representation. You see, God insists on keeping things tidy, putting things in *boxes*.

"So now we're getting to the good bit. You see, Prisoner, once the whole thing was set in motion, with Coffin regulating it, God expected it to be a matter of time before the whole thing went out of control. At which point one of two things would happen: Coffin's ego gets the better of him and all Life is obliterated. Or Coffin brings Death to a halt.

"As you well know, Prisoner, both have been on the cards. Trouble is, Coffin has been so indecisive that he only goes so far down any one road, with the irritating consequence that despite all the ridiculous and bizarre twists and turns that history stands testament to, the whole shooting-match was looking to be in serious danger of stagnating.

COFFIN MAKER   MARK L. FOWLER

"Neither oblivion nor immortality. So the Creator decided to spice things up a little. End the deadlock. Let the two extremes of Coffin's personality do battle. And so here we are, Hieronymus. *Prisoner.* You and I. Doing battle. Isn't it just the best thing ever?

"We – the Coffin Maker's extremes – locking horns? Nothing more than that. And by the same token, nothing less. The Coffin Maker at war with himself. And what makes the idea so sublime is that he hasn't a clue who we are or what's happening. And - and I find this the mark of exquisite genius - whatever the outcome of our uneven little battle, Coffin loses. It's either the end of the world or the end of Death. It amounts to the same.

"So you must be wondering about Gouge. Your philosophical brain will have worked out that I can't be the devil unless Coffin himself is part devil. Which leaves the colonel. Made not born. But made by who? *Not by me.*

"Was it you, Prisoner? Did you make the colonel? Are you the devil?"

The door burst open, knocking Hieronymus halfway across the room. Stunned, he turned to see Beezle standing in the doorway in all his scarred glory, holding up a single coffin nail.

"Enough mortals can pick locks with a good deal less. But back to our riddle: Coffin made Gouge - isn't it obvious?"

Beezle stepped into the room.

"Gouge is the latest manifestation of an evil that's been around since Coffin gave it life. Ironic, eh? He played about, tampering with this, messing with

COFFIN MAKER   MARK L. FOWLER

that. He brought them back to life, killed them off, restored them, sometimes giving the same corpse a hundred chances. Like playing with a wound, Hieronymus, one day it's going to turn malignant.

"And it did. Because somewhere in all of that messing, he gave life to something he didn't count on. Something he's never understood. And it keeps coming around. It's had countless names and now it happens to be called 'Colonel Gouge'. Difference is, this time evil finally made it to purity. This time it broke the shackles of birth and freed itself wholly from humanity. That's why Coffin missed it. And that's why it's so potent. I'd call it unstoppable. Can you wonder that God – or the 'Creator', if you'd prefer - wants rid of that old fool once and for all, whatever the consequences?"

Hieronymus' mind was spinning. Disorientation ruled the universe; what was up, down? He'd thought only of giving humans a better deal, but had meddled with the same magic that had brought evil into the world - no, it was worse than that: he was part of the Coffin Maker – part of what had brought evil into the world.

"Actually," said Beezle, "there's a certain poignancy to all this. For all the rubbish that's spouted about evil, it turns out that all along it's the product of Coffin's ridiculous arsing about. He never intended it, and didn't even realise he'd done it. Except, deep down, he suspected as much, but chose not to think about it – *denial*, that's what those idiots on Earth would call it - hence his paranoia at seeing his old practices being polished up. Isn't it just perfect, how it's all working out?"

COFFIN MAKER   MARK L. FOWLER

Hieronymus' mind, reeling with self-disgust, seized a moment of clarity.

"How come you know all this?"

"God told me," said Beezle.

"Why would He tell you? Why you and not me?"

"Feeling left out, Hieronymus? It's like this. God believed that He had set up an uneven battleground. That in a straight fight between Life and Death, the instinct of Life would prevail. He thought you would prove stronger, and He wanted to even up the fight. But all stories need a good strong ending, so how about this: In a few minutes, Doveman dies - in agony, of course. Zone Thirty-Nine collapses into chaos. Gouge takes control. He points Thirty-Nine's finest, most beautiful weapons at a hostile world, incinerating everything. Then he waits for the rest of the world's last, bitter reply. *Armageddon.* Beautiful, isn't it? Because no-one, absolutely no-one, gets to live happily ever after."

"Why?" asked Hieronymus.

"Is that all you can think to ask? What a fine philosopher you turned out to be."

"The end of the world," said Hieronymus. "Who benefits? What good is an empty, destroyed world to Gouge or to you?"

"Can't you see? Gouge is a product, a cell that went wrong. What good is a cancer, trapped inside the body it has destroyed? It is simply the nature of things, and the price to be paid for tampering."

COFFIN MAKER   MARK L. FOWLER

"No devil?" said Hieronymus. "No devil sending one evil soldier after another to spite God by destroying His creations?"

"You sound like a professor. A professor with his head stuck up his own philosophical arse."

"There is a devil behind this," said Hieronymus. "There has to be."

"Has to be?"

"Sometimes he sends a tyrant, sometimes a builder of malignant empires - and now he has sent a pure destroyer. This is just another stage in the battle - trying to outwit the Creator. If we really are the two sides of Coffin, hasn't God sent us to show the Coffin Maker that he - Coffin - has the power to choose?"

"Choose what?"

"Who to serve."

"What are you talking about?"

"Coffin has grown arrogant. Forgotten that even Death has to serve a master. God or the devil. Good or evil."

"Ha! You sound like an undergraduate now. Your logic is so frail. Once you accept the devil in your thinking, you don't know where the ideas are coming from - don't you see that? *What if God sent us?* you say. Coffin thought he recognised the handwriting - but Coffin knows nothing. Coffin likes to rewrite history in that stupid book of his. He writes about Eden, but he was post-Fall.

"Do you see the implication of that? *He was never even there!* He came afterwards. He's never seen the Creator, and he wouldn't recognise his handwriting if He wrote him a birthday card. So turn it around, as

COFFIN MAKER   MARK L. FOWLER

you must if you accept the existence of the devil. And what does it leave? Did the devil send Coffin the note? Does the devil know that Coffin will choose *me*? After all...it's *you* locked in this Tower."

"But..."

"But *what*, Hieronymus?"

"If Coffin was 'post-Fall', he couldn't have caused evil."

"If you want to believe that," said Beezle, backing towards the door, licking his lips. "Believe what you will, it doesn't look good either way. And what's not good for you is bad news for *them*. The glory of it is that it really doesn't matter whether you believe in God the devil or the fucking Sandman! But let's stick with tradition, just to get the point across.

"God wouldn't speak to me, but the devil might. Mr. D speaking directly to Coffin's dark side makes sense, don't you think?"

"You said there's no devil."

"I might have been lying. Toying with you. Whatever. You, the 'good' side, weren't vigilant. That makes it your fault, Prisoner. Tampering, for whatever rhyme or reason, turned creation malignant. I make that your fault again.

"Tough being the good guy, isn't it?"

The door closed, followed by the crack of metal breaking as Beezle snapped the coffin nail inside the lock.

Was Beezle right?

Did it matter which cosmology he chose?

Coffin had written of Eden, which made him pre-Fall. Which meant that he could have caused the

Fall. Yet how could Death have caused the Fall when Death was a consequence of the Fall?

It was too late for philosophy. Too late to sit and pick faults with the logic of the situation. Destruction was coming fast, descending on the world without mercy. If this page in the history of the world was too fantastic, then what of all the other absurd chapters that the world had come to accept as its heritage?

If there's no problem believing in a strange and tearful world revolving around a boiling star, and in the lives sustained in that world, and where the multitudinous paths of Life and Death have left the people of that world - why should one half of Death buck at any of it?

Hieronymus tried to step beyond the myriad of questions that Beezle had raised; tried to focus on the one thing that mattered now. For all questions about the universe boiled down to this: could he escape from the Tower and save President Doveman?

The sound of glass smashing interrupted him. He turned to see that the window was gone. At his feet was a fist of paper. He opened it and a dozen nails fell out onto the floor.

We really are behind the times here in the Kingdom of Death. Even humans have got so far as to believe that God might be dead. One more possibility for you: Coffin sent himself the note, the crazy old bastard. And one final thought for you to spend eternity chewing on: YOU'RE THE ONE RESPONSIBLE WHEN THE WORLD ENDS IN FIRE.

25: THE GREAT ESCAPE

President Doveman could hardly keep his eyes open. His Heaven on Earth campaign was wearing him to the bone. He sat at the writing desk in the Octagonal Room, where so many presidents had sat before him, preparing his twentieth address of the week. He would not use speech writers: it was *his* vision, and it would come from his own heart, styled by his own hand.

The words were blurring on the page. Heaven and Hell blending under tired eyes; energy and vision fading to rhetoric in a fatigued mind. His head was splitting. He was young to be president, according to the papers, but he was young by anybody's reckoning to be feeling so old. At last he let his pen stop, set down his reading glasses, massaging his pulsing eyes. His wife, busily running her sharp legal mind over yet another first draft, looked across. "Take a break, sweetheart. I want to yawn every time I look at you. The heart attack was your warning. You might not get another."

"Another warning or another heart attack?" Doveman held out his arms and beckoned her over. "No-one said Heaven on Earth was going to be easy."

The dutiful, the beautiful, the nation's first lady and favourite heart-shaped face, stooped to her heroic knight and administered the sweetest kisses. "Let me run you a hot bath."

Doveman smiled. "Never could refuse a pretty lady." He started to return her kisses, and then stopped. "Do you think I'm crazy?" he said.

"For kissing your wife, or for taking a bath?"

COFFIN MAKER   MARK L. FOWLER

"For trying to find Heaven on Earth through politics."

She struck a Socratic pose. "Now that's a tough one. Let me see. Do you want the secular response or shall I get changed and play Pope again? I know you like that."

He kissed her, teasingly. "You're medicine, honey, you cure all my ills. What could harm me with you around?"

"Tell you what; just to be on the safe side, I'll go up to the Big Wardrobe and get the papal outfit ready."

"I'm trying to be serious," he said, laughing.

"So am I."

"I'm not just another politician - another ivory tower idealist trying to make a noise, am I? I know, all the way down to my ass-bone, that religion and politics can work it out."

She ran her fingers through his hair. "You're a good man, and as sane as any politician I ever met."

"Steady with the praise."

Dog-tired as he was, her words lifted him. "You know, for all the bullshit politicians spout to get elected - and stay elected - I believe in what I'm doing five-hundred and five percent. I want people to know that faith doesn't mean looking forward to a life after death, it means *a life before* death."

She held up a finger to his lips. "You don't have to convince me. You've got my vote already."

"Maybe I'm a dreamer, and maybe they'll remember me for being the biggest meat head who ever took office."

"You never can tell with politics."

COFFIN MAKER   MARK L. FOWLER

"Maybe it's going down as the political suicide to beat them all. And there have been some."

She stopped him with kisses, this time falling long and slow. "You're a dreamer," she said, taking a breath, "but you're not crazy. You just need a long hot soak in a good hot bath... and then I'm going to show you the meaning of Heaven on Earth."

In the Tower, Hieronymus was moving with a fresh sense of purpose. He'd already tried using the coffin nails in the lock, but couldn't dislodge the one Beezle had snapped off inside the mechanism.

Out the window was a sheer drop. Under the floor was...the staircase.

What about the floor itself?

He knelt down and examined it. *Coffin wood.* Breakable, smashable, coffin wood. If he could displace one board, maybe, just maybe he could gain enough leverage.

Picking out a nail he tried inserting it between two floorboards, finding no purchase. The frustration quickly built and he ended up slamming the nail into one of the boards, barely scratching the wood. Furiously, he stamped at the floor, the coffin nail ready in his hand.

The boards wouldn't budge.

Breathless, and rubbing at a tender heel, he sat down to think. *"What have I got? A door with a broken lock, a smashed window, a handful of nails and the strength of a child. What does all that add up to?"*

He walked back to the door, rattling the handle angrily. What if he smashed off the handle? What

COFFIN MAKER   MARK L. FOWLER

would be the consequence of that? He couldn't seem to work out the implication, but decided it had to be worth a try.

Clumsily he kicked at the handle, kicking more with hope than aim. Wishing he was a man of action; knowing that anything was better than the hopeless waiting. "Come on," he shouted, "get angry. That's Beezle's ugly face you're kicking at. Make it count!"

Hieronymus focused his effort, and with a dozen purposeful kicks, the handle at last started to loosen. There was a working rhythm now, and as he lashed out, he felt the desire for blood building inside, numbing the pain in his foot. However fruitless the victory might ultimately prove to be, he was going to have that handle off that door.

It was coming. He took a breath, then set to wrestling the handle with his hands. It was giving. A few more kicks. The thing was stubborn, though. Weightier measures were needed.

He held onto the handle with both hands and walked his feet up around it, his entire bulk pulling back on it. There was a slow splintering sound. It was going, going - with a scream he launched backwards through the air, the handle still clasped in his hands as he landed.

For a moment he didn't stir, and it took a few minutes for the ceiling to come into focus. Then he crawled back towards the door, his head spinning so much that he didn't dare stand up. On his knees, he assessed the extent of the victory.

A handle-less door that remained locked. So now all leverage was gone. Great! The sum of his

COFFIN MAKER MARK L. FOWLER

knowledge, his fine reasoning brain, had amounted to a spot of mindless vandalism. Did he love humanity so much that he had to suffer from their failings?

In a few hours, all human thought, endeavour and accomplishment would be gone. Coffin was staring redundancy in the face and couldn't see it. Evil, in the shape of Colonel Gouge, was set to destroy its playground and God, the Creator - if He really was involved in any of this - had placed the cause of life into the hands of an impotent youth who couldn't lift a floorboard or break open a door to save the world.

Still holding the door handle, Hieronymus smashed it against the floor in temper. He felt something give.

The handle still held the bolt that had attached it to the outer handle, and the force of the blow against the floorboard had opened a split in the centre of the wood.

Leaping onto his good fortune, he began smashing the handled bolt against the floorboard, until the split had widened enough to get the metal bolt inside. Then he began levering out the floorboard.

It came out easily enough, and he started on the adjacent boards. Soon there was a space in the floor large enough to lower himself through.

Peering into the gap, he gave his eyes a minute to adjust to the darkness. Dimly he could see the staircase, a few metres to the right, though there was nothing to use to bridge the gap. Pulling himself back up, he pulled out more floorboards in the direction of the staircase, until finally he removed the board closest to the wall. Again he peered down. Now the staircase was only a matter of feet away, but there was still no way of bridging what remained of the gap.

The inevitability of heroic action dawned on him, and rested there uneasily. There was a risk, and a substantial one. He would have to lower himself through the hole, holding onto the remaining boards on one side only. He'd realised too late that he should have left the last couple of boards by the wall intact, then he could have held onto both sides to swing himself forwards. Now he would have to hang sideways, swing to gain some momentum, and then twist that momentum ninety-degrees towards the staircase.

He might still make it, but he didn't much favour the odds.

President Doveman was lying in soapy water, dreaming of a better world. He dreamt of a world where ordinary people had a chance of dying with their dreams fulfilled, dying in the knowledge that their children might live to find still greater happiness, passing the baton down the line. Already the people of his country were having children again. The live-for-today-and-to-hell-with-tomorrow culture was cracking and dissolving. The vision of a better world was raising the birth rate, breaking down the fear that had too long gripped the nation: fear that a prosperous nation in a dying world was still no place to give the curse of life to another doomed generation.

Yet this hope couldn't stay confined to the boundaries of his own people. Apart from the moral implications, it would be a narrow and ultimately self-defeating strategy. The point of his vision was its global application; there would be no limits of nationality. It was time that the outreach started in earnest.

A magnificent speech - perhaps the catalyst for the realisation of his vision - simmered in his mind; an address to the world: *Come and see what is happening here, because it can happen everywhere. We're all in this together. And together -*

A metallic snapping sound derailed Doveman's train of thought.

"Sweetheart?"

He sat up.

"Sweetheart, is that you?"

He could hear shuffling. Somebody was moving towards the open doorway. The blood was beating like a hammer across his temples. He gripped the sides of the bath, his eyes riveted to the doorway. Slowly a figure shuffled into view, bound and gagged.

"Sweet -"

Doveman pulled himself to his feet as another figure came into view. A shadow standing directly behind his wife, holding a machine-gun to her head. Again the metallic sound issued as the gunman flicked the safety catch, backwards and forwards. "Hello, Mr. President."

Doveman lurched forward, clutching his chest. His wife tried to scream and stumbled towards him, falling heavily against the side of the bath.

Doveman collapsed back into the water, his face lost beneath the foam.

His wife, stunned from the fall, quickly regained consciousness and looked up to see the gunman dragging her husband out of the water, then pressing

COFFIN MAKER   MARK L. FOWLER

down heavily on his chest, squeezing the water out of his lungs, breathing into his mouth. She watched in confusion at the sight of the man with a machine-gun strapped across his back, resuscitating her beloved.

Doveman's heart was beating again, and the gunman, still straddling the wet body, eased back to wait for the president's eyes to open.

When they did, the gunman pressed his face close to the bulging eyes beneath him, until the tips of the two men's noses were touching. "Take a good look, Mr. P. It's probably the only face that never made it onto those dolls of yours."

"*Gouge?*"

"Only to my friends. I've been hearing all about your plans to create Heaven on Earth. Well, I have a better idea, and I've invited myself to your country to promote it. It's called *Hell on Earth*, and it's going to be much more fun. I'm quite excited about it, actually. There's going to be rockets and firestorms and so many pretty colours. Oh, and a barbecue. And every living creature is going to be on the menu. I couldn't have you missing all of that, could I now, Mr. President, sir?"

Hieronymus lowered himself down through the floor. Already his fingers were burning as he started to take the weight of his body. There would, he knew, be no second chance. He started to swing, trying to gather some momentum before the pain in his fingers became unbearable.

Panic engulfed him.

COFFIN MAKER   MARK L. FOWLER

He was a fool and what was needed was a hero. He would fall to the foot of the Tower and rot there, while the world died screaming.

Beating back the waves of panic, he swung his legs higher. It felt like his fingers were on fire. It was now or never. He let go, throwing his weight toward the staircase, already losing height as the side-rail approached his flailing body.

He wasn't going to reach it. He was falling short.

The rail came up fast and he struck it with the side of his head.

Falling, he threw his hands out, catching the stone of the staircase steps, and clutching desperately as his fingers connected.

He was close to blacking out from the pain, holding on grimly by his numbing finger-ends. Inch by inch he pulled at the step, fighting it with his screams, every inch a new battle until, at last, and still not believing it so, he found himself on the step, sucking the stagnant molecules that sustained Death, back into his bleeding lungs.

He let the minutes pass before he dared to try and stand up, and when he did his legs were shaking so much that he fell straight back down, smacking his hip painfully against the hard stone. "There isn't time for this," he cried, then tried again, this time holding onto the rail. The pain in his arms matched the weakness in his legs and he slid back onto the unyielding stone. His eyes were filling. "Why me?" he shouted. "They deserve better than this."

COFFIN MAKER   MARK L. FOWLER

His words echoed around the walls and bounced back from the black stone to mock him. Giving up the idea of standing, he sidled downwards, as best he could, wincing as every thud added scorn to his battered body.

In the thickening haze of pain, Hieronymus looked on the final twist in the staircase as a cruel mirage sent in ridicule.

Only when he blinked in disbelief at the daylight glinting off the last step, did he believe again in freedom, the realisation forcing tears down his face. He tried again to stand, clinging to the rail, the blood driving through his legs and into his feet, like razor blades sailing his veins - and in agony he moved toward the light.

He was out.

Free of the Tower.

Coffin left the Dome with a glow in his bones. He'd put in a good session, nothing flash or too extreme, yet blessed with the spirit of craftsmanship. And now it was time to check how Beezle was getting along with the Gouge dilemma. No doubt there would have to be a little confrontation before the job got done, but if it came to it, he would not hesitate to use that ridiculous orange mop to drive the last nails home.

Glancing up at the Tower, he thought of Hieronymus. It really did seem a shame that talent should have to languish like that, but there were limits - and those limits had been woefully breached. A few more days up there, he thought, and I might pop in and have another chat, see if he's come to his senses. Perhaps, when this Gouge business is over, Hieronymus

COFFIN MAKER MARK L. FOWLER

might be a little more open to some good old fashioned common sense.

Back in his quarters, Coffin switched on the monitor and flicked around Zone Thirty-Nine for signs of Beezle's progress. It wasn't long before he'd tracked significant activity in the bathing quarters of the presidential palace. It seemed that security had been breached; the entire complex surrounded by Gouge's men.

Looks interesting, he thought. *A showdown? Two for the price of one?*

Focusing in on the bathroom, Coffin was met with a scene stamped diabolically with the mark of Beezle.

Gouge, sitting over the prostrate body of Doveman, hammering nails into presidential flesh.

In the corner of the bathroom, Doveman's wife watched, her mouth gagged, her limbs bound, a small battalion of armed men pointing guns into her face. Doveman was still conscious. There were nails buried into his hands, his feet, his legs. It looked as though the screaming had given way to a semi-conscious delirium. Gouge stopped to administer some resuscitation to the flagging president.

"This is fun," said Gouge. "I can see why those dolls sold so well." He turned to the president's wife. "Fun for *all* the family, what do you say?"

The resuscitation continued until Doveman's eyes were open again. Gouge held up a nail in front of him. "And where's this one going, do you reckon?"

The assembled battalion joined in the laughter.

COFFIN MAKER   MARK L. FOWLER

"Take a deep breath," said Gouge. "This might be a little bit sore."

Gouge placed the nail over Doveman's solar plexus. "Forget Heaven on Earth, my friend, and welcome to Hell. You should feel honoured, though, for you are the first of many."

The nail was hammered into Doveman's guts, Gouge leaping out of the way of the consequential projectile red vomit.

"What a lot of blood from such a little man," said Gouge, climbing back on board the writhing mess still clinging to life beneath him. He held another nail over Doveman's groin. "Won't have any use for all that where you're going." Then he turned again to the president's wife and sniggered, "Sorry about this, Lady."

The nail was driven home.

The president was again losing consciousness, and Gouge grabbed another fistful of nails and tried to capture the last of the potential for pain, hammering the nails furiously into Doveman's fading body.

Coffin stared at the monitor, watching in horror as Gouge turned for the last time to the First Lady, handing her a nail. "A souvenir to treasure always. To help you remember the good times."

Gouge was a shifting montage. Coffin had never seen anything like it. This wasn't human - didn't even pretend to be. He watched a thousand faces distort across the canvas of Colonel Gouge, becoming Beezle, becoming every tyrant and genocidal monster the world had suffered under.

COFFIN MAKER — MARK L. FOWLER

The Coffin Maker watched, transfixed.

The door burst open.

Coffin swung around, expecting to see the orange-haired demon racing towards him, hammer and nail raised in anger.

"Hieronymus?"

The broken figure of his abandoned apprentice stumbled into the room.

"You've got to stop him!"

Coffin looked at the crippled figure, compassion and anguish breaking free of their chains, as the slow trickle of truth at last started to solidify. Unable to speak, he raised his hand and pointed at the monitor.

Hieronymus looked into the nightmare.

Leering from the monitor was a grinning legion of devils crammed into the shape of Gouge. Taunting, goading. And under the stampede of cloven hooves, lay the body of President Doveman, leaking the last of its blood from the wounds of more than a hundred nails.

As the two stunned figures looked on the mesmeric grin of Colonel Gouge, they saw the face assume a final form.

The Coffin Maker staring into the terrible mirrors of his own metallic eyes, enduring the final act of mockery.

26: THE DARK NIGHT BECKONS

Hieronymus held out a fist, opening it to reveal Beezle's letter, retrieved from the ground outside the Tower. "Not more revelations, please," said Coffin. "Read it."

Hieronymus read as far as the second line..."*Even humans have got so far as to believe that God might be dead.*"

"Is he mad?"

"He suggests that you sent yourself the original note."

"Let me see that." Coffin snatched the note, the paper shaking wildly in his fist as he read from it.

"I think he's suggesting that we are to blame," said Hieronymus. "That you're in denial."

"Denial?"

"Of your true nature. That the devil is using you to outwit God."

"Outwit? How can you outwit something that's dead?"

"We have to be vigilant."

"By 'we' do you mean…me?"

"You have the capacity for good and the capacity for evil, the same as mortals."

"I have nothing in common with mortals!"

"I can only give you my interpretation."

"Then give it, for what it's worth. Give it and get it over with."

Hieronymus, his head swimming from exposure to the brutal images on screen, and from pain and exhaustion, did his best to sum up the complexities.

COFFIN MAKER   MARK L. FOWLER

"All of this - another episode in the battle between God and the devil. Gouge is not the devil, but one more of his legion. In my view the note came, directly or indirectly, from the devil. He took a risk showing you your good side, believing you would choose your dark side. It's my opinion that he underestimated your capacity for choosing good over evil. He knows that, as with mortals, it is easy to make evil seductive, evil being the naturally more virulent tendency; the good in us can become apathetic and we cease to believe that our choices can make a difference."

"Cut to the chase, Hieronymus. I'm tired."

"Beezle and I are the evil and good within you."

Coffin fell back in his chair, shaking his head. "When will I wake from this nightmare," he groaned. "Finish it, Hieronymus. Say what you have to say."

Hieronymus finished it. "The devil wants to win the battle for your soul. He wants you to believe the paradox: that the good part of you created evil. But that isn't what I believe any more than I believe that mortals created evil. I believe that the devil alone created evil; that he orchestrated the Fall of Mankind and the resultant mortal condition. And he clothed it with a deep guilt, because guilt does his work best of all."

"You're losing me," said Coffin.

"Okay, what it comes down to is this. Like mortals, you have a choice; and like them, you have a duty to be vigilant and combat evil at every turn - because what you choose makes a difference. This fight will go on to the very end. Every battle is significant on every level. When a mortal chooses *good over evil*, it

COFFIN MAKER   MARK L. FOWLER

makes a *difference*. Your choice is the choice of mortals, but magnified onto a larger screen."

"Stop," said Coffin. "You're telling me that the devil sent the two of you, and that the two of you are really me! The Creator didn't send the letter - the devil sent it. *Or I sent it to myself?* Is that what you're telling me?"

"The cosmology of which side of good and evil conjured us up is probably unknowable, and maybe it doesn't matter. The battle is inside."

"Inside me?"

"Inside all of creation. But in you..."

"Yes..? In me..?"

"In you it has found the ultimate battleground."

Coffin closed his eyes, and in the darkness he saw his mind splitting into two, the detached hemispheres walking away from him in opposite directions. As he called out to them to come back and not abandon him, the disembodied hemispheres took on faces, then bodies: one becoming handsome and noble; the other, ugly, deformed with hate, vowing vengeance on life; wanting to damn the works of the Creator and claim every living thing and then death itself in a final act of self-destruction. Dimly he hoped that what was happening on the inside of his eyelids was a dream. Deep down he knew that such a conceit was only wishful thinking.

He sat in silence as Hieronymus told him about Beezle's visit. About the other things that Beezle had said. When the youth had finished, Coffin bowed his head into his hands and wept.

COFFIN MAKER   MARK L. FOWLER

"There's still time," said Hieronymus. "We can kill Gouge, destroy Beezle."

Coffin looked pitifully at Hieronymus. "That thing...it had my face."

This much said he carried on weeping.

"It's not over yet," said Hieronymus. "You know the truth; you have the power to decide. But the clock's ticking. Beezle will be in the Dome already."

Coffin rose slowly to his feet and looked sadly at Hieronymus. "Know the truth? You're right, I do know the truth. It's over," he said. "Beezle's won."

Hieronymus held Coffin's shoulder as the old master started towards the door. "Haven't you heard what I've been saying? We have the power - *you* have the power. Beezle says you lose whatever happens, but he's wrong. The choice remains with you. Don't you want to show him that you alone control your destiny? Don't you want to show him what he really is - nothing more than an unfortunate part of *your* personality? The part that you're going to destroy."

"Unfortunate?" Coffin brushed Hieronymus' hand away and continued towards the door. Opening it, he signalled to Hieronymus to leave.

"Don't you believe me? Do you think I've made it up? Do you still think Beezle's going to carry out his orders and kill Gouge? That I'm plotting against you? What do you want me to say to make you see?"

For a moment Coffin gazed on Hieronymus with the eyes of a proud father. Calmly he smiled, and the tenderness that radiated stunned the young apprentice.

COFFIN MAKER   MARK L. FOWLER

"You expect me to believe a lot of very strange things, Hieronymus, and I do believe them. And that's why you've had to endure the tears of a sad old man. I'm feeling my age, and it's an age I would wish on no-one. I feel tired and sick. I can't keep up the pretence any longer. I don't understand what's happening even though you've just explained it to me. I'm hollow. I haven't the fight in me. That thing has my face and it's welcome to it. Let it mock; let it have its way. It feels like the end. Let whatever's going to happen, happen quickly. Let it be over. Let it be the end. I've let you down and I'm sorry. Please, go now."

Hieronymus looked for some remote spark in Coffin's eyes, but he saw only rusting metal. "You can't do this," he said. "You can't turn your back on them."

But it felt like talking to an empty grave, and he moved at last towards the open door.

"You deserved better," said Coffin, as Hieronymus limped through the doorway.

"The world deserved better," said Hieronymus, bitterly.

The door closed and the sound of weeping once more stained the dead air.

Hieronymus hobbled through the labyrinth of pointless complexity that surrounded Coffin's quarters. When at last he was free of it, he stood in the invisible, still void that passed for substance in the Kingdom of Death, looking over towards the Coffin Dome.

He thought of Beezle, assembling his forces. Imagined the billions of coffins that would have to be made almost simultaneously. For an instant he

COFFIN MAKER   MARK L. FOWLER

imagined Armageddon a sheer impracticality. For one glorious moment he indulged the thought that mankind would survive on the grounds of simple logistics: you can only make so many coffins at a time.

But then destruction was no more bound by the laws of logic than was creation. Philosophers could sit around all day thinking up grand-sounding reasons why existence was a logical impossibility, a paradox, nonsense - but there was to be no lasting comfort found in the cold laws of logic.

Logic left everything unsaid. The Coffin Maker alone had conducted slaughters on an escalating scale over the centuries with terrifying ease. There was always a higher gear waiting in the Coffin Dome. These were unassailable truths that made a mockery of all the laws of logic. On paper it was pure lunacy to imagine a single being managing even a single nations' catastrophes - let alone the solitary Coffin Maker conducting mankind's blackest days.

But then lunacy and reality were made for each other, and inside the Coffin Dome, whatever remained of reality was inevitably decimated as old records tumbled and new statistics burnt their way into the history books. What might appear to be a few pieces of wood and a few lousy nails, would more than see to the destruction of the human race.

All it took was the will to do it.

It was something akin to the loaves and the fishes; the feeding of five thousand from the most paltry of picnic baskets. Except this was to be no picnic.

Rather the ultimate expression of absolute madness.

Mass destruction.
Self-destruction.
Death's suicide.
The final slaughter...it was all the same with your head buried in the sand.

No opt-out clause for the Coffin Maker. No middle ground.

Good or evil? Either - or? Inaction was a choice; it held consequences. Moral neutrality - a mere illusion held together by the will to shed responsibility. Inaction would mean the snuffing out of the gift of life. The ground had been laid, and it would happen quickly.

And easily.

Because *all it would take was the will to do it*.

And Beezle had the will.

What was to happen could not be rationalised out of existence.

He was the master of his own destiny.

Yet a servant too.

And he had to serve something.

There was no escape.

No way out of the battle that was coming.

It was time to make a coffin.

What else could he do?

27: COFFIN SEARCHES FOR THE PERFECT SENTENCE

Inside the Dome, Beezle was gathering forces. Rigorous calculation showed that the Dome could handle it. Coffins enough for everyone, with an easy billion or so to spare.

It filled him with a profound sense of wonder. One of those funny things about the Dome, and equally, about the nature of time; the way both could flex to accommodate the demands of the moment. It seemed ludicrous that one being could simultaneously nail up enough coffins to accommodate a single air disaster, let alone conduct the entire destruction of a city. But all it took was the desire. If the desire was big enough, the world was small and frail enough.

As he watched the cargo of coffins chugging along the conveyor belts, it struck him that equal desire from the opposite direction could stop it all from happening. That was the way things were, the way they were made. To know more would be to know the mind of God. And what did technicalities matter anyway? Hieronymus was in the Tower, and Coffin - well, there wasn't much left of him to worry about.

As the machinery started to pick up the rhythm of the day, Beezle was moved by an awareness of the craftsmanship that had built this edifice of destruction, and even felt a twinge of admiration for the creative powers of the Coffin Maker. It was staggering to think that a clown could have built such a place, untold centuries in advance of this hour, somehow knowing

COFFIN MAKER   MARK L. FOWLER

the capacity to which it must ultimately perform under the guidance of his own dark side.

Recognising the dangers lurking within the transforming power of humility, he shook himself out of the thought, giving himself a talking to in the process. "You're beginning to think like Hieronymus. Beginning to hesitate like a philosopher. Before you know, you'll be turning into a handsome romantic fool, the Poet in the Tower, yearning to save the world and walk out at last into a glorious and heroic sunset.

"Well, there's only one cure for romantic illusion; one cure for philosophy and poetry: indulge them to the hilt. What has been the primary obsession of philosophers? *Death.* What is poetry's first inspiration? *Love?*"

Beezle laughed like a volley of gunfire. "I don't think so. And what's the final image the world deserves to see? God and His legion of angels descending from the Heavens?

" Sooo-rrry!

"How about an orange glow covering the horizon, looking as though I, Beezle, have fallen to the lost and desperate planet? That's more like it. And in the centre of that glow, an invitation, to each and every one of them, with no exceptions and no exclusions: *an invitation to their own cremation.*"

He raised his arms like a ballet dancer, but he spoke like a deranged cheerleader. "And so, with no further ado, let the march begin. The dance of fire awaits so take your partners please. A waltz into the flames, my friends, with a one-two-three-one-two-three...why, your hands are trembling you *dear, sweet*

COFFIN MAKER   MARK L. FOWLER

world. You've nothing to fear from me - well, that's not strictly true. But it won't hurt for long, and soon you'll be switching off the light, and closing your heavy eyes and settling down for a little sleep."

Beezle was dancing, tripping from machine to machine, flicking the levers, howling hysterically as the Dome sprang to life.

"In this kind of mood," he shouted above the growling, squealing cacophony, "I can squeeze time down to nothing. When the fun starts I can have it all done in the time it would take to craft a single coffin by hand. Think about that you poets and philosophers. Gorge yourselves on that thought while you wait for the party to start."

Coffin was staring blankly into his journal. He felt poignant, full of the labour pains of melancholy. There was poetry inside him and it was begging to be born. He wanted to sum it all up in a sentence. *One perfect sentence.* An epitaph for the entirety of time and creation. He wanted to say everything and he wanted to say it with words that could never be followed; words that would demand the final full-stop.

Trouble was he couldn't think of a single thing to say. All his ideas, his inspirations, seemed trivial now. Childish and senile. Where had it gone? What had become of the Coffin Maker? What had become of the Poet of Death?

The harder he thought, the emptier his mind became, until it felt like a thick blanket had been wrapped inside his head, soaking up whatever was left. One solitary, obsessive, circling thought remained: that

COFFIN MAKER MARK L. FOWLER

this was how it had always been. An empty-headed simpleton mistaking baby thoughts for profundity, and baby talk for poetry. And it had taken the History of the World for the truth to dawn.

The dawning of this truth *had* been the History of the World!

A terrifying gravity descended, one from which he would never break free. It would hold him firmly in the grip of endless emptiness. The page that was meant to contain everything, confirm everything, explain everything; the page that was meant to be the very apotheosis of everything - remained blank.

The weight of impotence bore so heavily on the Coffin Maker that he was soon weeping again, wetting the pages of his already forgotten masterpiece.

As the Coffin Maker wept, Hieronymus hammered nails into a coffin. And while he was hammering, he was holding a one-sided conversation with the Creator.

"So am I wasting my time, or is Beezle wasting his? Okay, let's try an easier one to get you warmed up. How about: if you sent two sides - the two extreme opposite sides - of Coffin's mind, or personality, or psyche, or whatever else you want to call it. If you sent those two opposites to come face to face with the very thing they inhabit, ie, the Coffin Maker - and if you sent them in the guise of apprentices, with not a clue to the poor old fool as to what's going on - does this mean that you have serious personality problems of your own? Does this mean that you have a very advanced sense of humour, specialising in the absurd? But above all, tell me: does it have a purpose? Couldn't the world have

COFFIN MAKER   MARK L. FOWLER

been destroyed by Gouge or saved by Doveman without any of this? Or is it that you can't resist the dramatic gesture?

"And why wait until now to split Coffin in two?"

He stopped hammering.

"*Or have you done this before?* No, you couldn't have done. There's nothing in the journal to suggest it. Coffin would have mentioned it. He can't break bony wind without writing about it."

Hieronymus began hammering again.

"So why now? Divine Comic Timing? Okay, so you'd rather not comment. But promise me one thing. When all this is over; when Beezle and I have sidled back into Coffin and he's running around looking for us; or when me and kissing cousin are locked up in the Tower forever so that extremes no longer form a part of Coffin's mentality - if that's possible; when whatever all this is leading to finally comes over the horizon, will you promise to let me into the secret, share the punch line?

"Even if it doesn't make any difference? You made me curious, just as you made mankind curious, and none of us, up here or down there, can stand another day of this wretched not knowing!"

He switched on the monitor. The last few nails were going to be crucial. There would be no second chances. Flicking the monitor over Thirty-Nine, he found an uneasy stillness.

A nation mourning its president?
Was time at a standstill?

COFFIN MAKER   MARK L. FOWLER

Was Beezle working Death so hard that all time had ceased?

Was the Coffin Dome smoking with the ferocity of his vision, and time crawling into the fire like a dying slug?

"Where are you, Gouge?" he said, swinging the monitor towards the presidential palace, finding Doveman's wife dying the slow tortured death of grief. The death that can last a lifetime.

Yet there was no sign of Doveman's corpse.

And no Gouge.

He scanned furiously, disorientated in time, bewildered in space. He sought out every conceivable hiding place and found nothing.

As he searched, he felt the world slowing ever more quickly, as though the emergency batteries were running down. People on the street were walking in slow motion, like they had left Earth and were breaking free of its pull. Voices were slurring. The Dome, thought Hieronymus, must be close to meltdown.

Still he could not find Gouge.

And still no sign of Doveman.

The prickly heat of panic was rising up the back of the apprentice. Maybe he should leave the search for Gouge and head to the Coffin Dome. Seek out Beezle and destroy him.

Hieronymus weighed up his chances, picturing himself - the limping, battered fragility of mere intellect, pitching itself physically against the deformed spirit of destruction that had the strength to smash the high-window of the Tower from the ground.

COFFIN MAKER   MARK L. FOWLER

It was absurdity on an apocalyptic scale. He wouldn't even limp half-way to the Dome before Beezle had lit the final fuse on the world.

He had to stay with the monitor and find Gouge. Find Gouge and prepare the final nails...

COFFIN MAKER   MARK L. FOWLER

28: THE STEEPLE AND THE PIED PIPER

Hieronymus found Gouge hiding deep inside the shadows engulfing All Saints. It was the last place he had thought to look and, he told himself angrily, probably the most obvious.

He'd swept the monitor across Thirty-Nine, coming within a whisker of cracking. Of heading over to the Coffin Dome, hammer raised, knowing in his heart that he would stand not a chance in combat, but having to do *something*.

The world was coming to a standstill from which it would never start up again. Eternal sleep; the eternal haunting of the ghosts of Armageddon.

Yet the stillness yielded a pattern; a sense of movement towards the spire of All Saints. Towards the spire that still pointed resolutely like a lonely finger.

Movement was becoming almost imperceptible, losing all shape. Yet like a slow motion flicker of breeze, the zombie-remains of human life pointed towards that immense spire.

Now he saw it.

Like a flag hanging from the top of the spire. Movement on the ground far below. Movement detached from the stagnating world. Movement that should have been clear as midnight sun, in contrast to the failing energies of a dying planet.

Hieronymus zoomed in the monitor.

At the foot of the church, staring upwards, pointing and laughing, stood Gouge's men. They had broken free of the restraints of the slowing world, conforming to a different set of laws - the *unnatural*

COFFIN MAKER   MARK L. FOWLER

laws of the universe. Their lack of nature had veiled them. But now the curtain was down, the flesh ripped back. There, bold and brutal, every colour of death dominating the monitor in the way that a matured and ready-for-the-endgame tumour might dominate an x-ray.

In front of them, on a mobile podium hastily erected, stood Colonel Gouge. He was speaking into a microphone.

As Hieronymus watched and listened, a gigantic cloud appeared to stretch itself over the extent of Zone Thirty-Nine, bubbling and blackening, while Gouge addressed the zombie-crowd still crawling towards the church like legions of dying ants.

"People - or can I call you....dregs? It wasn't so long ago that your president addressed you with a message of hope. Today I want to incinerate those hopes. Today I want to ensure that the hopes, the dreams, the ambitions of every single one of you are burnt to ashes."

Gouge scanned the multitude, his fingers drumming murderously on the lapels of his elegant frock-coat.

"Doveman might have saved you, if he hadn't been a politician. If he hadn't thought that destroying the fear of me sufficient for political power, he might have settled for nothing less than destroying the *reality*. He let you down, and now I am going to let him down. The flag of Doveman, President of Peace will, in a moment, be lowered forever.

"In a few minutes I will start to press some very important buttons. You are the lucky ones, the fortunate

COFFIN MAKER   MARK L. FOWLER

specimens, for you are about to go to war with the world. It will not be a war for you to worry your inconsequential brains over. I won't drag you through a boring repeat of what you call, 'The Great Wars'. Neither will I waste breath by giving it a number. And I won't fool about with one of those ridiculous wars of attrition that would try the patience of a saint."

He nodded towards the statue, and laughed, scornfully. "And believe me, I would never dream of putting you through the insufferable rhetoric of a *Holy War*. I'm not that kind of...animal." His face constricted like a coiling snake preparing to strike. "War has grown up. Come of age. It will not take long. Less peaceful presidents than Doveman have their buttons, too."

The snake-face grew claws and a stinging tail. "And what about me? Well, just to show that there's no hard feelings, me and the boys will stick around until the last few seconds, and then we're going to have a little cyanide party. You see, politicians like Doveman assume that all destructive impulses are governed by the will to gain power. But, like so many before him, Doveman was wrong. The end of the world is all I've ever really wanted. Even as a little boy it filled my dreams. A lesser man might have simply thrown himself off a cliff and done with. My motto though is: why be selfish? Why not take everybody else with you?"

The reptilian face distorted into a kaleidoscope of terrors, yet the voice retained its haunted charm, like cool honey running gently over scorched tongues.

"One last thought for you all. Do you want to know my earliest memory? I'll tell you anyway. It was

COFFIN MAKER   MARK L. FOWLER

listening to old Mumsy reading the story of the Pied Piper to me, night after night. She loved that story, and made me love it, too. She even used to invent variations, killing off people who'd upset her that day. 'It would be so wonderful,' she used to say, 'to be the Pied Piper. Or even the woman who gave birth to the Pied Piper.'

"It would indeed be wonderful to be the Pied Piper. And it *is* wonderful to *be* the Pied Piper. She had a sense of humour, did Mumsy. Some might say that she must have, giving birth to me, though they would likely find their mouths stuffed with high explosives if they were ever so discourteous. No, not even a woman as formidable as Mumsy can really lay claim to the honour of giving birth to the Angel of Death. No woman can. Some, you see, are not born at all; some don't know what childhood is.

"But let the poor creature keep her dreams. You know, I went through a phase of idolising that woman, just before I led her down to the Cage. You won't know about the Cage. Let's say, it was the place where I spent my childhood, such that it was. The place where I was fed to my heart's content on poisoned chocolates. And now Mumsy lives there, and I visit her from time to time, keeping her alive with wonderful stories of her real-life Pied Piper. Isn't that wonderful? Isn't that the finest story you've ever heard?"

Gouge's men clapped wildly and made election-style hooting sounds until their master quietened them with a mere flick of an eye.

"But the thing about Mumsy's stories that I liked the best was the way she always killed off everybody at

COFFIN MAKER   MARK L. FOWLER

the end. She used to say that it was the only way to end a story. She didn't even care to spare the Pied Piper, and of course she was right.

"Do I need to say more, my friends? Do I?"

He turned towards the spire, took off his undertaker's top hat and, sweeping into a low and theatrical bow, boomed, "Ladies and Gentleman, take your seats for the Show of Shows. Put them together one last time for the president. Please, lower the flag."

Hieronymus saw at last what hung from the steeple.

The impaled corpse of President Doveman, attached to a rope. Gouge's men pulling on the rope, forcing the dead body deeper onto the thickening spike.

He watched the naked corpse ripping apart, the pale flesh and bones falling from the spire, scattering to the ground.

Then horror turned to hope.

"Purity," breathed Hieronymus, *sotto voce*, grasping at the elusive truth. "Moral purity...survives death...is eternal...rare...powerful beyond measure...who are the purest..? the saviours..? those who pass the baton...pass the baton to...? ...the refugees from grief..."

His mind raced like a hurricane through world history, and through the remembered pages of Coffin's journal. He switched the monitor to Zone Six Hundred and Sixty-Six. A young boy, broken in half by the loss of his mother, was reading the book that his favourite uncle had given to him.

Coffin Maker.

The book Bishop Stones wanted destroyed...

Then *wanted*.

COFFIN MAKER   MARK L. FOWLER

"Excuse me for reading over your shoulder, little one," whispered Hieronymus.

The boy turned the page.

He read quickly and then closed the book, putting it under his pillow and turning out the light seconds before his father's head appeared around the door. Hieronymus watched the man enter the room and kiss his son's head.

The thought washed over him like a tidal wave.

"Against such evil as this...

...those who first recognised it."

Hieronymus took flight towards the Coffin Vaults, running headlong into a wall of pain and taking with him a hammer but no nails.

COFFIN MAKER MARK L. FOWLER

29: THAT ELUSIVE, PERFECT ENDING

Coffin was alternating between bouts of uncontrollable weeping and moments of resolve to write the definitive, concluding paragraph of Life and Death. A single sentence was too demanding now. It would have to be a paragraph, and might end up being a considerable one at that.

Still the page was empty.

And wet.

He had no idea that Hieronymus was once more entering the Forbidden Country, and if he had known, he might not have cared. It was too late for caring, too late for anything. What did it matter what efforts, struggles, last dramatic gestures took place in the final minutes? What mattered was that time was slipping by and the page still unwritten.

Drying his eyes he picked up his pen. The journal must be completed; the words found that would do the job. He squeezed his mind, searching for the stroke of genius that would close the book forever. Nothing came.

Inside the Coffin Vaults, a wild and insane inspiration was driving Hieronymus. "Poetic justice," he repeated, searching through the jungle of coffins. "*Poetic justice.*"

In the churchyard at All Saints, the flag of peace, in the ragged, torn jigsaw of the abused body of President Doveman, lay at the feet of Father Henry's statue. Gouge looked from under his arm, in a gesture intended

COFFIN MAKER   MARK L. FOWLER

to amuse the gathering. "I think the rain has stopped. It wasn't so long ago that it was raining better men than him. Looks like it's going to be a fine day."

He raised a finger, and the wheels of industry were instantly spinning in violent contrast to the slow motion of the surrounding world.

In the Coffin Dome, Beezle watched the monitor gleefully as Doveman's body sailed casually through the air, as time ground down towards standstill. His mouth pressed over the screen, he breathed, "Speed, Colonel Gouge, your time is here. *Godspeed.*"

In disconnected unison, Beezle and Hieronymus threw back their heads and bellowed out jubilant cries. For Beezle had breathed the final fire into the soul of Gouge, and Hieronymus had found the three coffins he had been looking for: Father Henry; Brigadier Browning; and an old man who'd fallen out of a tree, trying to rescue a cat.

The two ecstatic bellows, divinely different and unknown to each other, cut mysteriously into the thoughts of the Coffin Maker, who felt anything *but* ecstatic. He raised his head and listened. Was this it? The beginning of the end? Was this his last call to write the ultimate sentences and be done with it?

With new resolve, he racked his brains until his face became so crumpled it looked about to collapse over them. He picked up his pen one last time, giving it a ferocious stare - as though it alone was responsible for his lack of inspiration - before launching it violently

COFFIN MAKER   MARK L. FOWLER

against the wall. This much accomplished, he lowered his head and wept.

Hieronymus had the lid off two coffins and was working furiously at Father Henry's. Agonisingly the coffin nails resisted as he worked at them: prising, bending, hitting out wildly. Then slowly the lid started to give...

In the churchyard the extent of Gouge's personal security was descending. Helicopters hovered above the trees, encircling the church. Men on the ground stood two thick around the mighty gothic structure. All personnel outside the church, including the men in the helicopters, knew they would not be privileged to the precious capsules of cyanide that the chosen few would take inside. For them it made the depth of the sacrifice that much greater, as though missing the final bitter treat on the tongue transformed them into martyrs.

Every man had been hand-picked by Gouge; each had his curriculum vitae written and stamped in blood; each would give to the cause, proud to serve their lord to the end and grateful to disappear into the flames, in thanksgiving for the vision of eternal rest and peace and glory that they believed was theirs.

The few, the inner circle - they alone would watch Gouge press the buttons, and take their final, fast medicine with him. They were the lucky ones, for they would live to hear the last voice speaking the last words, pronouncing the world dead.

It seemed that the whole of Zone Thirty-Nine was here, watching in slow wonder as the clock of the world ticked towards oblivion, the dust of Gouge's address still settling like an acid over their spellbound thoughts.

And in three separate parts of the churchyard, the dirt around three graves almost imperceptibly shifted.

Leaving behind three opened coffins, Hieronymus moved as fast as his exhausted body would allow, stumbling back towards his quarters to drive the last nails into Colonel Gouge's coffin.

COFFIN MAKER   MARK L. FOWLER

30: DEATH KNEELS

A strange scene was unfolding in Coffin's room. The crying had stopped and a calmer, almost serene Coffin Maker was kneeling down, hands clasped, head tilted upwards, eyes closed. He was doing the thing he mocked mankind for doing.

"I have failed. I have let mankind down. I have let You down. I have tinkered around with death, treated it as a toy, a game for my own amusement. I have indulged myself on extremes to satisfy my curiosity. And now You, in Your wisdom, have sent those extremes that lie within me, to show me the errors of my ways. And still I have learnt nothing."

There was a long and heavy pause. When he spoke again, his voice was trembling.

"For those I have haunted and left lingering on a thread, forgive me. For those I have stolen away without thought, without reason, without pity, forgive me. When I have come down like a thief in the night and taken what was never mine to take...forgive me."

Another pause stretched out silently.

"I will not say they were blameless. I will not say that their own foolishness didn't add to their sufferings. But who showed them foolish ways? Who first haunted them with visions of earthly immortality and visions of glory? Who first planted the seeds of fear in their hearts? Did I make them mistrust You? Hate You? Abandon You? Did I do the devil's work without even realising that he – it - existed?"

Uncertainty swooped down on the Coffin Maker. "Was it really me who did these things? I'm not

COFFIN MAKER   MARK L. FOWLER

evil - I'm only death. I have no Grand Plan, no scheme. I do what I do, not having the intellect to make sense of it. I tried to fathom mankind, but their riddles are too complex. They're as divided as I am. Torn as I am. You didn't make them that way, surely. I shaped them. Death shaped them. All life is shaped by death.

"But tell me this: if I have been so incompetent, so cruel, why have You let me go on? Do You love me for the reasons that You still love them, despite the flaws and the curiosities that drive us? Do You love us because we are Your children still?"

A trickle of tears ran down to touch dry lips, and the taste was of rusting metal. Then fear rose inside, brutal and strong.

"Spare me. Have mercy on me. I can change. I can be whatever You want me to be. Just one more chance. *Please.*"

The fear didn't last. It came like a pang of indigestion, and was gone.

Coffin finished his prayer in a tone of quiet abandon.

"My journal is testament to my failure. I stand to be judged on it, though I no longer have the will to complete it. I am no Poet of Death and never have been. I hoped to redeem all my failings with one great paragraph. Put it all right on the last page. That, above all, illustrates the depth of my stupidity. Soon, when there is no more need of me. When my pathetic journal is read out over the ashes of humanity. Have mercy."

He stood, walked over to his journal and closed it. With enormous ceremony he laid his hand on the

COFFIN MAKER   MARK L. FOWLER

closed book. "It is done." A fountain of tears splashed across the back of his hand, and he let it.

At last he took his hand from the book and moved away. He owed it to Hieronymus and Beezle to be with them at the end. Looking around the room as though leaving it for the last time, he headed for the door.

In the churchyard, three figures were stirring out of the ground as life once more entered them. Not as skeletons did they come out of the ground, but as men, and each in his prime.

Father Henry didn't look much different than he had the day he'd given his last sermon. Indeed, in the absence of spare ribs and Stilton, he looked a good deal better.

Brigadier Browning was not the wheel-chaired old soldier who'd spent his last moments by the sea wall praying for peace, but a man earning medals face to face with cancers like Gouge, in half-forgotten times and places, under circumstances where war had been the only way of operating on such ferocious disease.

The Old Man came out of the ground not telling stories of centuries scored in cricket matches in days of war and peace, nor as the young man who had fought for freedom and justice alongside the brigadier; neither as the middle-aged man, embroiled in politics to make a better world, nor as the timeless educator who believed that the world was made for the living of everyone. He came out of the ground as the old man who had climbed a tree to save a cat, and who would have climbed the

COFFIN MAKER   MARK L. FOWLER

same tree and a hundred like it to save a single innocent human life.

The three men, the treasure of life restored to them, came out of the ground together, locking hands, forming a small circle outside the Great Front Porch.

"Isn't the irony magnificent?" said Gouge, his voice echoing through the cold stone splendour of the vast building. Everyone present agreed that, whatever the irony was, it was certainly magnificent. "Isn't the irony simply priceless - that this great gothic monstrosity called a 'church', should become the control room for the destruction of the world?"

All present agreed that it was an irony of absolutely the first order, and possibly beyond. "All the great moments in history have the hallmark of irony stamped into them."

The agreement was riotous until, satisfied, Gouge moved on from the monumental irony with a twinkle in his eye and a dribble of spit on his chin. "Well, gentleman, I do believe that we are ready to begin pressing the big buttons. But first, there are a few here amongst us who are not invited to the main feature. We thank them anyway for the part they have played in making today possible."

Gouge inaugurated a brief round of applause as he turned to the dozen men chained together by the main altar. A few feet from the terrified men, the last of a row of bright red buttons was being wired into position. The buttons would not have looked out of place if they had been stitched to the front of a circus clown's jacket.

COFFIN MAKER   MARK L. FOWLER

He looked lovingly at his buttons before turning with a look of mock pity, back towards the terrified men. "Obviously President Doveman couldn't trust himself to keep his hands off all those big buttons. What a puzzle you make together, gentlemen, with your pieces of apparently meaningless information. But together what a glorious picture you make. Pity you won't be around to see all the pretty colours that will result when all that partial knowledge comes together. You have another, more pressing appointment to keep now. Heads up, my friends. Or is that...*heads off*! Cheers."

He signalled for the main door to be opened, and the men led out to their fate. "Maestro!" he shouted towards the organ loft, where the quivering organist sat with a rifle levelled into each ear, wishing that this had been one day he hadn't arrived early, eager to perfect one of Bach's trickier fugues.

"Something slow," shouted Gouge, "*painfully slow.*"

The doomed procession shivered forward under the sound of the funeral dirge, towards the light issuing from the Great Front Porch. As they exited into the sickly daylight, Gouge said after them, "As a mark of my gratitude, I'm going to let you all have a nice play on my trampoline."

He looked again, lovingly at his big bright red buttons. "I wish Mumsy could have seen this, I really do."

31: A DEDICATION TO MUMSY

Gouge watched the president's men being led out to the trampolines, moving his hand over the first of the buttons. "This one I dedicate to Mumsy, natural mother to no living thing: Maker, raiser of the Pied Piper. To Mumsy!"

The sound of gunfire stole the moment. He spun around. "What's this?" He shot a vitriolic look towards the organ console. "Silence, damn you."

The dirge stopped at once, its miserable echo ricocheting around the church. Gouge waited for the echo to diminish, until he could hear the chattering of the organist's teeth. Outside, his army had turned its weapons on the three figures moving towards the open door. The men in the helicopters, who a moment earlier had been organising the lowering of trampolines, were joining the men on the ground, pumping thousands of rounds a minute into the three figures.

Still the three kept walking.

Through the entrance they came, and down the aisle. Solemnly, silently, like a dark parody of a funeral service.

Without the music.

Without the coffin.

"Who are you and what do you want?" spat Gouge.

The Three kept walking, close enough now to smell the venom on Gouge's breath.

"Who the hell are you?"

The Three stopped.

COFFIN MAKER   MARK L. FOWLER

It was the Old Man who spoke first. "Who are we? An old man, a priest and a brigadier - that's who we are."

Behind the Three, Gouge's troops had massed.

"We met a long time ago," said Brigadier Browning. "Before you were famous and I was...dead."

"We all died thinking of you," said Father Henry.

"Flattered," said Gouge, his eyes pulsating, ready to unleash the radiation building behind them. "You must be Father Henry. My apologies, but the service has been cancelled and we're waiting to close. I'm afraid you'll have to save your sermon for the next world."

"That's no way to talk to a priest," interrupted the Old Man. "It's time you learnt some respect. This is a house of God. Get on your knees and beg for mercy."

Gouge laughed. "Anything you say, Grandpa."

He turned to his commander for an urgent assessment of the situation.

"We've hit them with enough rounds to finish off a city," said the commander, the information echoing into triplicate before dying to a whisper amongst the pipes standing silent above the organ console. "We don't seem capable of making an impression, sir."

"I see," said Gouge. "Fond of the trampoline, gentlemen?"

In the Coffin Dome, Beezle had only one word on his tongue: "Hieronymus!"

COFFIN MAKER   MARK L. FOWLER

Picking up his hammer, he marched out to find him.

Coffin collected what was left of his thoughts and headed over to the Dome, to see it for the last time. He felt numb, tired, and alone. It felt like the End. This feeling, he thought, must be akin to dying; this emptiness something like the contemplation of the mortal abyss.

He wanted to be with Hieronymus and Beezle. He wanted to die (if that was what was to happen; if that was the way to describe the termination of Death itself) re-united with the separated parts of his being. He wanted to die whole.

With a sad glimmer of insight, his brain sucked at the idea that his crumbling mind was growing feebler because its two satellites were rearing up to some kind of zenith, and stealing the remains of his powers for *their* final battle.

He walked liked a lonely child into the Coffin Dome, not knowing what he would find. Hieronymus and Beezle might be engaged in a melodramatic arm-wrestle with the final lever; or standing back to back, walking ten paces apart with hammers raised.

Who cared how the last scene would play itself out?

Inside the Dome he found a poised silence. A hair-trigger that a cough, a smile, a tear might set in motion. "Where are my boys?" he said, daring the machinery to come alive. "What have you done with my boys?"

COFFIN MAKER   MARK L. FOWLER

He was down on his knees again, weeping, begging that they would come running back, holding hands; the three of them, back as one, together at the End; together to press the final lever - reconciled.

Let the world die its own death.

He wanted to die holding hands with his own.

Coffin stopped crying and looked at the levers. All set, primed. That would do it. That would bring his beautiful boys running. He stood, knowing what he had to do. He could manage that much. End it now. Forever. A good ending.

The right ending.

He caught sight of the monitor.

All Saints church - where else? Colonel Gouge - who else? Red buttons...he knew well enough the significance of those.

"What?"

Coffin's eyes almost rolled out of his head. Father Henry, Brigadier Browning and the Old Man were hoisting Gouge onto the altar, and five hundred automatic rifles were trying to intervene.

So Hieronymus had been to the Vaults again!
Using the forbidden magic.
The old magic.
His *magic*.

Now there was no telling how it would end.

Coffin left the Dome and moments later was standing outside, looking in all directions.

Not knowing which to take.

COFFIN MAKER   MARK L. FOWLER

On the monitor, unseen, the helicopters lowered trampolines, and the doomed started to bounce, slowly, rising gradually towards the blades.

As the dreadful screaming echoed in through the church door, the glitter of justice sparkled in three dead men's eyes, giving Gouge the unspoken promise of his first real lesson in the meaning of terror.

32: SKELETONS IN THE CUPBOARD

Hieronymus held the last breaths of Gouge in his hands. Five more nails and it would be over. He placed the finished lid over the coffin and picked up the hammer.
    Four to go.

In the race to find Hieronymus, the contest was unevenly matched. Coffin stood outside the Dome, surveying every possibility including the Tower. The last of his thin pragmatism had buckled and expired, leaving only a squadron of defeated thoughts to crowd his mind.
    Beezle, defined by action alone and loaded dangerously with the energy and focus of the metaphysically insane, could already hear the sounds of nails being hammered, and was racing like a demon to save his precious colonel.

Gouge was not amused at finding himself ceremoniously placed before the altar; neither was he impressed to find his body forced into a kneeling position. But he still found it in him to laugh, and laugh hysterically.
    With the narrow choices left to him of crying, begging or doing as he was bid (which would have entailed confessing his sins and asking for forgiveness) Gouge made his simplest decision since deciding to destroy the world. Rolling back a large head on a thick-set neck, he roared out a godless belly-laugh fit to make the dead quiver in their graves.

COFFIN MAKER   MARK L. FOWLER

Holding the last two nails in his hand, Hieronymus heard the sound of footsteps. He placed the nails, raised the hammer, and waited for Beezle to come bursting through.

    The wait was a short one.

Gouge's capacity for laughter was as inexhaustible as his desire for destruction, and he was roaring away still as the three shadows of All Saints took him from the altar and carried him back down the aisle towards the sunlight.

    He controlled his terrors well; didn't even try to summon his men, recognising the importance of a display of courage as solidly as he recognised his fate. He would remain the Pied Piper to the end, whistling a tune of merry laughter to the last. That the world might remember him with respect, and one day follow his path down to the Cage to meet Mumsy. Helping themselves, naturally, to his magnificent, endless supply of poisoned chocolates.

Beezle entered.

    Hieronymus, hammer raised, locked eyes with him.

    Neither moved.

    A twitch might bring the day to a close. At last Beezle broke the tension.

    "Two nails to go. You could have done it, but you waited. What do you want?"

    "How clever you are," said Hieronymus.

"If you call that clever you really have spent too much time with your head stuck up your philosophical arse. I'll ask you one more time: *what do you want?"*

"I want to finish off our conversation - the one that you started when you came to visit me in the Tower."

"Kind of me, wasn't it? Get many visitors, did you? Okay, as you wish." Beezle yawned. "Go on then. Let's get it over with."

"What I want to know," said Hieronymus. "If God really does confide his plans and secrets in you, surely He wouldn't want you keeping it all bottled up. It might unbalance you, all that Divine Knowledge running around inside that little mind of yours."

"There's a point to this?" said Beezle.

"If they all die, what becomes of you? Do you get to play around with the corpses for eternity? Full-time necromancy would suit you; you have the temperament."

Beezle acknowledged the compliment with a savage smile. Then edged forward. Hieronymus let the hammer nod in his hand.

"How many questions do you have?" asked Beezle. "This could get tedious."

"You seem to forget, I'm the one holding the hammer."

Beezle raised an arm. "So am I. Isn't that something? And *you* seem to forget that there's nothing to bargain with. You're going to hammer in those nails and I'm going to stop you, and no amount of pointless discussion will alter that. You know as much as I do. There. I think we're done."

COFFIN MAKER   MARK L. FOWLER

"Why should I believe you?"

Beezle shrugged. "Believe what you like."

The fire-headed youth threw the hammer, and then moved with such speed and agility that Hieronymus was overthrown in an instant, his own hammer knocked from his grasp.

While the two manifestations of his own inner turmoil fought to reclaim the hammers, Coffin was at last taking the correct turning, and heading at a steady gallop towards the sounds of violence.

Gouge was led to the trampoline, its canvas already soaked in the blood of the late president's men. If terror really had visited him, then it had been too frightened to remain in his company, and had gratefully fled.

They stood him on the trampoline. He wouldn't stop laughing. Even as the helicopter began its decent, he wouldn't stop. He looked down on the severed heads that littered the red-stained canvas, kicking a couple of them out of the way.

"Let's make some room around here. I've never seen such a mess. Nice day for a bounce, wouldn't you say? Care to join me?"

Then at last the laughter died. It wasn't the gore, and it wasn't fear that sobered him. Inexplicable rays of hope were gathering. Something, somewhere was saying that this wasn't over.

Father Henry was the next to feel the strange rays of twisting fortunes, yet to him they came not as an ally, but rather a force threatening to turn his resurrected bones to dust. In the midst of all this,

COFFIN MAKER   MARK L. FOWLER

Brigadier Browning and the Old Man held firm, oblivious to the unseen forces.

They held Gouge steady on the trampoline.

Beezle held both hammers and was already hearing the delicious splintering sounds that would follow once the blows began to rain down without mercy on the face of that *handsome* philosopher-child.

Coffin, at last approaching Hieronymus' quarters, and knowing that on the other side of that thin wall everything was being decided, hesitated, his heart executing the dance of trepidation, his ears straining at the groans and grunts within.

Gouge had replaced laughter with a smile. The rays of hope had brought his soul back to life, and what were three old corpses going to do about that!

He eyed the helicopter above him and the trampoline beneath his feet, and thought how wonderful it would be to watch the three witches fail the world under the whir of rotors. How wonderful to use their severed heads to bang down on those lovely big red buttons.

He waited for a drop or two more of this strange sunshine, not knowing or caring from where it came. Full of the magic, feeling magnificent and bloody, he would coin a dull old phrase one last time and get the show back where it belonged.

As Coffin's ears strained at the sudden silence, Hieronymus, pinned to the floor, looked into the face of

COFFIN MAKER MARK L. FOWLER

the hammers that hovered above his forehead. "As you're so fond of these little question-and-answer sessions, we'll have one more. A question each, for old-time's sake. Then we really must conclude our business."

The voice behind the hammers, thought Hieronymus, is the voice of victory.

This sounds interesting, thought Coffin, an ear pressed against the door, grateful that at least they were talking.

"I'll go first," said Beezle.

"Ah," said Hieronymus, "but if I answer your question, what guarantee have I that -?"

"*I'll answer yours*," mimicked Beezle. "You really do have shit upstairs, don't you?"

I don't like the sound of that, thought Coffin. I can see them falling out again.

"You see," said Beezle, "*now* I have no reason *not* to tell you the truth."

"But doesn't it follow," said Hieronymus, a frail plan forming, "that equally you have no reason *to* tell me the truth?"

Beezle narrowed his eyes. "Philosopher to the end, eh? Whatever, I'll still go first. The *Quiet Revolution of Death*, remember that? I want to know what the point was."

Coffin's ear was now squashed so hard against the door that it was practically impossible for him to hear anything. He silently cursed the solidity of the paper-thin timber, and quivered on the brink of knowledge.

COFFIN MAKER   MARK L. FOWLER

"I can tell you, but I doubt you'll understand," said Hieronymus.

"You can only do your best," said Beezle.

Hieronymus flinched in the light of the grisly gleam bearing down on him, then told the truth.

"Death should come when life has been lived, when the work is done, when the spirit is ready. Death should carry off a pile of bones, nothing more. Humans have an infinity of roads to travel, and sometimes the road is long and full of adventure, and other times it is barely a road at all. Once I thought that death could only be wrong and unjust and unfair, but then I saw that every day is different, and the whole of creation too complicated for such bald simplicity. Every life has its perfect day, and when the journey is over it should not continue. It's our duty here in the Kingdom of Death to recognise the day and work to it."

"How charmingly metaphysical," said Beezle. "But you know how Coffin hates metaphysics."

Outside the door, Coffin grimaced, and then frowned. He'd always thought metaphysics was something else entirely. He almost opened the door to ask. But remembering that he was seconds away from finding out the truth about Hieronymus' 'revolution', he let one curiosity give way to another, and waited.

"Let me put it more simply. Death is nothing to do with good and evil. It can be savage, but it can also heal. I wanted death to take account of everything. You look cheated. What did you want me to say?"

"You're not telling it all," said Beezle. "You're holding back."

"Okay, so I became too wrapped up in their sufferings. I tried to reverse the injustice of death when Death had acted irresponsibly."

"Whoever heard of Death acting irresponsibly?"

"*I* heard it, saw it, every time you picked up a hammer – every time you walked into the Dome."

The orange-haired youth tightened his grip on the hammers. It was going to be good breaking open that skull and watching those intellectual pools of pus running nowhere.

"So you believe you were tackling injustice? I think you are being too modest, Hieronymus. From where I was watching, I'd say you were *raising the dead.*"

"I did no more than Coffin had done. I realised, though, just as he did, that it was the wrong way."

"You realised it? Then why trip back over to the Vaults to raise the Three Musketeers? You know what you are? You know what you represent, really?"

"No. Tell me."

"*The skeletons in Coffin's cupboard.*"

Even as he stared into the face of the hammers, Hieronymus glowed with victory. "What paradox. The good side creating evil. And it all started so innocently. Breaking open coffins as I have done, with the single purpose of easing misery and despair. But then, as you rightly said, the Coffin Maker tampered and tinkered until evil was born out of the best of intentions. A good impulse corrupted. The road to Hell, as mortals say, paved with -"

"To hell with mortals," spat Beezle. "I want to know what you make of me. What you make of Coffin's

COFFIN MAKER   MARK L. FOWLER

so-called 'bad side'. Are you ready to bow to the superiority of your dark brother?"

"The bad side would never have thought of it. Why raise them if you didn't like them the first time around? The dark side of Coffin wanted them dead and done with. Nothing to do with evil, merely the instinct for destruction."

"Doesn't that make me the Angel of Mercy, come to put an end to all the misery in the world?"

"Maybe it does. I doubt the human race would see it like that. Life and Death have much to learn from one another, and you would deny them that knowledge."

"What are you talking about?"

"Human beings have an infinite capacity to learn - and if he'll only use it, so does Coffin. The contemplation of death informs life more powerfully than anything else, and it's a two-way process. Did the Creator tell you nothing?"

Beezle pulled his arm back. "When I've kissed you goodnight with these tools of the trade, and crawled back inside Coffin, what will it matter who told me what? I think it's time to end this conversation."

"But I haven't asked my question," said Hieronymus. "And I think it's a question that will surprise and fascinate you. After all, it has your future at heart."

Beezle eased his grip on the hammers.

"I need to show you something," said Hieronymus. "If you could just ease up a little on my arm..."

33: THE THIN PLAN

Hieronymus knew the plan was thin. So thin in fact that he wondered, if the world was saved by it, whether even Coffin would have the nerve to document it. Later, with hindsight, Hieronymus saw that the plan would never have worked if it hadn't been for Coffin, bumbling onto the scene like an actor late for the final scene, making it to the stage just before the last curtain fell.

Coffin had remained patiently outside the door, evaluating what he'd heard, wondering still what it all meant, and speculating what Hieronymus' question might be and the fruits of knowledge it might bear. Yet impatience grew quickly inside the Coffin Maker, and he'd soon had enough of the suspense; of trying to imagine what Hieronymus was showing to the dark apprentice.

And so as Beezle eased the pressure ever so slightly to let Hieronymus reveal what was in his hand, Coffin came tumbling through the door.

The distraction was enough for Hieronymus to thicken the plan decisively, levering the shifting weight of Beezle, unbalancing him, allowing an arm to come free before plunging the two remaining nails of Colonel Gouge's coffin deep into Beezle's left eye.

Beezle fell backwards onto the floor, screaming as the blood gushed out of the ruined socket. And while Coffin stood by the door, immobilised by the shock of what he was seeing, Hieronymus picked up a hammer from where Beezle had dropped it, moved across to the coffin of Colonel Gouge, and struck home the last two

COFFIN MAKER   MARK L. FOWLER

nails, dripping as they were with the remains of Beezle's shattered eyeball.

Gouge took his first gentle bounces on the trampoline, but uncertainty had grown in the hearts of the Three. A subtle sense of shifting power whistling through the graveyard, changing its tune even as Gouge began to bounce. He heard it too, and grinned, licking at his red mouth as he rose higher, full of mystical certainty that it was they who would be damned.

"You won't join me, gentleman?" he shouted, his head moving in and out of the whirring blades. "It's such fun up here."

Then something slipped and the light in Gouge's eyes went out.

The Three felt the burden lift. A balance broken. Gouge looked uncertain, no longer willing to get near the blades.

"Playtime over?" asked Father Henry.

Slowly, against his will, Gouge started to bounce boisterously. In a higher realm somebody was calling checkmate.

The last nail driven into Gouge's coffin, Hieronymus fell back. "It's done."

"But -" began Coffin, then turned to see Beezle stagger to his feet, clutching his face, running out through the door. "Where -?"

"Probably going to sign up for the Left Eye Battalion. He should be grateful. I've improved his looks one-hundred percent."

COFFIN MAKER MARK L. FOWLER

Coffin turned to the monitor. At the sight of the three resurrected figures he let out a subterranean groan.

"I'm sorry," said Hieronymus. "I couldn't think of any other way."

"How did you think of it at all?" asked Coffin.

"It was all down to a young boy reading a book."

"Book?"

"Written by the priest."

"You mean...?"

"Father Henry. What a genius."

"Genius?"

"I'd love to know how it ends."

The expression on Coffin's face was so wretched that Hieronymus couldn't help but lighten the blow. "You are the true hero of the day, though. And don't let anyone tell you any different. If you hadn't come in when you did, Beezle would have smashed my face into the floor and Gouge would have smashed the world into dust. You were in the right place at the right time, and if I wore a hat I would take it off to you."

"The world's saved?"

Hieronymus nodded. "Life and Death march on."

Coffin's face slithered towards a smile. "I was there when it counted."

"You certainly were."

"Perfect timing, don't you think?"

"Flawless."

"And the Creator thinks that someone with my talent needs apprentices!"

COFFIN MAKER   MARK L. FOWLER

Father Henry, Brigadier Browning and the Old Man stood in a circle, holding hands. They prayed for the people of the world, and for the enduring spirit of life. Then they asked that God would let them return to the ground so that they might continue their quiet preparations for whatever world was waiting for them.

But as their hands held tightly together, they started to tremble, then shake violently.

Hieronymus, seeing this on the monitor, turned to Coffin.

"Where's Beezle?" he asked.

Without another word they were heading, as fast as a broken body and a patched up heart would allow, towards the Coffin Vaults.

Beezle had to be in there, preparing to fight them with their own magic. Awakening the ancient dead, perhaps; trying to restore the potent magic of the darkest ages.

The Vaults were silent. No sound of lids being ripped off coffins. No sound of anything. Death reigned here, allowing no secret whispers. A single nail falling in the Coffin Vaults might set off echoes that would prove eternal.

All who had lived and died lay here; and all who still lived would one day rest here. The silence of the Vaults was like the end of the world, and the hush of the place had been known to unnerve even Coffin himself.

Like walking through a tunnel beneath an ocean, it gave the feeling that one infinitesimal crack might bring infinity roaring down from all sides.

COFFIN MAKER   MARK L. FOWLER

It was Hieronymus who broke into the stillness. "What fools we are," he said. "Of course he's not here. He's drawn us away. *He's with Gouge.*"

Stumbling back across the Coffin Complex, they feared the worst.

And that's what they found.

An open coffin.

Gouge resurrected.

"Well I never thought Beezle would stoop to this," said Coffin.

Time stood still outside All Saints. All that moved were four ghostly figures. Three against one: one against three. Neither side sure. Everything uncertain. All still to be decided in some unknowable realm.

How does a ghost die? Same way it made it to the halfway house in the first place: with a lid on its coffin. How do you stop someone taking the lid back off? How do you stop the game going on forever?

It was these thoughts that rifled inside Hieronymus. But there was no time left for speculative thinking. He prayed for clearness of mind and swiftness of action. Gouge had been freed from death. Beezle would be heading back to the Coffin Vaults to put the lids back on the coffins of the Three. They could do the same for Gouge, then trip back over to the Vaults to release the Three again, while Beezle crept back to release Gouge...

And round and round it might go until Gouge got near enough to those buttons to incinerate

COFFIN MAKER   MARK L. FOWLER

humanity. It had to end decisively, or it had all been in vain.

He turned to Coffin. "Okay, once you start this cycle of raising them, killing them, raising them - how do you end it?"

Coffin puffed up with so much pride he thought he might explode. *So Hieronymus didn't have all the answers. So when it finally came down to it, it would be the Coffin Maker himself who had the last say. It would take a craftsman. It would take a poet, The Poet -*

"Sorry to hurry you," said Hieronymus, "but I think I'm going to need an answer today."

"Only one way to do it," said Coffin. "Only one possible way."

"Yes?"

"Never imagined I'd ever need it. It's a simple enough method, at least in principle -"

"And what is it – this simple method? If you don't mind."

Coffin was in no hurry. It was good to be the one with the answers, letting out the wisdom a drop at a time. "You see, young Hieronymus, it's always been down to me to decide if and when to take off a lid and when to put it back. Never needed what we need now."

"Which is?"

"Fire. Destroy the coffin by fire. That'll do it - do it for good."

"Do we have fire?"

Coffin's face formed itself into a perfect blank.

Hieronymus closed his eyes and groaned.

"We could start one," said Coffin, trying to rescue his slipping moment of glory.

COFFIN MAKER   MARK L. FOWLER

"How?"

"You mean you know all there is to know about the world and you don't know how to start a fire?"

"Do you?"

"Never needed to," said Coffin, proudly.

"Well you do now!"

They found a few scraps of coffin wood, and began rubbing them together. At the same time Beezle hunted the Vaults for three particular coffins...

...and outside All Saints, while a stagnant world waited for the gods to decide its fate, the four shadows edged around each other, unsure of the odds.

"I think something's going to happen," said Coffin, rubbing furiously.

"Let's hope so," said Hieronymus, unconvinced.

Yet no sooner had the words left the apprentice's lips, than fire at last found its way into the Kingdom of Death, though it almost left before Gouge's coffin had even been singed.

The spark that was at last persuaded to become fire had sprung from Hieronymus' efforts, much to the irritation of Coffin, who at first proved reluctant to help Hieronymus fan the spark into flame, preferring to carry on his own efforts to win the imagined contest. It was only after much convincing - that the real glory lay in the very suggestion of fire; that in comparison to that stroke of genius, all glory in actually producing fire was a pale pretender to the throne of hero of the day - that Coffin felt easy enough about the situation to add his own lungs to the effort of keeping the precious spark alive.

COFFIN MAKER   MARK L. FOWLER

With Coffin's ego tended to, Colonel Gouge's coffin was crackling along nicely. Watching the fire licking eagerly at the wood, Hieronymus was struck by a thought. "Shouldn't the coffin be re-completed," he said, "I mean - with the lid back on?"

Coffin almost blushed. "I think you might be right."

Frantically they hunted for nails, the fire snapping angrily at their hands as they fought to place the lid over the burning coffin.

With the lid at last in place, they hammered at the nails through the intense heat, but with the flames still rising Coffin edged back from the inferno. "It's no good. It's too hot in there."

"We must finish it," said Hieronymus, taking on air before launching headlong back into the flames.

"No!" shouted Coffin.

It was too late. Hieronymus was in, leaving the Coffin Maker to stand helpless at the edge of the fire, listening to the sound of the hammer driving through the flames, taking home the final nails.

Father Henry raised his hands to Heaven when he saw the circle of fire spring around Colonel Gouge, though the Old Man remained cautious. "It isn't over yet. Gouge doesn't know he's defeated. He has to know it. Pray, Father Henry, *pray.*"

The fire crept steadily towards Gouge, already licking at his face; yet still no recognition of defeat registered among the ruins of his features, half-digested now by the quickening flames. With a passion beyond anything he had been able to achieve in life, Father Henry prayed, his voice rising with the searing heat.

The fire gathered over Gouge, but his voice continued to chisel the air, urging the dark gods to strike down these poor shadows and let him loose to finish his games of destruction. His ears had become cinders and his nose was roasting like a Christmas chestnut, yet the voice was relentless as his face melted into a grin.

A roaring wind rushed towards the flames, violently fanning them, and Gouge began invoking evil by its countless names, issuing a roll-call of the entire pantheon in a single breath. From the opposite direction, a different breath raced to meet its nemesis in the epicentre of the fire - two ancient winds locked together, fighting over precious centimetres, holding within them angels and demons of seemingly equal force and number, the fire holding steady, halting its consumption of Gouge, but not reversing.

Father Henry's praying hands were shaking apart, but the Old Man and Brigadier Browning heaved them together, forcing them back into the shape of supplication.

Above the roar of the two winds came Gouge's voice. "I would love to stand around and talk about ghostly things, but I have an apocalypse to attend to."

His words became incomprehensible as he addressed the dark gods directly, and the remains of his face assumed every form that evil has taken in the world, a million portraits flicking back through time with the urgency of a black tornado, resolving at last into the form of a serpent.

COFFIN MAKER   MARK L. FOWLER

As the serpent sang, the two winds still held each other in check, the fire wavering. Then the serpent changed into human form, addressing the Three in the calm, assured tones of a politician.

"This is the final phase," said Father Henry. "The most virulent. The most dangerous. Don't listen to the voice. The words will draw you, and once you have heard them you cannot resist."

The priest's eyes closed in a blind fever of prayer. "Keep my hands together. Don't let them slip."

The brigadier pushed at the priest's left hand, the Old Man at his right, while the shadows sought to separate them.

"Join in the prayer," screamed Father Henry. "Drown out that voice."

The Three wailed out a furious *Agnus Dei*, battling to blot out the silky rhetoric issuing from Gouge as he assumed the collective, distilled persona of history's most potent, most corrupt leaders. Yet despite the irresistible address, the seething invitation from the unholy legion, still no dark gods came to answer the call. Slowly, *slowly* the serpent resumed its slithering form, singing for the last time its awesome song of betrayal.

"He knows," said the brigadier.

The song was weakening, the venom draining out; for its failure, the serpent's fangs were being ripped from its head as it swung impotently, the agony building soundlessly, its raw mouth exploding with boiling blood, before crumbling and dissolving into a corpse, Gouge's corpse – a corpse beyond even the redeeming powers of the Coffin Maker's pliers.

COFFIN MAKER   MARK L. FOWLER

With a fury, the wild wind broke loose, ousting its opposite force, the flames crackling over the corpse of Colonel Gouge, blackening it to ashes.

The prayer stopped in Father Henry's mouth.

Silence.

Absolute stillness.

"It's over," said the priest at last.

The exodus began as Gouge's men fled from the churchyard in all directions. The Piper had been silenced, the children – young and old - of the world saved, while the bureaucrats, technicians and all associated servants of darkness were left to scatter like rats towards their own destruction.

The Three watched as the furnace stripped every morsel from the empty carcass. Watched until the flames finally died down.

34: THE HANDSHAKE

In the immediate aftermath Coffin's instinct was to seek out Beezle and break his skull open on account of all the trouble and inconvenience he'd caused. Hieronymus talked him out of it. After all, he told Coffin, it wouldn't be possible to hurt him more than they'd done already. Beezle was broken, spent. Why swat a dead fly?

"For the pleasure of it," said Coffin, though tacitly he agreed.

Hieronymus was in a bad way, though his spirits were high. And finding himself incapable of dying, he resolved to enjoy the victory as best he could. Yet his only company was the Coffin Maker, and *he* didn't seem at all sure of the victory.

"We saved a nasty war there, by the look of things. Don't suppose we'll be seeing any more of Colonel Gouge? Will we?"

"Don't suppose we will."

"Best keep our eyes peeled though, all the same."

"I agree."

"Belt and braces. Can't be too careful. What do you reckon?"

"I think that's fair advice."

"You don't think it's over, do you?"

"Do you?"

"I don't know what to think," said Coffin.

"For what it's worth," said Hieronymus, "I don't believe it's ever really over. It keeps on, relentless through the generations. As long as there's life, there's a job to do. Death feeds on life. It's how it is."

COFFIN MAKER   MARK L. FOWLER

"Do you think I caused all of this?" asked Coffin.

"All of what? *Life and Death*?"

Coffin shook his head. "I'm not that conceited. No, I'm talking about evil."

"For the record, I don't believe that a good intention can be the root of evil. We do bad things out of misguided intentions, but evil must come from somewhere else."

"The devil?"

"Perhaps. And if so, then one of these times, he's going to stop playing games, stop sending the troops. And when that day comes…you'd better have your eyes open."

He watched the thought jiggle around the Coffin Maker's brain, his face-bones flipping it like a pinball until the unpleasant flash of light in his eyes confirmed that it had been digested.

"So what do you think happens now?" asked Coffin.

"I was about to ask the same question."

"You're the philosopher."

"I don't understand everything that's happened any more than you. I think that's something else we have in common with mortals - along with our divided personalities."

"Your trauma hasn't affected your sense of humour, then?"

Hieronymus smiled.

"So you really don't understand it all?" asked Coffin.

COFFIN MAKER   MARK L. FOWLER

"Less than you, I suspect. After all I'm only one part of you."

"True," said Coffin, puffing up in spite of himself. *That's more like it*, he thought, the confidence returning like a flock of summer birds. "So what exactly are you having trouble understanding?"

"Well," said Hieronymus, "it's to do with the day of creation."

"What about it?"

"You met the Creator: what did He look like?"

"Why do you ask?"

"If Beezle and I really are parts of you, doesn't it follow that we must have seen the Creator too? I don't recall it, personally."

"Well, it was more a sense of Him, actually."

"What I'm getting at," said Hieronymus, "is that, when Beezle said he was told all this by the Creator - couldn't it have been the devil all along, setting it up? Beezle suggested the possibility himself, but what if he was deceived? What if the devil tricked Beezle into believing that raising the dead was the root of evil?"

Coffin, unsure of the implications, said, cautiously, "Go on."

Hieronymus went on. "Beezle gave the impression that he was one step ahead. Yet if he really is just a part of you – then how can he have all the answers? I mean...what if the devil tricked a part of you into starting all this? The Beezle part of you, of course."

"Of course," said Coffin.

"Isn't that what he does with humans? Tricks them, plays on their fears and uncertainties; their

COFFIN MAKER MARK L. FOWLER

curiosity, their weakness? Tries to turn them away from good - away from what the Creator intended?"

"Are you suggesting that he tricked me into sending myself that ridiculous note?"

"I'm saying that maybe we are all pawns in a greater battle."

Coffin cleared his throat, then cleared it again. "Interesting ideas, very interesting." Rubbing his chin and looking decidedly uncomfortable, he added, "Anyway, I think I owe you an apology. I should never have carted you off to the Tower like that. I ought to have conducted your trial more openly - I feel bad about the whole business."

"Trial?" said Hieronymus. "That was a trial!"

Coffin's hands were turning and twisting, one around the other. "So what would you say philosophy is then?"

Hieronymus, halfway between outrage at the notion that the farce in the Tower had constituted a trial, and laughter at Coffin's clumsy attempt at changing the subject, let it go and indulged him.

"Philosophy? Now let me see. I'd say that it's either the making or the undoing of everything."

"What's that supposed to mean? Or are you being philosophical?"

"Okay," said Hieronymus. "How about…an intellectual attempt to get at the bottom of things. The nature of things. And if I'm a philosopher at all, then it's only in the Greek sense - I mean of course the Zone One-Hundred and Ninety-Four sense."

Coffin acknowledged the correction but frowned at the rest of it.

COFFIN MAKER   MARK L. FOWLER

"What I mean is that I consider all knowledge relevant - science, art, theology; humans are trying to uncover how things really are. Like us they have been blessed - or cursed - with curiosity. They want to uncover the miracle."

"Miracle?"

"Of life."

"I see," said Coffin, not seeing.

"Problem is, where does it lead, finally? Is human life better or worse for its efforts at solving the mysteries? And how would anyone know? I think the bottom line is: we, like mortals, must choose carefully what we believe in, and do our best to understand the consequences and implications that follow from our choices. None of us can know everything, and we are bound to make mistakes."

Coffin sighed, wishing he hadn't started the whole thing up again. "So now you've told me all this, why doesn't anything seem any clearer? If the Creator really did tell Beezle everything, do you think that when - if - you two end up back inside me, his knowledge will become mine? Will your philosophy be mine too?"

"You don't hold much store by the devil theory?"

"I'm still not sure I believe in the devil."

"Leaves us with a heck of a burden of guilt if we don't. Maybe it does anyway. Scapegoats have always been handy, so why should the devil be an exception?"

Coffin's eyes twinkled. He could see the advantages, sure enough.

COFFIN MAKER   MARK L. FOWLER

"But to come back to your question," said Hieronymus, "I don't suppose you'll know what revelations are in store until the time comes."

Satisfied that at least he wasn't alone in his ignorance, Coffin decided it was time to bring his strange satellites together, and find out what the fusion might yield.

Inside the Dome all was silent. Beezle was on his knees. He had been weeping. Coffin, expecting to feel rage but finding himself instead overcome by a strange and powerful sense of pity, stood before the broken apprentice, respecting the depth of the stillness and letting tranquillity reign a little while longer. Then, at last, he spoke.

"Can't win them all, old son," he said, making a mental note of his wisdom and tact so that he could fully document it all later. "Can't have winners without losers, you know, and worse things happen at sea."

Since the whole business had ended, with the burning of Gouge's coffin, he'd found the old urge to write pulsing back; even raised his writing hand and massaged it in preparation.

There was no doubting it; the old poetry was returning. And how much greater that poetry would be when Hieronymus and Beezle were back inside him, full of knowledge and treasure. Oh, yes, the best was still to come for the Coffin Maker, with his babies back inside him. Already his words had that fine resonance – the mark of the true, the original, the unique.

The poet was back.

COFFIN MAKER   MARK L. FOWLER

"Buck up, lad," he said. "It's time to make an old man happy."

In the graveyard at All Saints, three figures headed back towards their graves. And like three old friends walking home, there came a point where they could go no further together. Kneeling down, they silently offered their private prayers of thanksgiving, and when they had finished, it was Father Henry who spoke.

"I hope God won't be too hard on Doveman. He did what he thought was right, and from good intentions. He just didn't understand the nature of the beast."

"I think history will find him lacking," said the Old Man. "An idealist and a pursuer of votes: in short, a politician."

The brigadier nodded his agreement. "But his death will secure his immortality, and a certain noble dignity. The inexplicable death of Colonel Gouge will be the subject of endless speculation, but ultimately who but Doveman will be mentioned alongside it? Certainly none of us. If we'd done more in life we wouldn't have needed this nightmare in death."

Father Henry took a hand of each and formed a circle. "Let Him lead us safely back to quiet graves."

After a chorus of *Amen*, Brigadier Browning said, "It was a girl, a little girl. The moment Gouge fell and was consumed by flames, I saw her, in my daughters arms, healthy and alive. A new generation, a new chance allowed. I have never seen anything so beautiful."

COFFIN MAKER   MARK L. FOWLER

The brigadier, laying to rest the notion of the emotionless ghost, started to bubble up. As Father Henry comforted him, the Old Man said, "We came back and finished what should never have been allowed to get this far. We can rest now. Our wars are over. God bless the living and the dead."

"I think we should pray for Bishop Stones," said Father Henry.

He caught the look of his friends, and squeezed their hands.

"He has an important job to do, and I think he has learnt much since our last encounters. Perhaps my book wasn't such a good idea, coming from a clergyman. But I've been looking in on young John, and reading it doesn't appear to have done him any harm. Matter of fact, I saw him turn over the final page with a tear in his eye. That boy needs to cry."

And so a short prayer was offered for Bishop Stones, and for John, and then the three friends returned into the ground, silent and alone.

Beezle followed Coffin back from the Dome, remaining a suitable distance behind to reflect the depth of his shame.

Back in Coffin's quarters, Beezle took his place next to Hieronymus, and the two kept their remaining eyes to themselves and their thoughts unspoken as Coffin tried his best to make the air ring with poetry, waxing interminably about the spirit of reconciliation.

At last the words petered out, and Coffin briefly warmed his bones over the embers of Colonel Gouge's still smoking coffin, which he'd had Hieronymus drag all the way there.

He beckoned his apprentices forward, holding out warmed hands, touching the smashed eye of Beezle and the scalded face of Hieronymus with equal tenderness, before slowly drawing a hand from each and clasping them together.

"I want you to forgive each other and shake hands," he said, pleased with the gravity of the ceremony, and already wondering how he could do it justice later with his pen. "In the true spirit of reconciliation, we'll have an appropriate word from you both."

He looked first at Hieronymus. "Nothing too philosophical, young man."

Hieronymus said, "Love them."

"Bit short," said Coffin, but seeing that Hieronymus had spoken his last he turned to Beezle. "Your turn."

Beezle said, "Hate them."

Then, having no choice but to go on with the charade, Hieronymus and Beezle shook hands and in a second were gone.

COFFIN MAKER   MARK L. FOWLER

35: THE DIVINE PLAN

For some time after the departures, Coffin waited for the revelations to come. But nothing came. Hieronymus and Beezle had left as quickly as they had arrived, but without the scent of violets and the stench of rotting flesh.

Coffin felt no different, experienced no strange sensations. There was no knowledge. No wisdom.

He waited in ecstasy, joy, hope and finally despair for them to give him a sign.

Nothing.

He called after them, hunted the Coffin Complex high and low for them. They were nowhere to be found. His questions remained unanswered, the Divine Plan unscaled. He took his anger to the left ear and tore it down, and did the same to the right ear. This done, he went back to work.

Back to the promise, at least, of solitude.

Later, when the world was settling down to the single beat of Coffin's hammer, and the Dome was humming along like old times, the Coffin Maker sat down, his pen hovering over the virgin landscape of a blank Page One. It was time to begin again. A fresh start. A brand new journal. This time there would be no mistakes. The old journal was nothing more than a book of notes, photo-snaps of history. It was time for the real poetry to begin.

But where to begin?

A double obituary, maybe? *In remembrance of Hieronymus and Beezle.* Or a self-portrait, perhaps?

COFFIN MAKER — MARK L. FOWLER

Again, a very mortal tendency. Painting himself as nothing more than a metaphor for mankind's divided self? Explaining himself out of existence with all the conceit and pimply profundity of an undergraduate?

He brought a bony fist down heavily on the desk, attempting to frighten the wretched thoughts from his head. "Hieronymus. Whatever he was, he's me again. Somewhere in here. Nudging me towards the act of mercy. Letting Mrs. Jones see her grand-daughter married; extending Mr. Smith's remission to get him to the 'Holy Land' of Zone Five-Hundred - though why anybody's death-bed ambitions would run to that hell-hole remains one of the mysteries of the mortal world."

He took a moment to compose himself.

"Will my boys never stop fighting? Beezle wants me to make it rain every day down there..."

He let his pen descend onto the page. A dangerous corner was approaching and Coffin took it at full speed.

I love them. I hate them. That's how it is. That's how it will always be.

With a smile he put down his pen. How majestic the words looked on the fresh white paper. How beautiful and profound. What a fine start to a new era. What a fine start to the New Dawn of Death.

He might have thought that enough poetry for one day, and been content to spend an hour in the Dome. Yet an impulse caused him to take another look at what he'd written.

Already the words had soured on the page.

COFFIN MAKER   MARK L. FOWLER

He reached for his old journal and flicked through the centuries. It was everywhere. Practically his signature. Here he would find - *I love them;* there - *I hate them.* The two phrases coming closer together as time passed, until they'd sat together unashamedly on the page, the way they were sitting now at the head of his lovely new journal, not even blushing at their own perverse union.

And now it was ruined, this brave new beginning - and it was the Creator's fault. Oh, if he hadn't let his anger rise at His manipulations.

If he hadn't let himself become incensed, thereby glimpsing, from out of the corner of an eye...

...the *Divine Plan*.

The Coffin Maker stopped the thought.

Trembled beneath it.

A great moment was arriving as all great moments arrive - without trumpets.

He gave the thought time to snap back at him, mocking him with its triviality. Yet the thought only grew until the Coffin Maker became at last convinced that this thought was the one he had been waiting for. The thought – the very one – that would herald a new – the real - beginning.

Words fine enough for Page One of his new book.

He wrote,

I am the Poet of Death. I have fathomed the Divine Plan and know Your secret heart. Why You created Life and stalked it with Death. Why You sent me two halves of myself. What drives You.

COFFIN MAKER   MARK L. FOWLER

Coffin raised his pen triumphantly over the page, savouring the delicious anticipation. Able to contain the thought not a moment longer, he let it loose.

The essence of the Divine Spirit is humour. The culmination of the Divine Plan...

ETERNAL LAUGHTER.

Coffin sat back and tried to laugh, though he was far too excited.

Good and evil. The battle within. The battle outside. It's what keeps it all rolling along. And You want to keep the two balanced to extend the joke. You named me Coffin *and laughed until You ached. You sent two halves of myself to torment me and Heaven and Hell were deafened by Your roar. You watched me trying to make a fresh start. Trying to learn from it all. Causing structural damage to the universe laughing at how I've spoiled my new book. So what now? Another punch-line brewing? Did You intend me to change? Do You want me the same? Does it make any difference? Why won't You tell me!*

Anger exploded out of the Coffin Maker. Anger at the rotten truth of it.

That he didn't know a damned thing about anything except making coffins.

He looked up from the page. *What was that?* His eyes raged into the gloom. At last, satisfied that

COFFIN MAKER   MARK L. FOWLER

there was nothing in the room but himself, his journal and an aching contempt, he scratched into the page,

Was Hieronymus right to believe in the devil? Did the devil send the note? Should I address him directly in future? Or am I so crazy from an eternity of doing this job that I wrote the note myself? No God No devil just plain insanity.
    Is God the devil death life good evil all rolled up into me and multiplied by the billions who roam the Earth? Why am I thinking like this?

Coffin switched on the monitor. Zone Six-Hundred and Sixty-Six. A young boy sitting alone, reading his late uncle's book.

Doveman dead; Gouge destroyed; Hieronymus and Beezle gone.

The Coffin Maker looking into the screen, watching the boy. Reading over his shoulder...the boy turning around, nervously...but finding nobody there...

...And so the Coffin Maker went back to work, his boys inside him, and the world went on turning until the next time. And the souls of the dead rested that night though they would keep a close watch on the precious lives of those who still walked the Earth...

...The boy could feel the tears welling up and he let them go. When the spasm of grief has subsided he turned the page. Father Henry hadn't quite finished.

COFFIN MAKER   MARK L. FOWLER

...It goes without saying that those who - either by circumstance or inclination - find themselves inhabitants of what the Coffin Maker would call Zone 666...well, they'd better keep a weather eye; for one day all that darkness is going to find its natural home, and Coffin none the wiser when the time comes...

...The boy was laughing when his father came into the room. This time he didn't try to hide the book, instead offering it, his father promising to read it...

Coffin switched off the monitor. "Is that what I'm reduced to - a character in a book written by a dead priest! *You had one hell of an ego, Father Henry, and if you weren't already dead...*"

He walked back to his desk, replacing his new journal with the old. Leaving a single-line space from his last entry, he wrote,

Business as usual. I love them I hate them.

Then it happened.
　　Like the time before.
　　An object falling past his window.
　　This time the Coffin Maker knew better. He sat watching the note hit the ground, and didn't move, not an inch.
　　More mockery. More tomfoolery. Somebody up there running low on ideas.
　　Coffin watched the note lying motionless outside his window, letting his thoughts wander around it for a while. What harm could that do? A little idle

speculation about the answers it might contain; the truths, the secrets - where was the harm in that? Time, space, the meaning of life and death - all there, all explained.

Am I, the Coffin Maker, really able to choose? Or are my thoughts preordained? Will the world end through war, or will mankind learn lessons only to be finally confronted with extinction through a cosmic event - or unforeseen developments in the nature of natural disease?

Built in obsolescence. And what would be the crueller? What would be the smellier?

What would get the biggest laugh?

And am I making the same coffins, over and over? Is life a child's slate - get into a mess with a sum, a picture, with whatever you hoped might be, then the slate's wiped clean and you start again somewhere else, as someone else? And is that infinitely cruel? Or infinitely kind?
    Or just infinitely funny!
    He pressed his face up against the window. The note - it might contain anything. It might foretell...anything.
    The Creator planning a journey that would take His creations even deeper into the realms of the absurd?
    Planning to send the Coffin Maker...
    ...*what*?
    He could stand it no longer.

And went out to collect the note.

EPILOGUE

At the end of an extraordinarily long shift, in which the personal apocalypse was managed more than a million times, Coffin relaxed in front of the monitor. Nothing in the world or about the world seemed any different. Nothing had changed. They were all asking their God the same old questions:
Will you let Mummy/Daddy live?
Will you end this/that war?
Will you end this drought/famine?
Will you let Jack/Jill see his/her son/daughter married?
Will you let Nancy receive her letter from the Queen?
Will you let the soul of Brigadier Browning rest in peace - and let his daughter see the christening of her little angel? *She's still getting over the death of her father. She seemed to be doing so well.*

Coffin's eyes widened; felt his insides shift an inch on either side. "I may just do that."

Instantly there was a stab of pain from deep inside.

"Beezle getting restless in there?"

A different kind of pain retaliated.

He smiled, in spite of the discomfort.

"My moral conscience stirs. I'll have to think about this one for a while, boys."

...Will you give Lu another chance?
Will you save poor David? His father needs help. He's going to end up killing that boy.
Will you let Ixa learn to forgive before she ends up drinking herself to death?

COFFIN MAKER   MARK L. FOWLER

Will you look out for my son? He's a brave boy, and seems to be coping well. But I fear for the long years ahead, because a child needs his mother, and I pray you will give me the strength to raise John into a man that his mum would be proud of. And thank you for the life of Father Henry, his wisdom and love, and for the book he wrote which has given strength and comfort to his beloved nephew.

Coffin sneered.

Will you allow Nazwah to see his daughter graduate?
Will you give Vinda the chance to see her homeland one last time?
Will you let me live forever?
Will you bring them back?
Will you this, will you that, will you...?

Coffin turned off the monitor. "Don't know why they keep asking. He does whatever He likes. Whatever gets the biggest laugh up there."

Returning to his journal he wrote,

Curious feelings. Beezle and Hieronymus. Missing them. I feel their presence but they tell their secrets silently. Feeling lonely. Feeling old. Send me a sign. Something. Anything. Soon.

Restless, he switched the monitor back on and watched the worthiest of Zone Thirty-Nine lower President Doveman into the ground, close to the statue locally referred to as *Old Henry*, though officially titled *The Unknown Saint*. It was the wish of the late president's wife – still clinging to life, defiantly, despite the pummelling of grief - that Doveman be buried there.

COFFIN MAKER   MARK L. FOWLER

The occasion filled the churchyard at All Saints with a huge gathering, most of whom seemed to be trying hard to look important. Politicians. Churchmen. City Fathers. Television crews...

Coffin listened to ramblings about international terrorism and the need for ever tighter security. Listened to speculation about the contenders for office. Listened to so much crap on so many themes that it seemed to him more a free-for-all exercise in ego-tripping than a funeral.

Bishop Stones broke the mould by actually mentioning Doveman and saying a prayer for the dead man's family.

"You certainly do a better funeral when there's a camera present," conceded Coffin.

The bishop prayed that the good work started in bringing a mood of genuine reconciliation between Church and State, might continue and build. He finished his prayer, much to Coffin's disgust, with the ridiculous - and not remotely original - suggestion that the "bloodless revolution that this great nation has started might offer a vision that the whole world might one day see fit to embrace."

"Ha," said Coffin. "Doesn't care who he steals from!"

Then it was the turn of a rather bulbous looking priest – clearly Father Henry's replacement, and an obvious contender for some late-night feasting - to issue a few brimstone-tinged warnings against complacency, calling for vigilance and prayer in the "never-ending battle against the Evil One."

Coffin yawned.

COFFIN MAKER   MARK L. FOWLER

It was time for his Round the World.
Should he bother?
Nothing of consequence was likely to develop so soon after recent events.
Yet old habits died hard in the Kingdom of Death, and so the Coffin Maker settled to the task in hand, seeking re-assurance, perhaps, that everything really was back under control.

Seven-Hundred and Seventy-Seven zones later, Coffin was trembling, though not with laughter.

Zone Six-Hundred and Sixty-Six. How could he have missed it? Another tumour erupting on that sick planet. And not just any tumour but by the look of it the mother of all tumours.

And he'd caught that wretched child reading again. Father Henry's final words from that infernal book.

...with the warnings unheeded and the world seemingly incapable of change, it could only ever be a matter of time before the evil one itself arrived...and in his home town...in the zone bearing his number...

"Hogwash!"

Coffin remembered the note with its dancing lights. Comprising of three numbers.

666

Suddenly it made sense. It could only happen in a place with all the sixes. How many threes in 666? If Coffin had learnt anything, anything at all, it was that the number Three, and all that it contained, was cursed. And by extension any place with those many threes hiding in it was bound to turn sour.

As far as he was concerned that was the top and bottom of it!

Coffin peered back into the monitor.

The boy was reading Father Henry's postscript.

...The future lies with you, John. The subsequent hero. The sequel beckons...it always does. So step up to the plate, my brave young soldier, and keep the flame alive and burning...run with it, my son...

Coffin is reading over your shoulder...understanding nothing.

The Coffin Maker, unamused, shut down the monitor. There was work to be done...

Lightning Source UK Ltd.
Milton Keynes UK
UKOW04f1302171114

241730UK00001B/52/P